SHADOW DANCING IN THE U.S.A.

SHADOW DANCING
IN THE U.S.A.

Michael Ventura

JEREMY P. TARCHER, INC.
Los Angeles
Distributed by St. Martin's Press
New York

The author is grateful for permission to quote from the following:

"Ballad of a Thin Man" (Bob Dylan) copyright © 1965 M. Whitmark & Sons. All rights reserved. Used by permission.

"Rock & Roll Never Forgets" © 1976 Gear Publishing Co./ASCAP.

F. Scott Fitzgerald, excerpted from *The Last Tycoon*. Copyright © 1941 Charles Scribner's Sons; copyright renewed © 1969. Reprinted with the permission of Charles Scribner's Sons.

Reprinted by permission of Schocken Books Inc. from *Voodoo in Haiti* by Alfred Métraux. Copyright © 1959 by Alfred Métraux.

Nathanael West, *Miss Lonelyhearts & The Day of the Locust*. Copyright © 1938 by the Estate of Nathaniel West. Reprinted by permission from New Directions Publishing Corporation.

Wild Style Subway Rap 2 by Grand Master Caz, copyright 1983 by Wild Style Productions, Ltd.

"Do You Believe in Magic" by John Sebastian, © copyright 1965 Alley Music Corp./Trio Music Co., Inc. All rights administered by Hudson Bay Music Inc. Used by permission. All rights reserved.

Library of Congress Cataloging in Publication Data

Ventura, Michael.
    Shadow dancing in the U.S.A.

    1. United States—Civilization—1970–   —Addresses, essays, lectures. I. Title. II. Title: Shadow dancing in the USA
E169.12.V46 1985   973.92   85-16852
ISBN 0-87477-372-5

Jeremy P. Tarcher, Inc.
9110 Sunset Blvd.
Los Angeles, CA 90069

Design by Thom Dower

Manufactured in the United States of America
10 9 8 7 6 5 4 3 2 1
First Edition

For Jan, who wasn't fakin'—
whole lotta shakin' goin' on—

Contents

All activity is cultural activity. A church is a smile ... a walk is as profound as a system of judging.
—Imamu Amiri Baraka

The point is, to live everything. Live the questions now. Perhaps you will then gradually, without noticing it, live along some distant day into the answer.
—Rainer Maria Rilke

Preface

Most of these essays began as installments of my "Letters at 3 A.M." column in the *L.A. Weekly,* but they've been expanded a good deal and most have been substantially changed, so that more than half of this material hasn't been in print before. This is no collection of articles except in the sense that the articles were, from the first, intended as bits of this book. I'm deeply grateful to the readers of my column, especially for the letters, written both to the editor for publication and to me personally. They helped give this writing a context and a direction, and no writer could ask for more from his readers.

As solitary as the act of writing is, nobody uses words in solitude. A book, though signed by one person, carries the presences of many. To name the many whose presences I've felt in this writing would be an impossibly lengthy list to inflict on strangers, but some specific thanks are necessary. Thanks, then, to my father Michael and my mother Clelia—his gentle, questing intelligence, and her fiery, visionary intelligence, which never met except in their children; to my foster family, the Laws; to Donald F. Carlo and John Judson, two superb high school teachers who taught me the craft of prose; to Jeff Nightbyrd, who had the faith to give me my first writing gig, on the *Austin Sun,* when I hadn't a credential in the world, and whose friendship has informed my writing ever since; to Paula Latimer, who supported me through that first year or so when writing took all my time but could not pay nearly all the bills; to

Ginger Varney, a comrade in the craft, for everything; to Michael Berger, David Rosenthal, Dave Johnson, Butch Hancock, George Howard, Dixie Howard, Janette Norman, and Big Boy Medlin, whose thoughts spurred many of mine; to Jay Levin, editor of the *L.A. Weekly*, who prints styles, thoughts, and forms that go beyond the givens of journalism; to Laura Golden and Hank Stine, who wanted this book to happen, and to Jeremy Tarcher, who rolled the dice; to Brendan McCambridge, who helps my writing in ways I'm sure he'll ask me about someday; to Mike Rose, Helen Knode, Hank again, Jan again, Jeremy again, Jeff again, Michael again, Laura again, and Julie Reichert, for invaluable work with the manuscript; and to Robert Bly, whose work and example have been crucial, to me and to so many.

More names should be here. They know who they are. In a novel by Doris Lessing, *Briefing for a Descent into Hell,* the narrator is gripped by an epiphany wherein he says, "I *am* my friends." He means this in the most profound sense possible. So do I.

Michael Ventura
Los Angeles
June 1985

Introduction—It's 3 A.M.
Twenty-Four Hours a Day

3 A.M. An impossible time to read a newspaper. A book—perhaps. The television. Or you listen to music, or drink in silence, or listen to the breath of the sleeper beside you—a sound that sometimes comforts, but just as often, if you're willing to admit it, fills you with a nameless unease; you know that person both well and not at all, and there are times when you can't tell which is which. Or there's no one else there, and there isn't going to be. Either way, the night can feel like one huge parking garage in which you can't remember where you left your car.

Sometimes you don't know if your wakefulness is or isn't a fear of dreams, and you wouldn't be sure of what to do if you knew. But what you are doing—standing in the dark, full of conflicting emotions—isn't that what the whole world's doing now? A world tossing and turning, restless with fresh and disturbing impulses, trying to redo itself, rethink itself, realign itself, and trying to live up to its troubled and inarticulate sense of new realities.

That's what everybody's complaining about, not that the world's asleep but that it can't sleep any longer. It's been awakening for about a hundred years now. And people are arguing about exactly what time it is on the historical clock. The anti-nuclear activist Dr. Helen Caldicott, is right about nuclear weapons but wrong about the historical time of day. She says it's ten minutes to midnight. But it was ten minutes to midnight about a hundred years ago, before the discovery of radium and the publication of *The Interpretation of Dreams*; before Einstein's theories and before motion pictures, and light-bulbs and airplanes and cars; before the first cornet solos of Buddy Bolden and before Picasso's *Demoiselles d'Avignon*. By now the world's clock is at about 3 A.M. of the new day, the new civilization. For the new day doesn't start at dawn, the new day starts at midnight.

The new day starts in darkness.

Right now it's 3 A.M. in whatever we will call that period of human history that comes after A.D.

When your clock reads 3 A.M. it's a time of separate-ness, of loneliness, of restlessness. Nothing on television, nothing in the newspaper, nothing much anywhere sug-gests that our restlessness, felt so privately, is part of something huge, something alive all over the world: a many-headed restlessness that is the shaky underpin-ning of nothing less than a worldwide transformation. We all know that technology is marrying all the races and places of our world into a pulsating, panicky whole that is far from knowing what to do with its (with our) imposed unity; and we sense that no culture on earth utilizes more than a small portion of the human brain, the human capacity (perhaps it's this unused part of our-selves that's making us so restless). But the new can't grow in what's already used up. It has to grow in what longs in us, in our loneliness and our restlessness. We make a mistake when we sidestep and placate these feel-ings, for only in the raw and unformed parts of ourselves —only in this bewildered area within—is there space for the new to take root.

This may not be what you want to hear in your par-ticular share of 3 A.M. So you pour a drink, maybe, and flick on the TV with your remote. Twenty-four-hour news, twenty-four-hour rock videos, twenty-four- hour movies. Here in L.A. you can get the 6 A.M. children's shows in Chicago (the Three Stooges doing in fun what you often wish to do in anger) or the early morning religious programming in Atlanta. You flick through about forty brief bursts of images, flick through them again, and flick them off. The silence is worse now. And if you go to sleep your psyche will provide its own swirl of images. And if you walk out the door—but perhaps you're nervous about taking a walk at 3 A.M., even though your neighborhood is certainly not the worst. And the world is in exactly the same state you are, though it tries to dignify its panic with the word "history."

Who can say where the history of the world and the history of an individual separate? No matter how personal our individual sense of urgency is, that urgency is amplified in a feedback effect by a world that is able neither to meet us nor to leave us alone. No one can make a separate peace. That much is clear. For there's nowhere to hide anymore. The wilderness is washed with acid rain, and human viciousness can strike in the deserts as well as in the cities. There is no land anywhere—no city, no household—that is not touched by the common tumult. One of our most pressing *personal* problems now is how to meet the astounding, intrusive, and dangerous realities presented by an electronically instant, planet-spanning environment. How do we turn the noise of information into the coherence of vision?

Plainly nobody is going to do it for us. Whether a resonant, resonating world culture evolves out of all this cacophony is strictly up to us—all of us and some of us and each of us, at one and the same time. By a culture I mean a living web of thought that contains, rather than is contained by, the particulars of the environment. For right now we are surrounded, and intruded upon, by our technological environment, and culture as we've known it has been shattered. Its pieces are still alive but there is no longer a sense of a whole. We long for, we search for, we are trying to create, a new culture that can make sense of, and give human proportion to, the technologies through which humankind is now evolving.

That's an easy thing to say and a difficult thing to live. Yet one doesn't *decide* to live out these concerns. We live, and these dilemmas come at us from the depths. There is no such thing anymore as minding your own business. And that fact is part of the nature of the problem, of the environment, and of the changes it has wrought in us.

In such a world, 3 A.M. can suddenly strike in the middle of the afternoon.

This book has been written in the hope that it might contain a few pages that could satisfy at 3 A.M. Most books today simplify a theory into an artifact and attempt to market that artifact for mass consumption. Here, there is no overall, cover-all theory applied from cover to cover. That kind of forced unity seems false to me. It is not the world we live in and I doubt that it resembles the world we're approaching. How could there be a single subject or theory for a book meant to be received by our 3 A.M. restlessness, whether that restlessness strikes early in the morning or in the brightness of afternoon? For at 3 A.M. you're apt to think of anything, and anything you think of is apt to take on numinous properties. It may be your marriage or world politics; it may be a rock'n'roll song or the homework assignment your kid showed you last night; it may be thoughts of sex or images from a movie you saw weeks or years ago; it may be memories of the sixties or fantasies of the future. All of that will be in here, as one's consciousness shifts backward and forward through a world that, in turn, shifts around and within us as we pry through ourselves.

But the book has a pattern, as all books must. That pattern is simply to begin with thoughts of the intimate life (marriage, sex); to the social life (rock'n'roll, mass movements); to media, then to history, then a vision of the present, then a vision of the future. The book makes a spiraling, circular movement, then, from the intimate outward.

That is all the unity that seemed realistic or possible to me in a world where we are so scattered and desperate.

I think of the movie *Invasion of the Body Snatchers,* and how when the townspeople fell asleep their bodies were duplicated by alien "pods" from outer space. Only if the hero and heroine could keep awake could they resist being taken over by the body snatchers. In just that way, our consciousness is in danger of being overpowered by the surrounding cacophony. We have got to keep awake till the dawn of the new culture that *must* be taking shape out of all this chaos. Or is that a rash hope? Since only the future can answer us, we must keep faith with that future.

But faith is too abstract a concept for most of us now. I like to think of it as dancing. For this is a time of tremendous movement, and dancing is the embracing of movement. Within a dance there are many changes and there is the necessity to remain centered within those changes. We dance among shadows and we cast shadows as we dance. *And something moves within our movement: the unity of the dancer with what is danced.* Such is the dance of the self with the outside world, and the dance of the self with our inner worlds. The thought dance, the love dance, the work dance—the grace we strive for, and the sense of movement that is sometimes all that keeps us alive.

Survival is a frightened word. Think of it as dancing. The new day starts at midnight. We have to dance till dawn.

A DANCE FOR YOUR LIFE
IN THE MARRIAGE ZONE

It is good knowing that glasses
are to drink from;
the bad thing is not to know
what thirst is for.

—Antonio Machado, translated
by Robert Bly

Marriage is the most dangerous form of love. Count the casualties and you know. It turns many people to stone. We all have seen that. Our society is cracking under the weight of many stone-lives. We all know that. But will we, or will we not, discover all that a man and woman can be? Marriage is not the answer, but it is the most demanding way to *live* the question.

Don't *ask* questions. Live them.

That is the unrelenting demand of an active inner life. If we shirk that demand we begin to turn to stone.

So here are speculations on a flux, a life, a dare, that I sometimes refer to as "my marriage." They are the notes of a man who, only a bit more than two years ago, joined in "wed-lock" (the phrase is not without its sinister echo) with a woman and her young son. The notes of a man who, at the time, only dimly realized that in marrying with these two others he was marrying no less than—everything.

"Everything," in Greek, is the word *pan,* and *pan* is

what they called the wildest, most elemental of the gods, the god least subject to placation—the god that was never housebroken. No wonder they sang and danced at that wedding!

Our life leads separate lives.

I am "married," as they say in this world, to Jan, who is "married" to me—"two old fuckers," as she puts it. She, forty. Me, thirty-nine. And Brendan, eleven now (her child but, as I find myself putting it in conversation, "our boy"). It is now, as I've said, two years since I married these two people and they married me—three separate acts. Three very different inner ceremonies—Jan's, Brendan's, and mine—taking place within the one ceremony that joined us. Or that symbolized our joining. For in marriage symbols often come first: first the instinct to join, then the symbolic joining, then the relentless reality of trying to join.

So far the above would be described by most systems of thought—psychological, sociological, whatever—with the phrase: "The two of them [or the three of them] are married."

A pathetically useless phrase for the description of any reality I know of. We'd best leave it behind right now. For one thing, it implies that there are only three people living in our apartment.

But, living in this small apartment, there are, to begin with, three entirely different sets of twos: Michael and Jan, Jan and Brendan, Brendan and Michael. Each set, by itself, is very different from the other, and each is different from Jan-Brendan-Michael together. But go further: Brendan-Jan-Michael having just gotten up for breakfast is a very different body politic, with different varying tensions depending on whether it's a schoolday or not, from Brendan-Jan-Michael driving home from seeing, say, *El Norte,* which is different still from driving home from *Ghostbusters,* and all of them are different from Brendan-Jan-Michael going to examine a possible school for Brendan. The Brendan who gets up at midnight needing to talk to Michael is quite different from the Brendan who, on another night, needs suddenly to talk to Jan, and both are vastly different from the Brendan who often keeps his own counsel. The Michael writing at three in the afternoon or three in the morning, isolated in a room with three desks and two typewriters, is very different from the Michael, exasperated, figuring the bills with Jan, choosing whom not to pay; and *he* in turn is very different from the half-crazed, shy drunk wondering just *who* is this "raw-boned Okie girl" moving to Sam Taylor's fast blues one sweltering night in the Venice of L.A. at the old Taurus Tavern. The Jan making the decision to face her own need to write, so determined and so tentative at once, is very different from the strength-in-tenderness of the Jan who is sensual, or the surefooted abandon of Jan dancing, or the screeching of the Jan who's had it up to *here*.

I can only be reasonably sure of several of these people—the several isolate Michaels, eight or fifteen of them, whom "I" pass from, day to day, night to night, dawn to almost-no-longer-dawn, and who at any moment in this much-too-small apartment might encounter a Jan or a Brendan whom I've never seen before, or whom I've conjectured about and can sometimes describe but am hard pressed to know.

So in this apartment, where some might see three people living a comparatively quiet life, I see a huge encampment on a firelit hillside, a tribal encampment of selves that must always be unknowable, a mystery to any brief Michael, Jan, or Brendan who happens to be trying to figure it out at any particular moment.

And *who*, on this hillside, subject to its many winds and weathers, *who* among these loyal but often nomadic manifestations of Jan, Michael, and Brendan, *who* among these people is "married"?

Some are. Some are gladly and enthusiastically married, with, as the wonderful old phrase goes, "abiding faith." Some are married but frightened, nervously married, hesitant as to their capacities, their endurance. Some are hostile to the marriage. Some are too crazy to be married. Some just go about their business, it doesn't affect them. The hostile and the crazy and the unconcerned may be in the minority (though there are days when it doesn't feel that way), yet they exist, they speak with our mouths sometimes, they break a dish now and then, they make a bad joke—they even have bad dreams. As the parts that are gladly married have their good and bad dreams.

I think of a Henry Miller line in *Tropic of Capricorn*: "The labyrinth is my happy hunting ground." I am beginning to see what he means. In this labyrinth, I have found that on days when I feel far-off from Jan, and she feels rejected, it is not Jan whom I'm rejecting at all, I am rejecting *the parts of me that feel closest to her*. That is a very different bowl of gumbo. It indicates a very different sense of, and object of, responsibility.

And I can only guess, yet, at how many Jans there are whom I haven't yet seen naked. They are the "other women" I've been interested in since I met her. As there are Michaels *I* haven't encountered yet, and who only come to life, surprising me, in "her" presence, in the presence of some Jan or other.

I *feel* a leader to all my selves whom I call "I." It was *his* idea, this marriage! Most of the others cheered him on, a few tried to shout him down. But always this whole motley crew is in my consciousness, in all its motliness, when "I" say, "I am married."

There have been times during our marriage when I have heard all our inner people laugh at once. That is marvelous. And nights when they have all rested within the same sleep. (That is more rare by far.) And days when this entire hillside of selves seems to follow "the three of us" down the street as though a great festival is taking place, and only we know of it, yet its psychic exuberance "adds its light to the sum of light" (in the words of one Billy Kwan). This luminous, virtually religious sense of one's inner life radiating into and nourishing the outer, wider world—I have felt it before, but never so strongly as in the context of this thing we rather lamely name "marriage." And the converse: the sense of dread when I feel us failing, not only the dread of the private failure but the sense that we are failing more than ourselves, that we are failing a world that needs us not to fail. Failing not the crumbling world that is, but a world that some of us feel is struggling to be.

I think of the Sioux medicine man Lame Deer when, as an old man, he cried on a hilltop to his gods for a sign that he had not entirely failed them. That sense is not dead in all of us, though we may be shy to speak of it in ourselves and suspicious of others who do. It applies to marriage in the sense that marriage doesn't only join two people, it links their inner quests—the quest of each to share in, and build on, the sense of *becoming* in the world, the feeling that this era is struggling to transform itself into another, more fulfilling era. If only one of a married pair can succeed in taking part in this transformation, both will feel a hollowness.

There are many who are not interested in contributing to the world's transformation, but there are also many for whom such concern is an enormous, if often unadmitted, pressure, and we live in a society that hardly names this feeling, much less honors it. But even if one person in a marriage feels this dimension, the marriage takes on the burden of the concern whether named or not.

This is one of the many ways that a "relationship" can feel so much more free. A relationship is defined as it goes along, with a lot of subtle and not-so-subtle negotiations as to what is and what isn't the other's business. Inner quests may, or may not, be part of that negotiation, whichever choice or compulsion dictates. The special thrill of a "relationship" is to select one or two (rarely more) of one's many selves, and play them out with someone who is doing the same. Sometimes the self being lived out in the relationship is shallow, or wonderful but severely limited, and the relationship ends quickly; sometimes it goes deeper, so that as time goes on more of one's inner selves participate, coming into the presence of both relating I's. A serious relationship usually ends when there are more secret selves participating than your mutual intentions can bear to accommodate.

A marriage puts you in a very different existential position. A man and a woman, in a marriage, are not offering each other only their favorite, *or* most convenient, *or* most needy selves to partake of. You marry everything, like it or not. If you're living together and not married, it is still not quite the same—though there is a great deal invested, the door is still metaphorically open. Whereas marriage puts a lot more pressure on the psyche, because whether or not people say "till death do us part," thousands of years of heritage have made the vow implicit. This is what marriage *means* in our collective consciousness, if not in our modern ceremonies, even now. So if we get married yet are still trying to follow the ways of a relationship, we feel undermined by the massive cultural vow we have ingested without wanting to. We feel closed in. Sooner or later, we feel dread.

Jan and I let the vow stand, said it out loud with our joined voices, as though to let our inner tribes of selves know what they were in for: "till death do us part." We instinctively felt what we began both instantly and painfully to share: that, willingly or unwillingly, we had each married *all* of the other, including parts yet un-guessed at.

Marriage *is* this inclusive act, like it or not. You will not make it something else by saying that you want it to be something else. You will not make it something else by *believing* it should be something else. Life is not so simple. The psyche, collectively whole yet enormously varied within you, is not so easily contained. The very fact of *being* married will act as the catalyst to make your psyches both the subject and the object of the mar-riage. You can face this, and feel as though you're lead-ing a dangerous, even adventurous life; or you can avoid it, and gradually feel more and more unanswered by the presence of your mate.

When two people "get involved," each usually has a clear (if usually nonverbal) idea of what he or she needs for the next stage of his or her growth. Virtually every serious relationship or marriage is a partially conscious means by which this "next stage" is achieved, is grown. Crisis time comes when one or both of them have pretty much exhausted this more-or-less-intended stage of growth in the other and are trying to figure out if they can accompany each other through yet another signifi-cant stage. We are living in a society in which there are few things more rare than two people accompanying each other through more than one significant run of growth.

The idea of marriage flies in the face of this. It is, depending on your viewpoint, a gallantly or foolishly un-realistic challenge to one's own future. Looked at this way, it's a damned silly way to treat yourself. Fortu-nately or unfortunately, there is a phenomenon we've not yet alluded to which short-circuits these consider-ations. It is referred to somewhat vaguely as *love*.

We love before we know. Love comes first, and in

order to answer its questions we have to love further. The fling turns into an affair, the affair turns into a relationship, the relationship turns into a marriage. For many people today the process of the relationship has been the first stage of growth; marriage is then an attempt at a second stage. Then a sad thing often happens: instead of really trying to stake out a further unknown territory, many try to adapt how they've grown already (the first stage) to what they feel are the conventions of marriage. This is usually an unmitigated disaster.

As it happened, Jan and I went straight from fling into marriage. We decided to marry within ten days of meeting each other. This saved us the relationship stint of getting to not-know each other, which usually and sadly consists of people trying out their various selves on one another, compulsively and/or intentionally, testing for commitment. That's necessary for one stage of life, but like many people our age we had each done that many times. We decided: this time no tests. Dance to the music.

Marry it.

Were we marrying each other or marrying the impulse? *Good question.* A question that can only be answered after it's too late. Fine. For love is nothing if it's not faith. Nothing.

When Brendan was born, almost nine years before Jan and I met, Jan had sent out announcements with that old blues refrain:

> *Baby I learned to love you*
> *Honey 'fore I called*
> *Baby 'fore I called your name*

Love often occurs "in this wise," as the old phrase goes. As though love is *for* "calling the name." And certainly "to be loved" is to feel one's name called with an inflection that one has never heard before.

So we found ourselves sending out wedding invitations that went:

> *Come on over*
> *We ain't fakin'*
> *Whole lotta shakin' goin' on*

Odd, now, to think how small a sense of foreboding we had at that Jerry Lee Lewis verse—though we've only "come to blows" (revealing old phrase, isn't it, with its odd sense of formality?) once, and she struck first, broke my glasses, and I hit her then, one time, and she slumped against the wall, both of us feeling so soiled and ugly and wrong. How many bitter, gone grandmothers and grandfathers stood in the room just then, cackling their satisfaction at our shame? Hers, Irish; mine, Sicilian. Both of them traditions that did not teach us to forgive. To learn to forgive is to break with an unforgiving past.

Pause at the word: "for-give." "For-to-give." Forgiveness is such a gift that "give" lives in the word. Christianist* tradition has tried to make it a meek and passive word; turn the other cheek. But the word contains the active word "give," which reveals its truth: it involves the act of taking something of yours and handing it to another, so that from now on it is theirs. Nothing passive about it. It is an exchange. An exchange of faith: the faith that what has been done can be undone or can be transcended. When two people need to make this exchange with each other, it can be one of the most intimate acts of their lives.

One thing that forgiveness is, is a promise to *work* at the undoing, at the transcending. Marriage soon

---

*Following the lead of James Hillman's work, I'm going to use "Christianism" in place of "Christianity" and "Christianist" in place of "Christian" wherever possible in an attempt to get around the enormous bias for the religion built into our very language.

enough gives all concerned the opportunity to forgive. There have been enough broken chairs, broken plates— and one broken typewriter, my beloved old Olympia portable manual, that I'd had since high school and smashed myself—to testify to how desperate can be the joined desperations of all the Michaels, Jans, and Brendans. Whole *lotta* shakin' goin' on, and on and on, and sometimes when you are trying to break through the hardened crusts inside you and inside each other, some dishes and typewriters and furniture might go in the process.

The most odious aspect of goody-goody, I'm-OK-you're-OK dialogues is their failure to recognize that sometimes you have to scream, slam doors, break furniture, run red lights, and ride the wind even to *begin* to have the words to describe what is eating you. Sometimes meditation and dialogue just can't cut it. Sometimes "it" just plain needs "cutting"—or at least a whole lotta shakin'. Anyone afraid of breaking, within and without, is in the wrong marriage. Let it all go. Let the winds blow. Let's see what's left in the morning.

And *that* is "the solace of marriage"—a phrase I've heard in several contexts, but am otherwise unable to comprehend. The discovery of what is unbreakable among all that's been broken. The discovery that union can be as irreducible as solitude. The discovery that people must share not only what they *don't* know about each other, but what they *don't* know about themselves.

Sharing what we know is a puny exercise by comparison.

And did I say there were only myriads of Jans, Brendans, and Michaels encamped in the firelit cavern that appears to be an inexpensive old wood-frame duplex south of Santa Monica Boulevard in Los Angeles? Life is not so simple as even that. What about the raging mob we refer to, politely, as "the past"? Nothing abstract about "the past." What has marked you is still marking you. There is a place in us where wounds never heal, and where loves never end. Nobody knows much about this place except that it exists, feeding our dreams and reinforcing and/or haunting our days. In marriage, it can exist with a vengeance.

Bloody, half-flayed, partly dead, naked, tortured, my mother really does hang on a hook in my closet, because she hangs on a hook in me. Occasionally I have to take her out and we do a rending dance, tearing each other bloody as we go, and the stuff splashes happily all over—all over Jan, several of the many Jans, and several of the many Brendans, and then run for the hills, my dears, for I am in my horror.

One of my several, my insistent, horrors.

We are all, every one of us, full of horror. If you are getting married to try to make yours go away, you will only succeed in marrying your horror to someone else's horror, your two horrors will have the marriage, you will bleed and call that love.

My closet is full of hooks, full of horrors, and I *also* love them, my horrors, and I know they love me, and they will always hang there for me, because they are also good for me, they are also on my side, they gave so much to *be* my horrors, they made me strong to survive. There is much in our new "enlightened" lexicon to suggest that one may move into a house that doesn't have such a closet. You move into a such a house and think everything is fine until after a while you start to hear a distant screaming, and start to smell something funny, and realize slowly that the closet is there, alright, but it's been walled over, and just when you need desperately to open it you find yourself faced with bricks instead of a door.

In our cavern on this hillside in this apartment, there is quite a closet, where my hooks hang next to Jan's, and to Brendan's—it's amazing how many you can accumulate at the mere age of eleven—which are also there for their good and harrowing reasons.

This is one reason it's so odd to "see the parents." Can't comment on marriage and fail to mention the in-laws. Odd to see them, because you've seen them already hanging on hooks in your closet, and the beings splayed on those hooks are so removed from these aging, well-intentioned, confused souls who are the actual people. Actual, older people who are powerless, really, because they cannot act in their own names any longer. The past acts through them, no matter what they try. All they can do is hope to change that past. That is, to transmute its effects. Which is not impossible, but is so very rare.

So it is, as I say, odd to see your mate's parents because you know them already, intimately, as archetypes in your mate's sleeps. To assure this archetype that, yes, you really do love her fried chicken, is to enter a realm of comedy in which even the Marx Brothers might be frightened to cavort.

And so the horrors and the joys of what we foolishly call "our pasts"—we would more accurately call them "our sleeps"—blend, and we live the strengths and lacks of what we were, and that also is marriage. "Your people will become my people," goes the old vow, and it is inescapable in the sense that I am speaking of.

For a marriage to be a marriage, these encounters do not happen compulsively or accidentally, they happen by intention. I don't mean that the encounters with all the various selves and ghosts are planned (that's not possible, though they can sometimes be consciously evoked); I mean that this level of activity is recognized as part of the quest, part of the responsibility each person has for him/herself and for the other.

Which is the major difference between the expectations of a marriage and a relationship. My experience of a relationship is two people more or less compulsively playing musical chairs with each other's selected inner

archetypes. My tough street kid is romancing your
honky-tonk angel. I am your homeless waif and you are
my loving mother. I am your lost father and you are my
doting daughter. I am your worshiper and you are my
goddess. I am your god and you are my priestess. I am
your client and you are my analyst. I am your intensity
and you are my ground. These are some of the more gar-
ish of the patterns. Animus, anima, bopping on a seesaw.

These hold up well enough while the archetypal
pairings behave. But when the little boy inside him is
looking for the mommy inside her and finds instead on
this particular night a sharp-toothed analyst dissecting
his guts? When the little girl inside her is looking for
the daddy inside him, and finds instead a pagan worshiper who wants a goddess to lay with, which induces
her to become a little girl playacting a goddess to please
the daddy who's really a lecherous worshiper and . . . little girls can't come. Or if a woman is attracted to a ma-
cho-man who is secretly looking to be mothered: when a
man's sexual self is in the service of an interior little boy
it's not surprising that he can't get it up or comes too
quick. Or they're really not *there* at all, they're mastur-
bating, really, men in their little-boy psyches for whom
the real woman is just a stand-in; while the woman who
happens to be in the same bed, an extension of their
masturbation, is wondering why even though the moves
are pretty good she doesn't really feel slept with. And
why he turns away so quickly when it's done.

On the other hand, teachers fuck pupils with excitement, analysts fuck clients with abandon, and people
seeing each other, in bed, as gods and goddesses light up
the sky—but the psyche is a multiple and a shifting entity, and none of these compatible pairings hold stable
for long. The archetypal mismatches soon begin, and
then it's a disaster of confrontations that can take years
not even to sort out (it would be *worth* years to get it all

sorted out) but simply to exhaust itself and fail. And then the cycle starts all over again with someone else.

My experience of a marriage is that all these same modes are present, but instinctively or consciously it becomes a case of two people running down each other's inner archetypes, tackling them, seducing them, cajoling them, waiting them out, making them talk, 'fessing up to them, running *from* them, raping them, falling in love with some, hating others, getting to know some, making friends with some, hanging some in the closet on each other's hooks—hooks on which hang fathers, mothers, sisters, brothers, other loves, idols, fantasies, maybe even past lives, and *true mythological consciousnesses* that sometimes come to life within one with such force that we feel a thread that goes back thousands of years, even to other realms of being.

All of this is what we "marry" in the other, a process that goes on while we manage to earn a living, go to the movies, watch television, go to the doctor, walk on the Palisades, drive to Texas, follow the election, try to stop drinking, eat too much Häagen-Dazs.

Obviously, if two people are completely oblivious to this level of life, they cannot live consciously on this level of life. If *one* person is oblivious, life can't be lived at this pitch. (Though this is a level that works its ways *whether or not you're aware of it;* it is, in Lawrence Durrell's phrase, "the life of your life," and most people thrash around on its surface, the puppets of their needs, hardly guessing.) If two people are in competition with each other then this sort of responsibility toward each other's inners cannot occur. (This sense of women and men in competition is a common notion now, and I don't necessarily mean career competition, nor do I mean that people pursuing the same careers are necessarily in competition.) Nor can life be lived at this pitch if one person is trying to tame the other. Nor can it occur if people are trying to live up to an ideology, whether it is a Christianist ideology, an it's-time-to-live-happily-ever-after ideology, or a "liberated man/liberated woman" ideology. Sooner or later your wife is going to come prancing through the living room with the flayed undead carcass of her ex-husband or her lost father, and you're going to be slipping on their psychic slime, and watch out, mama's boy, that bitch wants to *dance,* to dance with her horror, and you better be able to give her something more *present* than a Marxist or New Age or fundamentalist ideology.

With volatile people much of this is surprisingly out front, given the eyes to see it. But the same stuff goes down with sedate, quiet couples. It just happens more undercover, and is harder to spot. Worse than harder to spot, it's harder to feel, because it's not so specific. But it is, after all, the mannerly Anglo-Saxon peoples who started a new religion partly to institute divorce and who fought hundreds of years of religious wars partly to keep a Protestantism that allowed divorce. It is their descendants in America who have largely made divorce a legal institution. Even so, roughly a third of the murders that occur in America take place within families. These forces can remain unknown, but they are never unfelt.

Statistically, there are many more violent crimes per capita within families in the United States than there are in any other nation. When you consider that this is the nation most responsible for the stability of the world's economy and that this nation—*these families*—elect leaders who have the power to end all life on this planet, you may agree with me that this issue of what might constitute a dynamically sane marriage is as crucial as wars in the Third World, economic justice, and nuclear survival. These situations are certainly and umbilically linked.

Which brings me to my main point: *There may be no more important project of our time than displacing the Christianist fiction of monopersonality.* This fiction is the notion that each person has a central and unified "I" which determines his or her acts. "I" have been writing this to say that I don't think people experience life that way. I do think they experience *language* that way, and hence are doomed to speak about life in structures contrary to their experience. This contributes to the pervasive and impotent sense of bafflement that very quickly can turn to violence.

Marriage, for instance. Our conventional concept of marriage came out of the life of feudal Europe, a life so strictured that it likely evoked only two or three of the selves within one person on any given day. The higher thinkers and artists of the time knew most of what we know about the psyche—their cathedrals prove it. And the worshipers had a virtual chorus line of saints they could react to with their various selves. But they worked six days a week, they went to bed at dark, they were married and often had families by the time they were fifteen, and their life span was often not much more than forty years. Except for the church and the holidays, there were next to no external stimuli outside of the daily grind. We are still speaking their language. We are still structuring thoughts—envisioning reality—with their grammar. But our lives are totally different.

Modern society *can be defined as a barrage of stimuli haphazardly evoking many conflicting selves daily in every individual.* These selves—as our art proves, from the Pyramids to Homer, from the Bible to Chartres and the present—have always been alive and only restlessly asleep in our race; now they've been awakened by a cacaphony of simultaneous and constant calls. Yet most Western thought—most psychology, socio-economic theory (both leftist and rightist), feminist theory, to name a few—labor under a model of the human personality as outdated for contemporary life as Newtonian physics was to relativity physics.

This meditation on marriage has been based on another model of the psyche entirely: *the notion that we have not a single center, but several centers; that each of these centers may act independently of each other; and that each center has in turn various active aspects, or shadings; and that all these centers are unified more by an atmosphere, an overall mood and rhythm, than by anything as stolid as a "central command post" called an "ego" or whatever.*

There *is* a central awareness; but awareness is not control. Confusing awareness with control is the mistake Western thought has been making for centuries. It is tempting to call this awareness many things—one's ego, one's character, one's personality—but those words are just screens onto which we can project what we most need and want to be, projections that change depending on which inner self we are expressing and acting out at the moment. A new model of the psyche must take this unifying urge into account, and presume that its impulse is fundamental to us; but a new model of the psyche must go beyond this impulse and envision the inner multiplicity which this impulse strains to unify. It's as though the reason this impulse is so strong is that there's so *much* within the individual to unify. *For too long Western thought has mistaken the impulse to unify for the entity itself (the psyche) that needs such an impulse because of its very multiplicity.* The central "I" is not a fact, it's a longing—the longing of all the selves within the psyche that are starving because they are not recognized.

This notion is certainly not original with me. You can find it, in various forms, in the novels of Doris Lessing and Lawrence Durrell, in the teachings of the Sufis and the Zens, in the art of Picasso and Bosch, in the poems of Ovid and Lorca, in the writings of Gurdjieff

and Laing and Jung and Marie-Louise von Franz and
James Hillman. Here is a passage of Laing's *Politics of
Experience* that gets at it in terms similar to, and pos-
sibly clearer than, mine:

> *Consider the metamorphoses that one
> man may go through in one day as he moves
> from one mode of sociality to another—family
> man, speck of crowd dust, functionary at an
> organization, friend. These are not simply
> different roles: each is a whole past and
> present and future, offering different options
> and constraints, different kinds of closeness
> and distance, different sets of rights and obli-
> gations, different pledges and promises.*
>
> *I know of no theory of the individual that
> fully recognizes this. There is every tempta-
> tion to start with a notion of some supposed
> basic personality, but halo effects are not
> reducible to one internal system. The tired
> family man at the office and the tired busi-
> nessman at home attest to the fact that people
> carry over, not just one set of internal objects,
> but* various internalized social modes of be-
> ing, *from one context to another. (Laing's em-
> phasis.)*

My description, as compared to Laing's, is—well,
more Catholic than Protestant, more the Tarot than the
I Ching. No matter. The important thing—as important,
I believe, as relativity proved to be; indeed this may be
the only way we can cope with relativity—is that many
are at the beginning of a theory of personality that will
gradually overwhelm the monopersonality model that
still warps the West's vision, for that is a model as
inadequate to a more accurate perception and experience of what we are as Newton's mechanical-universe

model was inadequate to charting any but the grossest, most obvious movements of the universe.

It is crucial to every form of human effort that we forge a model of the psyche that is closer to our hour-to-hour experience, because, in the long run, as a society, we can share only what we can express. Our institutions don't match our experience, and that is causing chaos on a world scale. It is likely that these institutions won't match our experience until we can articulate our experience in more accurately contemporary terms. Marriage is only one of those institutions.

Remember Charlie Chaplin and Paulette Goddard walking away down the road at the end of *Modern Times*? They're broke. They're vulnerable to any circumstance. Their walk is almost a dance. They're on their way. That's the image of marriage that keeps *this* married man going. For us, marriage is a journey toward an unknown destination. The "solace" possible is to be reasonably certain you're not going backward, not uselessly covering the same terrain again and again, not circling one another in one place.

Sometimes, of course, you find yourself walking backward, facing where you've been, blind to where you're going—interesting, disorienting, and infuriating, but it happens. Sometimes you're pushing each other over impossibly steep, sheer terrain. The metaphors, from this point on, could be as endless as the road. The important thing seems to be to not kid ourselves about the destination. We don't know it. It is not "security," which is impossible to achieve on planet Earth in the latter half of the twentieth century. It is not "happiness," by which we generally mean nothing but giddy forgetfulness about the dangers of all our lives together. It is not "self-realization," by which people usually mean a separate peace. There is no separate peace. "While there is a soul in prison, I am not free," said Eugene

Debs once upon a time, and that goes for all sorts of prisons, psychic as well as walled, and it's as true if you're married as if you're not. Getting married won't stop it from being true. Until we accept the fact that technology has married us all, has made us one people on one planet, and until we are more courageous about that larger marriage, there will be no peace, and the destination of any of us, married or not, will be unknown.

The mission of marriage in our age is to live out the question, How far can men and women go together? Because they must go wherever it is they are going *together*. There is no such thing as going alone. Given the doings and the structure of the psyche, there is no such thing as *being* alone. If you are the only one in the room, it is still a crowded room.

Marriage creates a field between two people in which these issues can be lived out, lived through. This, of course, happens or tries to happen willy-nilly in any serious connection between people; but it is the focus and inner mission of marriage. That is the danger of marriage, and its very danger is its hope and the measure of its importance.

In this sense, marriage is on the cutting edge of this culture now as it may never have been before. What men and women may or may not become is being tested in its crucible.

So . . . I get up to look for matches for my cigar before I re-read all this and send it in, and Jan says, "I hope it's not like the first draft."

"What do you mean?"

"I hope they know we *laugh* sometimes."

In laughter my writing is weakest, and she knows this better than anyone.

"We laugh a lot," I say.

"Not in the first draft."

NOTES ON THREE ERECTIONS

If you're ever in Los Angeles, drive to the end of Wilshire and face the sea. Something stands in your way—something that purports to be a statue of Saint Monica herself. As to who Saint Monica was, the statue gives no clue; bullet-shaped, the stone stands without expression or gesture, giving nothing, asking nothing, and seeming to absorb any light or glance with no return reflection. The piece has an air of wanting to be ignored and it gets its wish. It is as though the sculptor had been frightened by his own idea. Plainly, whether he knew it or not, his idea had been to sculpt the image of a woman onto a phallus.

Walk around the statue. From behind, it is an erection plain and simple and only slightly abstract. From the front, a woman of minimal lines has taken her place within, or on the surface of, the penis. The conception is so phallic that once seen this way it is difficult to see it any other way, if indeed there was any other.

I think of lines from the poet John Yau:

Memory going one way
the body another. Something wedged in
between.

This minor sculptor was wedged in between, exercising
his limited gifts while all but unbeknownst to him his
psyche went back, far back, to the Neolithic era and
beyond. In that day, it was not unusual to sculpt images
of the Great Goddess onto carvings of the erect penis.

There were no gods then. Only goddesses. It would
be thousands of years before the race would begin to
sculpt male gods. Neolithic humans apparently felt little
maleness in divinity. Or put it another way: intense
spirituality brought forth from them female images. Or
another: for a long, long time in the youth of humankind, flashes of the spirit were felt primarily with the
feminine aspects of both men and women.

We can only guess at what they meant by carving
the Great Goddess onto the cock. Was it the Goddess
tattooing her claim onto the very maleness of men? Was
it the man finding a passion in sexuality that couldn't be
wholly satisfied by the physical, a yearning in him for
something of the spirit to mix with his passion? Or was
it the meeting not only of the divine and the physical,
but of the masculine and the feminine *cohabiting the*
cock itself? An idea to reckon with. If the cock is also
feminine, then where does "feminism" hide and where
does "macho" run?

We have made such easy distinctions in our society,
and they suit so conveniently our prejudices of the moment. But simplicities like "feminine or masculine" and
"straight or gay" are shallow beside these ancient
stones. Robert Bly cites experiments in England that
show that if a man suckles an infant regularly, after a
few weeks his breasts will start to give milk. That secret
was there all the while in those crude stone statues of
goddesses on phalluses.

For us these can't be statues of precise meaning and shouldn't be. "Precision" in such things means to focus on one possibility while ignoring others. Rather these are statues of the cock as a metamorphic possibility—a capacity to leap from meaning to meaning within the flesh itself. Very different from the singular thrust that "erection" means for us. Think of it rather as raw goddess-stuff and raw god-stuff that, like water from a fountain, hovers in a pillar at the height of its flight, keeping its huge erect form while engaged in continuous transformation.

But these are just words circling the image. Once the image gets into your consciousness it has its own life and doesn't need explanations so much as it needs to be savored, remembered. What is important in the image of the goddess etched onto the penis is that male and female energy meet in the cock without either one losing essence or form. And the first thing to "do" with such an image is to realize that we already embody it, no matter what we've forgotten and what we hide from ourselves. The erection, which the feminist and the macho alike have seen as such a one-note, one-purpose organ, is less a sword than a wand.

So, as an unknowing representative of ancient consciousness, that rather sad statue on Ocean and Wilshire transcends itself and becomes a piece of psychic archeology. We have many a neolithic stone in our heads. One of Freud's first and most important discoveries was that "in the subconscious there is no Time." Jung extrapolated from individuals to the entire race, using Freud's insight as a passageway down which he went to find the collective unconscious and his demonstration that ancient archetypes of thought live their own lives through and with us. Not that we are possessed, but that we are connected, and that the rhythms of our wills are often ancient dances.

Take that piece of stone, sandblast out "Santa Monica" and chisel in "Erect Male Member, Featuring Goddess" (marvelous word, *member,* a member of the group that is the person, a member both connected and somehow independent)—*then* people would stop and contemplate that statue. Or laugh at it—which would at least be a beginning, a step away from the monolithic notion of male sexuality in which we're all, men and women, equally trapped.

Put the Neolithic phallus beside another phallic image, this one some 17,000 years old: a painting in the innermost of the ancient caves at Lascaux, France. Deep in what is considered to be Lascaux's holiest vault, a wall painting depicts a bison hovering over a stick figure of a man with a birdlike head and an erection. This is thought (by such as Joseph Campbell and William Irwin Thompson) to be the earliest known depiction of a shaman. The birdlike head is thought to be his mask. His erection is taken as a sign that he is dreaming—for men very often get erections while dreaming. The shaman, who is reclining, is thought to be dreaming of the image of the bison that hovers over him.

Here again is an image to remind us of what the sexual deliberations of the last twenty years, mostly feminist and gay, have largely ignored: that an erect cock has more meanings than sex; that the act of ranging through realms of the psyche, which we call "dreaming," and which is how the psyche generates its images into composite sequences to give us signs, this act, too causes erections. In fact, given the time we spend sleeping, it may not be too outrageous to say that dreaming causes *most* erections. Which is to say that there is something of the dream in every erection. The dream's complexity, its lineage, its imagery, and its metamorphic possibilities.

Go further and say: every erection is, in effect, a

dream. It rises from a dream, it is sustained by a dream, it seeks to penetrate a dream. Rilke wondered often in his poetry whether lovers ever truly touched. There are the man and the woman and all that each is and all that they want to be and all that they pretend to be and all that they think they are and all that they seek in each other, and all of that is present in *every* coupling, making every coupling a veritable orgy! And the link through which all these aspects pass, the connector, is the erection. Again: the wand.

The shaman sleeping his vision in Lascaux, his vision seeming to hover above his hard-on, sleeps in us as well. We may have forgotten him, we may not like to think about him, but he dreams on, and his cock is also ours. What has happened to us, denying these subtleties of the cock? We've attributed all the mystery to the cunt, that's what. Projected it there, and then resented it there, because we had so little of our own. But the cunt has its own great claim on mystery, it doesn't need the inflation we men give it by denying what's inherently within us. It's a sorry way to be men, to live without our own physical mystery.

Who can say how much this denial's hurt us? And who can say how much it's wounded our world? Sexism is the need to suppress the women we secretly fear, and why do we fear them unless it is the suspicion that they contain mysteries, and therefore powers, that we can't equal? And while the mysteries aren't only sexual, the emblems of these mysteries certainly are. I am saying that men would have much less to fear of women if we were open to the equally sexual emblems of our equally mysterious natures.

In white men, this denial has been a cause of another horror: the racism that has plagued the world in the 500 years that European whites and their American descendants have sought to dominate it. We have looked upon black bodies, especially male black bodies, with utter horror for half a millenium, and why? Christianism has taught us that the body, per se, is wrong and that to deny the body is right. Christianism has saturated us with an iconography in which white is good, dark is not. It was a program for hate. When we came upon peoples who were not only dark but who moved with a suppleness that whites had denied in themselves—who were *in* their evil bodies without denial—then everything we'd denied in ourselves came to face us. It was unbearable. For many, it still is. Rather than waken the sleeping shaman within our own cave, we ravaged a world.

We enslaved and hated and killed with the power of our own impacted mysteries. We were mad. A thousand years of denial had made Europeans restless enough to leave their homelands, and ruthless enough to seek mastery of everything. Peoples who hadn't denied as much, who were content with their homeland, and who wanted not mastery but the slow evolution of their traditions—these couldn't stand against the white jihad. We were like a horrible dream of the sleeping shaman within us.

He slept but was not dead. He has been stirring for a while now, half-awake, opening his eyes. In some men he speaks. In some he dances. He has enough mystery of his own, enough power, enough darkness in his light, not to fear or envy anybody else's. The ancients of Lascaux knew that you had to crawl down and down and down through the stone in yourself to find him, and this is something some of us are painfully learning to do. One thing that he will teach us is the ways of the wand.

To find the third erection, drive down the eastern coast of Mexico, where there are few Anglo tourists, and stop in one of the little towns about midway between Brownsville and Tampico. There are no flashy sights to see. These are simply working towns. Walk around in the early evening and go into one of the workingmen's bars (if you're a man—females aren't approved of here).

There's usually a pool table, sometimes someone playing music, or a TV or radio. Mostly it's just a bar, no frills, just men drinking beer and talking. But on the walls you will often see two images. One is a crude wall-sized drawing of a *Playboy*-pinup-like woman (often not a Mexican woman) tied down, bloody with torture, being raped by some huge man, often an Aztec-like Indian. On the other wall, sometimes the opposite wall, there is likely to be a brightly colored drawing of a flying cock—often a winged and phoenix-like phallus rising out of flames.

Those genial, grizzled, work-tired and sweaty men drinking their *cerveza* are living between those two images. Most of us are. The incongruity between the men and the pictures would be almost comical if we didn't know that those pictures are painted on the inside of their skulls as well. On the one hand you admire how unselfconscious they are about it all—how readily accessible those images are in their lives. Most supposedly sophisticated peoples have to dig a lot harder to unearth the same material. On the other hand, you have to feel for how without consciousness they are—bearing the weight of a culture that is somehow both tumultuous and changeless, exhausted by a struggle for survival that reduces them to a dependence on symbols that make it more difficult for them to survive. They drink their beer every night under the images that could help free them if they weren't too leaden with fatigue—in every sense, on every level—to think beyond what they've been given, to feel beyond what they know.

The winged cock: is it a symbol of disembodied sexuality that will claim no responsibility and that wants no love, hence justifying and making possible the torture on the opposite wall? Or is it an unconscious counterpart to an equally unconscious image of torture, a vivid and poignant image of male sexuality trying to transcend the very walls on which the pictures are painted?

Both, I suspect. Here is the price of the macho code, yes, but that is too easy to say. What creates a macho code? Here is a household matriarchy governed economically by a societal patriarchy that emphasizes being "a strong man" while denying men power over their lives or their work. Which means that there is no place for these men to be men. In work they are mules. And the home is the woman's domain. And so they are powerless except in their bars. And there they have no power but to play games, to talk, to pose, to get drunk, to fantasize. They don't paint pictures of their bosses and politicos being buggered because they would be arrested or shot, and most of them are too savvy to let themselves be so easily murdered. They can only burst their limits in that other place where they feel powerless, their homes. Their families. Their women. Their children. It is a miserable and vicious circle—no different from North America's ghetto bars and redneck bars. It is only that in Mexico it is more stark and less self-conscious, and both those qualities give us these wall paintings.

The rape is a fantasy of power over the women, the home, obviously; yet on another level this usually Aztec rapist is torturing an almost-white Mexican woman, so this is also a fantasy of the ancient spirit of Mexico making Europe and the United States pay for their sins. It is no wonder that this is the only place where these men can relax; it is the only place where their rage is expressed honestly, however passive that honesty has to be.

And the winged cock flying from the flames—the one that I remember most vividly was so brightly colored, and its lines were so full of energy and movement, that you couldn't mistake its joy. Here was every metamorphic possibility set loose. Here was the rush of wings a man can sometimes feel in his pants. (Not to mention how a woman may want to feel it flying within her.) And here was the flaming psyche it rises from. Here was the wand in its power. And, yes, that power must be grounded to be genuine, to be able to replenish itself. But we separate too easily the idea of being grounded and the "pure" idea, as the psychologists would call it, the idea of flying free. I think of how these concepts live together in a verse of Robert Bly's:

> *A dream of moles with golden wings*
> *Is not so bad; it is like imagining*
> *Waterfalls of stone deep in mountains.*
> *Or a wing flying alone beneath the earth.*

A flight only occurs, after all, in relation to a ground— and what else is an erection but a rising, a flight, and then a settling down to ground again? Bly's "wing flying alone beneath the earth" is such a resonant and satisfying image because within it the contradictions exist without needing to be put to rest by some compromise between them, some resolution. There are nights of love-making that are like flying beneath the earth.

The penis, which offers the same passage to piss and jism, to dead waste and creation itself, never resolves its contradictions. That's apparently not what it's here for. The wand, far from being the monolith the West has made of it, has many lives that exist at once; its flesh is a medium of paradox, potent by virtue of the possibilities it calls forth.

There has been much talk, in these eighties of ours, about masculinity and about the possibility of a masculine movement through which men would begin describing themselves in a more full, more vital way than they yet have during the reign of Christianism. If this dialogue or movement is going to have some social force, it will have to have at its core a discussion of male sexuality, as feminism had at its core a discussion of female sexuality. I've offered these images of erections as a small part of a large beginning.

For certainly the weakest, silliest aspect of feminism—which for the most part has been an overwhelmingly beneficial movement—has been its description of male sexuality. It was a description that assumed a monolithic, monointentioned erection; it was a description that equated the ejaculation of sperm with coming. The three images here—and there obviously could have been many more—should be enough to suggest the many secret passageways within an erection. As far as the question of male "coming"—it is an immense and untried question. Ejaculation is a muscle spasm that many men often feel with virtually no sensation but the twitch of the spasm. To ejaculate is not necessarily to come. Coming involves a constellation of sensations, physical, psychic, emotional, of virtually infinite shadings. Coming may *sometimes* or *often* occur at the moment of ejaculation, when it occurs at all. *But many ejaculations for many men happen without any sensation of coming.*

Until a woman understands this she doesn't know the first thing about male sexuality.

Nor do many men. There is ample evidence in face after face that, as there are women who have never come, so there are men who have often ejaculated but never come. And they likely don't know it, as many women never knew it until a few began to be vocal about such things. These men live in a terrifying and baffling sexual numbness in which they try the right moves and say the right things but every climax is, literally, an anticlimax. It is no wonder that in time they have less and less connection with their own bodies, and are increasingly distant from the women they want to love.

Feminism has also gotten a lot of mileage out of the mistaken notion that men can't fake coming the way women can. Men can't fake the ejaculation of sperm, of course, but we can fake muscle-spasms, hip-jerks, and moans as well as any woman can. During an agonizing period of premature ejaculation, I ejaculated almost instantly upon entering but, remaining hard, I didn't let on but kept right on going through the motions, faking the muscle spasms and moans of orgasm when the woman had (or faked) her own. Several male friends, when questioned, admitted having had similar experiences.

How are men and women to know of these things when they're never spoken of, and when even in literature you can search far and wide for a worthy, complex description of what it may be for a man to come. You don't find it, for instance, in Henry Miller. He describes brilliantly how it feels to be a cock inside a cunt, to truly enter and *be* there; he describes his perceptions of women coming; and he is truly brilliant at writing of the shaman's dreaming erection—often he seems to write out of the center of those dreams themselves; but he never, in all my reading of him, gets inside his own coming. Nor does D. H. Lawrence, who is so fine at expressing the longing of the phoenix-like, winged erection. Their narratives stop before the ejaculation, pass over the experience of coming with some summary phrase, and continue after it.

Mailer gets close, once, but not in one of his novels—where, considering his aesthetics, his glossing over the issue is unconscionable. But he did it in an essay, a brief passage in his thought-sparking book *The Prisoner of Sex*. After chiding feminist writers (a brave move in 1971) for their "dull assumption that the sexual force of a man was the luck of his birth" he writes of " ... orgasms stunted as lives, screwed as mean and fierce and squashed and cramped as the lives of men and women whose history was daily torture ... comes as far away as the aria and the hunt and the devil's ice of a dive, orgasms like the collision of a truck, or coming as soft as snow, arriving with the riches of a king in costume, or slipping in the sneaky heat of a slide down slippery slopes ... "

A few sentences onward he gives one of the sentences of his life: at orgasm, he says, "the eye of your life looked back at you then. Who would wish to stare into that eye if it was poorer than one's own?"

Who indeed. We are all paying the price of such moments. We pay for our own and for each other's. Men and women alike. Yet there are times when the eye of your orgasm, the eye staring back at you, matches your own; and times when it is richer than your own, leading you on to what you may yet be.

A single suggestive passage about male orgasm in years of sexually explicit literature is a poor showing. Doubtless there are more floating about, but not many, and they're hardly known and apparently unremembered.

We men, who have never spoken of such things, are squarely to blame for the consequences of our constipated silences. What more than spasms is to be expected of our entire culture of adult men who are frightened to wear colors during business hours? The neatly knotted tie is all that's left of our desert shawl and shaman robe. Most American and European businessmen, aped by businessmen all over the world now, still walk around in the black-and-white and brown-and-white color variations of celibate monks who spent a thousand years frightened of nothing so much as of all the imagery that might rise out of an erection.

One example of a reaction to the color fear are rock stars like Prince who, for all his childish and sexist lyrics, is on the cutting edge of these issues right now because he is bringing colors back to men. Or at any rate, back to boys who will one day be men. The hot-colored styles Prince inspires reflect the spectrum of the psyche much better than gray flannel.

There are many who would like the needed innovation and advances to occur on a more sophisticated and enlightened level than, say, Prince works on. But that is a luxury we can hardly afford. We are desperate people, and must take our signs as they come, whether from a rock star, or a sullen statue on Ocean and Wilshire, or a painting in a cramped cave, or a mural in a Mexican bar. They are the work of men, and so they are ours.

The body is such an immense place. We take so long to find our ways across it. And each of us has so many bodies. Sometimes they drag behind us, and we feel encumbered and earth-laden. Sometimes they race before us, making huge decisions in our name, while we scramble to catch up—and sometimes we call that "sex." And we know so little about these things. And one of the only ways we can test the little we know is to speak of it.

WHITE BOYS DANCING

You can *say* anything, but you can't *move* any way. White people tend to think they know things if they can say them. That's the assumption at the root of our education. It's an assumption that pervades everything in Western life and has long been our standard of superiority. Yet, though pushing forty, there are still some of us who are uncomfortable at parties where people don't dance. What else is a party for?

"Watch a man move," a (white) woman I know once told me, "and you don't need to ask him his life story."

"Can you tell how he'll be in bed?" I asked. And her rap went something like: "It's fun to guess, but naw—too many things enter into *that*. You can tell if he's got *talent*, but talent doesn't mean anything—screwing's like anything else, plenty of people with talent can't *do* much. Dancing—dancing is more how you've lived and where you've been, than how you screw. We're not far enough along yet for screwing to be ... *representative*, you know? It still says most about our hang-ups. Dancing is what you *might* be when you get to where you're going. Wanna dance?"

The class of white males who've called the shots for so many years, maybe they've *said* it all—but cruise the clubs some night to watch the white boys move. They want to be there—why else would they be there? But the stiffness in the legs . . . feet that seem hardly to move by themselves, as they're hoisted up by the jerky crane of the thigh . . . arms just waggling or moving in half-hearted punchlike jerks, in accompaniment to a kind of hop . . . or flailing arms, with the torso swaying in awkward hula-hoop motions, having no more than a coincidental relation to the music . . . and the face: having to concentrate *so hard* on the little that's going on, and hardly ever smiling . . . and some shake violently, music the merest excuse, as though trying to shake life into atrophied limbs.

Which is, of course, what we're all trying to do. Maybe it's what rock 'n' roll is for.

The descriptions are painful because the process is painful. You've got to call it dancing; what else is there to call it? But if the band weren't playing, if there were no women, no booze, no late-night juices flowing—strip it all away and just watch the middle-class white boys move, and most of what you see is a desperate, rather brave effort to claim their bodies for the first time.

This ain't aerobics. With aerobics and sports the movements themselves may be challenging, but they aren't psychologically threatening. With aerobics you may or may not get healthier, but with aerobics you do not leave the world of white Christianist assumptions for other, entirely different, and possibly revolutionary ways.

For what *happens* when they start playing that music, in whatever dive or fancy joint?

It's an instant environment. One-two-three-rock—

and you're there, *in it*. The rules of your culture are changed that instant, done away with. The new rule is: you can move, and you can move any way you want to.

A very new rule, that. Not how dancing was with the twenties' Charleston, the forties' lindy, or white-folk and cowboy dancing taken without much variation from northern Europe. Those dances mimed the patterns of their cultures; specific moves, to specific rhythms, only certain moves allowed, and boy leads girl. But sometime in the fall of 1958, a couple of years after Elvis Presley's "Heartbreak Hotel" had broken the air-waves wide open for rock 'n' roll, a new kind of dancing hit the Italian slums of New York. We didn't know that blacks had been dancing like this for hundreds of years. We didn't know anybody had *ever* danced like this. The first time we saw it in our neighborhood, it was a guy we called "the Weasel"; he was dancing with the memorable Maria Tombino, doing something sexy that looked like fun and was called the slop. In the South it was called the dirty bop, sometimes the sherry bop, and often the nigger bop. It was all the same.

It was the first time we saw people dance without holding hands. With no set step. Which meant that there was no leader. We didn't articulate it that way, that's just the way it was. Weasel was picking up Maria's signals, just like Maria was picking up Weasel's. That came naturally with this kind of dancing. The improvisation, the rhythm, the intensity, the freedom, the equality: *there* was a new culture. There were the only politics that ever held *me*. There was the paradigm for something new in America that could matter.

We were just a bunch of thirteen-year-old kids. We were feeling, not thinking. But the attraction was immense, and soon we were all dancing the slop.

There was something of a slinky shuffle recognizably the slop, but you had your own riff on it or you were nobody. And your face danced as much as your feet. It wasn't the breathless concentrated look of people doing the fifties' version of the lindy (a holding-hands fast-dance that was seen on "American Bandstand"). With the slop faces were playful or bored or tough, a come-on or a come-off-it, sexy-feisty or sexy-deadpan (memories of girls with faces floating as unconcerned as the moon over bodies that undulated, rippled and bumped—and they sure didn't learn to dance that way from their mothers, yet it had somehow been there all along).

After a few months of slopping, everybody was just doing their own no-hands dance. From now on the twist, the monkey, the mashed potato, the swim, and the bump would come and go, but each dance was incorporated into that individual style which was what dancing had become.

You could move any way you wanted.

We didn't know we were doing something new in white culture. We didn't know we were rejecting maybe 3,000 years of patterned white dancing. We'd never seen a ballet with its stiff torsos and tense grace. We didn't know we were taking the principles of Isadora Duncan, Martha Graham, and Merce Cunningham—all the gurus of uptown high art—into the street or that we were getting these principles from the same place they'd gotten them, Africa and the West Indies.

Appropriately enough, the first record that Weasel and Maria slopped to was the flip side of Mickey and Sylvia's "Love Is Strange," a tune called "I'm the Monster Rock'n'Roll," in which a gravelly voice growled with great authority, "Ah'm duh mon-ster rock'n'roll, duh louder they scream duh bigger Ah grow," or words to that effect.

On the East Coast the slop-style dancing didn't get out of the slums till around 1961, when the twist caught on. Of course, the twist was as patterned as any kind of traditional dance, but in its excitement well-brought-up suburban children stopped holding hands when they danced, and they didn't start again when the twist wore off. They were dancing like us by then—or trying to. The change was permanent. Each individual dancing with each individual to a music that was their own. Thirty years later, you can go to any rock club anywhere and the dancing is fundamentally the same free-style pattern that began back then. Thirty years have developed infinite varieties, but, except for the brief lapse into disco in the late seventies, what is danced is still individualistic, still free style.

In most cultures that we honor enough to study, the dancing that everyone does—not just the dancing that the few do—has been considered of paramount, even religious, importance. If our anthropologists had discovered the same sort of change in a non-Western culture, many books would have been written about it by now. Only in a culture like ours, a culture that tries to put everything in its mouth, thinking nothing important unless it can be said—only in such a culture would such a fundamental change go virtually unheralded by the "intelligent" voices of the time.

"The Whole on high hath part in our dancing. Amen. Whoso danceth not, knoweth not what cometh to pass. Amen." So says Jesus in the Gnostic Round Dance, an early "testament" that the followers of Paul discarded when compiling the "new testament" which codified their authority. Jesus's feeling for dance does not comfort a need for centralized authority. I have also heard it translated, in much better English, as "He who doesn't dance does not know what happens."

Back in Brooklyn we were finding out what happens. Our bodies had been set loose. Still within the limits of the dance floor, yes. For only as long as the music, sure. But for the first time in the world of the Western white there was a *social form* that enabled us to be in our bodies, watch other people be in their bodies, even talk to each other through our bodies. The only limit used to be indecent exposure and that's not really a limit anymore in some places. There wasn't anything you had to learn and there weren't any standards to scare away the timid. If they were scared, they were scared of the boys, or of the girls, or of their own bodies, but not of the dance itself, because it asked nothing of them but to be danced. Here was an echo, though they didn't know it, of an old saying from Zimbabwe: "If you can talk, you can sing. If you can walk, you can dance." That was rock 'n' roll all the way. For the first time there was an accepted social form of the body that mixed both sexes, as sports never did; wasn't confined to capital-D artistic Dance in the ghetto of "art"; and didn't ape the worst patterns of the culture (like rigid steps and the boy always leads the girl).

It isn't very surprising, when looked at this way, that the rush of excitement generated by this new form of being together would gestate into a youth movement that for the next fifteen years would roll at full momentum, giving tidal-wave force to the civil-rights movement, the antiwar movement, and the feminist movement. All of those would grow like cultures in the petri dish of the unity-of-feeling (not harmony certainly, but unity) that the music and its dancing created. Even now, what is called "pop music" these days is still powerful enough to give young people an environment in which to experiment with life away from the rules and ways of their elders. And we still don't know whether other society-shaking waves may roll out from what they're doing.

This is not to defend the shallow glop that has constituted so much of rock 'n' roll/pop. But the disc jockey Alan Freed knew what he was talking about in the late fifties when he said that this was a music "destined to make history." He should have. His dance show on TV, "The Big Beat," was the first television show in the country on which blacks and whites not only appeared

together but danced together—even danced *slow* together. This was before many of our colleges and our
lunch counters were integrated. And these weren't carefully selected, acceptable blacks, or whites either. These
were street kids. There's good cause to believe that this
was the major reason the FBI and the police hounded
Freed.

And there is no need to defend rock 'n' roll against
those who complain about how loud it is and how much
noise it makes. Rock's noise has been necessary to break
through the crust of self-consciousness accumulated over
these last three thousand years. So that a place long
asleep in us would wake. In the instant environment of
rock, the literally deafening noise cancels out the rest of
the culture. The culture is based on "In the beginning
was the Word," on what can be said, but the music starts
and you can't *say* anything. It's too loud to talk by.
Either you move or you watch other people move or you
watch the performers. There's no way to go but out of
the culture and into the beat.

And remember that this music got a lot louder as it
was played more and more by suburban WASP kids. The
genres of rhythm and blues, rockabilly, and soul music
—basically poor-white and black forms, both urban and
rural—aren't all that loud. (Certainly they're no louder
than a big band of the swing era, and often not nearly as
loud.) But WASP families don't scream in their houses.
When they argue, things tend to get tensely, unbearably
quiet; screaming is taboo. So when their children play
music, they play it *loud*.

Once you go out of the society and into the beat,
transformations occur. Revelations flash, whether you
enjoy them or not. And the culture itself is seen bare in
the flash.

Watch the white boys dancing. Most white men of
the securer middle classes don't have what they call in

rock 'n' roll "the moves." They are singularly graceless. But many of the white women of the same class aren't. They move pretty good, on the whole, especially in comparison with their men. And the people who can *really* move are the street kids—poor whites and Latins as well as blacks—who invent the dances and keep them alive. The mystery, then, is: what do most middle-class white females and most street kids have in common? Because their affinity for the same moves proves that they share something which the white middle-class men don't have.

No matter what level of society a woman's from, her primary awareness right from the first is of her body. She's not necessarily conscious of this, but that doesn't matter. From her earliest memories, what she puts on her body and how it moves is how she's judged. Judged all day, pervasively, no matter how enlightened she and her friends are. Her very survival, the jobs she gets, the people who accept her, is a matter first (and most brutally) of her body. In living rooms, in the girls' room in junior high, in offices, clubs, and while crossing streets, she's looked upon and judged by men, and women, again and again and again, hundreds of times a day. As she learns the dangers of having a female body today and the effects she can produce, she learns to control the signals it sends and receives with a subtlety that is so much a part of her she rarely need think of it. Learning the power of her body, how easily she can be noticed, what a stir she may make in the air as she passes, is fundamental to her knowledge of herself. Whether she likes it or not, this awareness of her body must become so pervasive for her that it ceases to be "awareness." She simply breathes it.

No surprise then that most middle- and upper-class women look graceful on a dance floor, at least when compared to their men. Their men think about their bodies only when hurt, hungry, or horny, or in relation to the mechanics of sports or aerobics. When the music starts, with all its fluidity, they're at a loss, while the women have learned the constant dialogue between a body and its world that is called grace. The difference in the nature of the middle-class male's and female's physical experience is mind-jarring.

But out there on those mean streets, the male experience of the body is as intense as that of the female. Any male growing up on the street is always aware of one overpowering fact: at any moment he may have to fight. The street only asks one question, and asks it again and again, every day: How tough are you? How much can you take? And how do *we* know?

On the street a man's body is an object as much as a woman's. He is always being watched, or feels he is. His moves must be as minutely measured, as delicately shaded as any lady's ever were. At the extreme, your moves can get you killed or save your ass. And on the street, things can get extreme at any moment. You have to show the street, at all times, just how tough you are. And it has to be precise: too much, and somebody a lot tougher than you may feel they have to take you to keep their status; too little, and they take you for sport. You shade your moves for who you're with and where you are, and if you walk around a corner and, like the Springsteen song says, things get real quiet real fast, you shade your moves for what you think your chances are. It's a reflex. And if the girls are watching you, or you want them to watch you, you shade your moves for them. Because boys parade their sex on the street just like women do. Street kids preen. So their repertoire of stances grows. It's not surprising that when the music starts, these boys know how to move.

We are faced with a paradox no liberal will enjoy: danger makes for grace. How to explain to a technocrat that his man-child moves like a constipated aardvark because danger is part of the body's food, and his child has been starved?

So no matter where we dance to rock 'n' roll we're dancing in the street. Just like Martha and the Vandellas once sang. Or as Archie Bell and the Drells put it some twenty years ago, "We not only *sing,* we *dance* just as good as we walk!"

Not just that the toughness of rock comes from the street; or that its dances and its rhythms originate there; or that its greatest innovators and interpreters started poor and tough and streetwise; but this: when rock shouts down the culture, then the music itself is the longest of the mean streets, all sex and quest and provocative moves with a beat, and the beat goes on. A street with enough extremes to keep it interesting; a street, over the last thirty years, with jungle-dense variety; and always the tense dialogues of bodies, even when those bodies don't know what they're saying. A music that inspires the flesh in cities that deny the flesh. And doesn't an empty dance floor feel like a deserted street?

Or say that the music cut a street through the whole society, so that something of what was best in the slums and the tin-roofed shacks made its way out, uptown, and into the suburbs, the small towns, the farms, shaking up everyone, invigorating so many, and giving people who never had it before a chance to find their own body's special grace.

The bitterness is that it's a one-way street, and no gift remotely comparable or life-giving was passed back to the slums.

THE *BIG CHILL* FACTOR

The sixties. We lived their din and now we live in their shadow. Virtually every aspect of the New Right's program, both social and political, attempts to turn back what happened to us in the sixties. And everything the baby boom generation does now is seen in relation to what it did then, whether transcending the sixties or—the most damning phrase these days—"stuck in the sixties." In either case the sixties now often seem . . . embarrassing. Extreme in all things, naive, passionate, sincere, shallow, experimental, rebellious, foolish, committed, fanatic, visionary, long-haired, dope-hazed, multicolored, polymorphous perverse, apocalyptic, uprooted, uprooting, and invoking more spirits than it wanted or had guessed existed or could ever handle. The sixties were a "movement"—and we should take "movement" here to mean literally a *moving,* an enormous moving, where suddenly we were living in the biblical terms of "The last shall be first"; "Seek and ye shall find "; "What good if ye gain the world and lose your soul." As a "movement," it was both quintessentially middle-class and furiously proletarian. One thinks of Huey Newton and Bobby Seale as Greil Marcus described them in *Mystery Train,* "drawing up [the Black Panthers'] statement of aims and demands while playing Dylan's 'Ballad of a Thin Man' over and over."

> *You walk into a room and you ask*
> *Is this where it is?*
> *And somebody points to you and says It's his*
> *And you say What's mine*
> *And somebody else says Where what is*
> *And you say Oh my god am I here all alone*
> *And you know somethin's happenin'*
> *But you don't know what it is*
> *Do you*
> *Mister Jones?*

To think of that, and to think of the flower children, believing every manner of esoteric claptrap that could justify whims that had been created by a childhood of commercials preaching instant gratification—and yet they were brave enough (we forget that it took bravery) to put their flowers into the barrels of M-16s that they knew (they weren't *that* naive) could, as a last resort, be fired against them, offering love where love had never been offered, never been thought of, never been considered a possibility. For a while they seemed to know what love was. A very short while, here and there. A summer in San Francisco, a spring in New York, a concert on somebody's farm where even the redneck police were impressed with their gentleness and genuine goodwill. And then they forgot what love was, or they were overwhelmed by what everyone else already knew: that love was not enough. That love invoked complexities which only maturity could handle. They were not ready to be mature, and why should they have been? They were, above all other things, young, and they were living out their youth as nobody had ever dared.

You tend to forget just how much raw energy was loose in the air then, and you don't quite believe your own memory: that sometimes, then, for weeks on end, we actually thought (1) that we were living in the Promised Land, the New Age, the Other World, (2) that it was everything we had ever imagined it could be, and (3) that everyone was going to join us in its promise as soon as they saw how good it was. There was, hovering over everything, a possibility larger than the tedious makeshift that had been called "daily life." Simply to be alive then, to be part of the demographic bulge called the war babies, meant that *somewhere someone was working out a vision.* Somewhere people more or less your age, people who might conceivably welcome you in their effort, whom you might even run into on the street (which often happened!), were trying to *practice* whatever fool idea, passionate thought, or cosmic vision they thought themselves capable of. You yourself could be doing nothing about such things for the moment, and maybe you never had and never would, yet through some alchemy of the time somehow you were part of their hope and they were part of yours.

There were in that era intimations of a freedom so fantastic that every definition, everywhere, felt questioned by it. And didn't Janis Joplin and Mick Jagger, Jim Morrison, James Brown, and Jimi Hendrix, enact for us live onstage just what *freedom* could mean when pushed to the limits of its ecstasies and dangers? Wasn't each performance a topographical map in space-time of the lay of the psychic land at the extremes of human possibility? If you'd invented Joplin or James Brown for yourself on acid or in the workshop of sleep, you'd have thought an amazing lesson had been given you *that* trip.

The Sioux once sent young warriors to the mountains alone, and they were not to come back until they'd dreamed their names. They were protected by the instruction they'd received in how to survive and in how to interpret dreams. We had mostly had instruction in how to be like everyone else, only more successful, and in how dreams were not important. So when, as an entire generation, we made everywhere we went a mountain on which we were trying to dream our names—we were messy, out of hand, easily distracted, out of our depth, full of shit, half-assed, and in deep trouble. But all that sound and all that fury, all that silliness and all those trips imprinted on everyone who was there and on everyone who came after the notion that humankind has far more dimensions than had been admitted for a very long time. It is a simple and utterly disruptive notion. Some people have been trying to live it out and a lot of people have been trying to forget it ever since. Because once you admit it—once you *really* admit it—nothing is quite the same. And that notion, at that time, was admitted in too many ways by too many people ever to be forgotten entirely.

As it was all coming to an end I wrote a kind of note to myself which I wouldn't read again until a long time later, a fragment of clarity on a cacophonous night: *We know now that our dreams are not going to come true. Are never going to come true. We have learned that our dreams are important not because they come true, but because they take you places you would never have otherwise gone, and teach you what you never knew was there to learn.*

Some comments among several college friends, men and women active in the sixties, who have since become very comfortable:

"I feel I was at my best when I was with you people."

"When I lost touch with this group I lost

*my idea of what I should be ... At least we
expected something of each other then. I think
we needed that."*

*"I'd hate to think that it was all just—
fashion."*
"What?" another asks.
"Our commitment."

*"Sometimes I think I've put that time
down, pretended it wasn't real, just so I can
live with how I am now. You know what I
mean?"*

*"I think I've been too slow to realize that
people our own age, with histories just like
ours, having gone through all the same stuff,
could be dishonest and back-stabbing sleaze-
balls."*

The above quotes are from the most sustained, coherent scene in a film called *The Big Chill,* written and
directed by one Lawrence Kasdan. It came at a point in
Mr. Kasdan's career when he had a lot to answer for. He
had just written a script about white profiteers having a
grand good time robbing the holy artifacts of ancient
peoples *(Raiders of the Lost Ark),* another that cheap-
ened the ideas of mysticism and initiation into a fantasy
of easy outs for the good guys *(The Empire Strikes
Back);* and he had written and directed one more in the
long line of American mystery films that suggests that
people capable of sexual intensity must therefore also be
capable of cold-blooded murder *(Body Heat).* It's no wonder that he's feeling contrite—and *The Big Chill* is, if
nothing else, a contrite film.

What is remarkable about it is that two years, now,
after its release, successful young professionals who
went to college during the sixties still talk about *The*

Big Chill. A reference to its title serves as a reference to a conversation they might have had, or had wanted to have but probably didn't. Which indicates that *they* feel contrite. Among other things it indicates that the evasions of the film are widespread evasions, deeply rooted and worth looking at.

The film is an extension of the "Tonight Show" in more ways than one, the least of which is that it was produced by Johnny Carson's production company. This is fiction as talk show. Seven old friends gather for a weekend to mourn the suicide of an eighth, and they talk. Not the involved, sometimes desperate verbal ventures of friends who need to make crucial judgments about themselves and about each other, as Louis Malle captured in *My Dinner with Andre.* *The Big Chill* is talk in the Carson format, pithy sentences (those I quoted are among the longest speeches in the picture) wherein nothing serious can be said without being followed immediately, compulsively by a one-liner. Any exchange of serious dialogue is closed with a deflating joke.

We can't blame this entirely on the film. It is what passes for "manners" in many circles, standard party style. On the other hand, these people are so trapped by this style that the suicide of a friend doesn't put a dent in it. The lack of feeling in the film isn't so remarkable. Many films, and all of Lawrence Kasdan's, lack genuine feeling. What is remarkable is that people are hungry enough for some resolution to the sixties to endure this film's lack of feeling, often more than once, *in order to feel spoken to* about this hole in their lives.

The sixties are symbolized by the dead friend, Alex. A brilliant scientific mind, and apparently the instigator and leader of their group during the days of demonstrations, music, and drugs, Alex is the only one among them who never chose to go straight. This is interpreted by the others, finally, as failure. He had all that talent and never *did* anything with it. He kept searching for a

self he couldn't find. *Their* failure is in not making him
see the error of his ways. Alex is dead. The sixties are
dead. Alex is dead because he never realized that the
sixties had died. It is never suggested that not being
able to "join" this society might have involved a moral
stance which Alex was neither able to forgo nor, finally,
to live with. Because what, in fact, would he have
joined? Who are these others who not-so-secretly resent
Alex's inability to go their way?

Harold, who has made a fortune selling jogging
shoes; his wife, Sarah, a doctor, the success of whose
practice we can guess at by the huge estate she and her
husband live on; Sam, who is the star of a glamorous
private-eye TV program; Michael, who was going to
"teach black kids in Harlem"—the only mention of
blacks—but who is a gossip reporter for *People* maga-
zine; Meg, a lawyer who was going to defend the poor
but enjoys lucrative real-estate law much more; Karen,
who married a very dull businessman—instead of one of
her fascinating friends—for the security; and Nick, a
Vietnam vet whose wound has made him impotent and
who deals drugs and doesn't give a shit, or tells himself
he doesn't. He gets to define the "big chill" of the title,
which is nothing less than that this is a cold cruel world:
"Well, wise up folks—we're all alone out there and to-
morrow we're going out there again."

It is not that none of them have been true to what
were no doubt some pretty naive ideas of what to do with
their lives. It's that none of them found anything, none
of them give any evidence of ever considering anything,
except naive idealism on the one hand and a no-holds-
barred rush for money on the other. You can still consider yourself a righteous person because everyone
knows idealism isn't feasible, and what's left? Money.

Here are adults stuck in a convenient either/or system that lets them completely off the hook. Never does
anyone express the idea that they have to take responsi-

bility for the world they live in. "Responsibility" is defined as making money. Where would these people be without their one-liners? The humor of the film is not merely to entertain; it is all that makes these barren existences watchable.

Which leaves us with the film, and somebody's need to watch it. We can blame *The Big Chill* on Kasdan and that hydra-headed entity, Hollywood—it certainly doesn't have to reflect on *us*. But the fact is that large numbers of people have felt that it fulfills some need in them. Justifies them, somehow. Expresses them.

> *And you ask what's mine*
> *And somebody else says Where what is*
> *And you say Oh my god am I here all alone*

And you do. And maybe you are. And there was little in the sixties experience to prepare you for life on those terms except its music (and the music was a lot). It is a giveaway that *The Big Chill*'s soundtrack is mostly some very good but not very threatening soul songs—the Temptations, Aretha Franklin, Marvin Gaye. One Rolling Stones song, which of course is "You Can't Always Get What You Want." Dylan, Morrison, Joplin, Hendrix, James Brown, the Jefferson Airplane, the Buffalo Springfield, Crosby, Stills & Nash, the Band—and, for that matter, almost any other song by the Rolling Stones—are noticeable by their absence. The characters may not have reacted to it but the audience would have had to. These musicians expressed a far more complex vision of existence than *The Big Chill* is willing to concede anyone of the era ever felt. But that still leaves us with an audience that is willfully forgetting, willfully twisting, something that was very important to them once upon a time.

It's not that this is new or even that it's shocking. Most people in most generations chicken out sooner or later. The film makes its objections to such behavior only in order to rationalize those feelings by its conclusion. The film is intended to *reinforce* the idea that there is no middle ground between idealism and a flaunted materialism. It is intended to make you forget that both stances, idealism and materialism, are childish yearnings for total and instant gratification. They are each the shadow of the other, and neither has anything to do with growing up. To grow up is to be responsible, and responsible does not mean "successful." It means, at least in part, that one of the things you're responsible for is your world, and in one way or another you have to find a way to fulfill that responsibility. The world is an ongoing act of creation, and you are part of that act *whether you accept your role or not.* If you deny your creative role, you are creating denial. You are spreading the power of compulsive powerlessness that powers the American machine. And how you fulfill your creative role—"Your mission, should you decide to accept it"—is *your* problem. Nobody can answer that for any of us. D. H. Lawrence once pointed out that the life-giving force can be in anything:

> *As we live, we are transmitters of life.*
> *And when we fail to transmit life, life fails*
>   *to flow through us ...*
> *It doesn't mean handing it out to some*
>   *mean fool, or letting the dead eat you up.*
> *It means kindling the life-quality where it*
>   *was not, even if it's only in the whiteness*
>   *of a washed pocket-handkerchief.*

If there was one such pocket handkerchief in a film like *The Big Chill* ... but there isn't. So an audience—innocent only by virtue of its refusal to consider the consequences of its life-style—finds in the film a permission to be increasingly lifeless. For these characters are dead to the world. They can make all the jogging shoes, real-estate deals and television series they want, but every day they just become more a part of the very thing they're accumulating wealth to defend themselves against.

Which is the fate of most Americans—our baby-boom generation in particular.

So *The Big Chill* pretends to be an exercise in nostalgia when it is really an exercise in surrender—both for the people who made it and the people who decide they can see themselves in it. This is a terrifying thing to be brought to, but it is terror in the style of the "Tonight Show," where the next wisecrack and the next commercial always waits, and nothing is so awful as a moment of silence.

The *Big Chill* factor, then, is the erasure of memory, the surrender of identity, and the installment, in their places, of an all-purpose, nonthreatening nostalgia.

In an age when media overpowers the unwary and infiltrates memory, it becomes more important every day to pry your memory from media and to live with your own past instead of the past that is being sold collectively as an artifact.

Memory is never an answer, but memory can sometimes pose the needed questions. There is, for instance, the question of our political tactics and our silliness in the sixties. It is important for the next generation to remember that ours never translated its visions of freedom into an effective politics.

This is not to imply that the politics (either radical or mainstream) were exactly *in*effective. The radical antiwar, civil-rights, and feminist movements educated Americans about America—it was the most important period of self-examination that the country as a whole had undergone since the movement to abolish slavery. We will be a long time living with, reacting to, and implementing that education. Nor could the mainstream liberal politics of the day, the big-spending programs now in such disrepute, be called ineffective. At the time, most of the country believed Lyndon Johnson was right, and that if we only poured enough money into our national wounds—poverty, racism, injustice—those wounds would heal. The money flowed, and instead of a salve on our wounds, it was salt. All that the great expenditures of the Great Society did was to show us where and how much we hurt. Johnson's programs didn't work nearly as well as we all naively hoped they would, so the effort has been considered a failure, but this is our infantilism that expects something to go away just because we pay for it to go away, thinking that money could be a substitute for the changes we need to make in ourselves. We haven't considered it a victory that the Great Society's awkward and often failed programs caused us to begin to live, instead of to hide, our pain. Or that American life began to be lived at a depth it had never before attempted to cope with.

That's not what we were paying for. Yet to bring the national agonies into our national consciousness—which those programs very successfully did—was the crucial first step in a healing that must inevitably take quite some time.

Still, that's a long way from what we generally mean by "politics." As an exercise in memory, as opposed to nostalgia, let's think of the election of 1968. Nixon is remembered for his landslide victory in 1972, for Cambodia, Vietnam, China, and Watergate—but not for how closely he squeaked by in the election of 1968. We can see how devastating were the assassinations of Martin Luther King and Robert Kennedy earlier that spring. They were the national figures who could have mobilized "the sixties sensibility" into votes. Nixon, who almost lost to Hubert Humphrey, could not have stood against Kennedy. And we can see how shallow were the tactics of the young radical leaders who gave Nixon the election by refusing to participate and urging that the rest of us not participate either, in the hope that breaking the Democratic party would leave room for the creation of a new, more radical party. But everybody was young, and all-or-nothing was far more appealing, emotionally, than gradual change. As a generation we were, and we remain, as hooked on instant gratification as the television sensibility we despised.

It is hard to fault any human being, of course, for neglecting to vote for Hubert Humphrey. That was a race between a pig and a rat. One left the voting booth—having finally, after endless discussions, voted for Humphrey—feeling that the act had been *physically* ugly, the psychic equivalent of dipping one's hand into a vat of warm mucus. It came out dripping of collective ills.

Humphrey was a pig, looked and squeaked like one. Not the pejorative "pig"as we used it then, meaning cops and capitalists (cops whom we, too, called when in trouble, and capitalists whom we would yet become). No, Humphrey was a porcine soul whose impressive legislative record was the work of an able and sentimental bureaucrat who was nonetheless a weak and not very moral man. There was the Senator Humphrey of the helpful liberal legislation, and there was the Vice President Humphrey who praised Vietnam as "a great adventure" and all but literally kissed Lyndon Johnson's rump. And there was the Humphrey who, in 1950, had proposed a bill that set up detention centers for American radicals. The bill passed, seven camps were built, the only peacetime American concentration camps (in the original, pre-Nazi use of the term) since the first Indian "reservations." Humphrey's camps weren't used, finally, but they were nonetheless his camps.

Still, some of us voted for him. Our thought was this: American voters did not have the right to be fastidious. The stakes were too high, and we would not be the ones to pay the price. At the time we were dropping napalm on Vietnamese civilians—our government was using our money to make the stuff, we were making it in our factories, it was being dropped by our friends and neighbors. Humphrey was far more likely to end those murders than Nixon, if only because he was more susceptible to public influence. It was disgusting to vote for him, but did we have the right to compare our disgust to how it felt for napalm to boil a child's skin? To bear our disgust might have been the least we could do.

For many of us who once were and may still be radicals, our sense of decency had been curdled by events into nausea, and this nausea had rendered us politically impotent. While "the worst," as Yeats had it, "are filled with passionate intensity," and still are. To proceed in the face of one's own nausea is a kind of courage no one ever told us about, but it is the courage we needed and still need.

God knows we had every right to vomit. At that riot of a convention in Chicago, Humphrey kissed the television when he won the nomination. The man *kissed* a *television screen*. It is almost a virtue that he did it shamelessly, knowing that he was being photographed by another television camera. While outside his hotel the police were beating hell out of everybody who didn't have a uniform on.

Beware of your own innocence. Innocence offended too often results in paralysis. "The children of the sixties" were shocked at the behavior both of police and of presidential candidates. I confess, here is where I began to part company with them, for I was less a child of the sixties than a child of the streets. And it must be admitted that in the Bronx, in Bedford-Stuyvesant, in East Harlem and Harlem and the East Village, we who had been children on welfare in the fifties watched the Chicago riots with a mix of furies, sometimes as angry at the demonstrators as we were at the cops and the Democrats. We were angry, yes, but anger wasn't a thing we'd learned in college. We'd been angry all our lives. We were the statistics the college kids quoted. We were the hunger, we were the violence, we were the illiteracy, we were the crime. So, watching that convention, it must be admitted that for some of us our anger was laced with satisfaction, for "the Chicago treatment" was part of our daily bread. It came down on us for the way we looked, the way we talked, the way we walked. It was impossible to find a family among us whose young men had escaped it. Not long afterward my mother's kitchen would be filled with cops clubbing my brother into unconsciousness while she screamed. So it was with some satisfaction that we watched the well-off kids learn the hard way, which for us had been and would continue to be the only way. And it was with contempt that we viewed their shock and their tears. They had been trying to tell *us* about America, and yet they had been so protected from America that they now had the luxury of shock. Their mothers' kitchens were safe, we thought. (As it happened, we were wrong. Their kitchens were almost as full of ambushes as ours, different in style but almost as damaging—they had been sheltered too much, so as they grew older their need for comfort would trivialize most of their best impulses, leaving them empty and without dignity. But we had no way of knowing that then.)

Yet we had marched beside these college kids, and would again, for even in our bitterness we knew that they were making leaps of awareness that few individuals, much less whole generations, ever made, and they were doing it with real courage and purpose. Was their "Don't trust anyone over thirty" a premonition of how comfortable they'd become when over thirty themselves, how much fire they'd lose? How little there would be to fear from them after they got what their parents had wanted for them all along—security, success, a stake in white America. And would we have been a little less condescending to them, a little less macho toward them, had we been able to see, for instance, that Eldridge Cleaver would attend the 1984 Republican convention as a Reagan delegate—that Neil Young and Jerry Rubin and so many others would join the Reagan camp. We saw their traps so clearly, and our own so badly, which is to say we were very much alike, middle and lower classes, doomed alike to using our insight into others as a shield against seeing into ourselves.

Fast-forward through the summer, to within weeks of the election, October 2, 1968, Mexico City. "Student unrest," as the media calls it, had been going on there as it had all over the world that year. But Mexico was especially uptight, because for the first time it was being treated internationally as a grownup—it was being allowed to stage the Olympic Games. This heightened the Mexican government's self-consciousness about its students, who were demure when compared to those in other parts of the world. In the words of Octavio Paz, "the Mexican students did not propose violent and revolutionary social changes, nor was their program as radical as many groups of German and North American youth. It also lacked the orgiastic and near-religious tone of 'the hippies.' The movement was democratic and reformist, even though some of its leaders were of the extreme Left."

On that day in October, thousands of Mexican students gathered at the Plaza of Tlatelolco for a meeting (not a demonstration). At the end of the meeting, when they were about to leave, the plaza was surrounded by the army, and the soldiers opened fire. It was a massacre. The English newspaper *The Guardian* is thought to have the most reliable figure on the number of dead: 325. Thousands were wounded. Thousands were arrested, many of whom remained in prison, without trial, for many years.

If our political consciousness in North America had *been* a political consciousness, instead of an incoherent and emotional rebellion that never stopped long enough to think very hard, the Mexican massacre would have sent us into the streets by the thousands and into the voting booths by the millions, realizing that the ugliness and stupidity of our government was still the ugliness and stupidity of a functioning democratic society—at least democratic in comparison to any other. Because the Right perceived this, and we did not, the Right firmed its power then and has fundamentally kept it ever since.

But the Mexican massacre barely dented North American consciousness then and is largely forgotten now. If we had felt solidarity with those students, if we had by the thousands called on our government to demand an accounting by the Mexcian government; if we had even simply pulled out of the Olympic Games in symbolic revulsion—but how could a nation that was napalming civilians pretend to be horrified by anything?

Yet, if we had done virtually anything, North American eyes might have begun to open to Latin American realities, fifteen years before the choices we now all face with Nicaragua, El Salvador, Guatemala, Honduras, and Mexico. Open eyes change history. The very fact of awareness changes history. Who knows what would have happened if that moment had been seized?

I make these notes for the future, not in regret at the past. As that era is every day rewritten by a nation embarrassed and frightened by its intensity, as its immense cultural advances are taken for granted and as "the children of the sixties" are blamed for the crimes of its old men, it is instructive to understand what our actual mistakes were.

Fast-forward again, past Nixon's tiny election margin, a man allowed to win by people who couldn't bear the nausea of voting for Humphrey; past Nixon's massive escalation of the bombing of Vietnamese and now Cambodian villages *even though his own CIA and Pentagon continually reported that the bombing was having no military effect, and in fact was having, in the CIA's view, a negative effect, strengthening Vietnamese resistance.* Why did he continue to murder? For if it was not military, then it must be called murder. Because the U.S. was not winning on the ground, and he wanted the *image* of winning, and that image was the B-52 cascading firestorms on civilian villages. He seemed to believe that the Vietnamese and the Cambodians would react to the image as much as to the destruction. Watergate was what Nixon went down for, but this mass murder was Nixon's real crime, as it had been Johnson's: murder as a form of public relations.

What Nixon had most in common with the people who demonstrated against him was that they understood, and they were avid about, each other's public relations. We reacted on the same level on which he bombed, both sides caught in the mood of the time. The secret bombings of Cambodia, kept secret even from Congress, illegal and certainly an impeachable offense, became public in the spring of 1970. Students again led the protests. In Kent, Ohio, several frightened National Guardsmen fired rifles at unarmed students, and four white kids died. Within days more demonstrators—blacks—were killed in a similar and apparently not-so-accidental incident in the South, but there was nobody to take an amazing photograph and the event was swallowed up, even at that time. Many black activists had been killed in police raids in many places at roughly that time, and white college students seemed to take this for granted.

The demonstration in Washington against Nixon's Cambodian murders was impassioned even more by the Kent State deaths. Were they going to start shooting at *us* with impunity now? Nobody knew. Anything seemed possible. My friends and I played the Jefferson Airplane's *Volunteers* album over and over again, piled into a car and went to Washington. We didn't have any weapons, but we had crowbars and such tools placed strategically around the car. We didn't intend to be taken quietly, if we were to be taken at all, and we didn't intend to let the police beat on us as they had the kids in Chicago. The Mexican student movement had folded after the massacre; after the Kent State skirmish, it seemed essential to show the government that they were going to have to shoot a lot more of us before we'd back off. We didn't know we were going to one of the last great demonstrations and that in fact the Kent State shootings were going to be enough to signal the end of *that* era.

There was one moment in that demonstration that still stands out, for me, from all the moments in all those years of demonstrations. Thousands of us walked in a mob up a street adjacent to the White House, with "One-two-three-four we don't want your fucking war" pulsating out of us like amplified heartbeats, when near the head of the procession, if it could be said to have a head, a skinny, pretty blonde girl got up on some tall guy's shoulders. You could see her up and down the street. How she started leading the chants, I can't remember. It happened by virtue of the fact that she was the only one that everybody could *see*. It certainly wasn't premeditated, but it got so *she'd* shout a chant and the rest would follow, thousands perhaps, hundreds certainly, "Hey hey USA, how many kids did you kill today?" and she'd yell the next chant and we'd yell it louder.

Could it have lasted for even five minutes? I don't know. It was the sort of intensity wherein you lose your sense of time. The mob suddenly had, if not a leader, at least a figurehead. And a female figure—*very* rare in those days. Like our own Chantal, the singer who inspired the revolution in Genet's *The Balcony*. A yearning ran like a thrill through the street, a moment of real mob-ecstasy unlike the orderly, heavy sense of companionship and momentum usual in the huge demonstrations, and as we chanted and followed that blonde, nearing a White House barricaded with troops (we would learn later that Nixon wasn't even home), someone near me yelled, "This could be *it* muthafucka if she says *Go* I say *Go* we *GO!*" And for a giddy, hovering moment it looked as if that could happen, we could rush the White House. It occurs to me now that it would have been a futile gesture, whether or not Nixon had been there. No doubt many of us would have been shot. And the White House propaganda machine would have turned the gesture against us. But I didn't care much about those things right then. The White House was still pretty faraway and we never would have made it, but the raw release of the act was almost unbearably attractive. For that moment that girl—and she was no more than a girl—may have been the only person with real power in the whole movement, though I can't say for sure that people in the same march but a block or two away were even aware of her. Those demonstrations were like that.

The moment passed. I had gotten close to her and I saw her face as she slid off the tall guy's shoulders. She was very, very frightened. She had felt our anger focused through her, flowing through her, and she couldn't bear it. Who could have? I said something to her but she looked right through me, and there was no mistaking the shaken expression on her face: she hated me, she hated all of us, hated us for the fear she was feeling. And that march went the way of all marches while she lost herself in the crowd.

And thinking of her now I think of that Bob Seger song: "Come back, baby—rock 'n' roll never forgets." But I don't expect her to come back. We had exhausted the *image* of the demonstration. It was never really enough, and we had treated it as though it was more than enough. And fifteen years later it is still an image too worn to shock or motivate. The Right perceived then that there was no substitute for grass-roots organizing and steady, plodding work. They had always been good at plodding, so only seven years after Watergate their most rabid representative took power. It is all the more amazing, in the light of the Right's massive power, what far-reaching changes the radicals and visionaries of the sixties instituted with no more power than the power to make noise.

The most joyful noise we made—and it may yet go down as the most joyful noise *ever* made in North America—was at Woodstock, where, thank the gods, someone (Michael Wadleigh, bless him) had a camera crew and would do the job of seeing that the weekend didn't pass entirely into legend. Otherwise, by now, the reality that the film preserves would have been pooh-poohed as exaggeration. In that last summer of the sixties, several summers past the first and short-lived "summer of love" (it didn't last quite a summer), everything that had been wonderful, everything that had been visionary, the quintessential joy of that collective impulse that we all felt with such private heat would gather on a hillside for a few days as though to transmit its remembrance into the future. For future generations, "the sixties" would be distilled into that long weekend that was further compressed into two hours of film. Everything that went into the making of something like *The Big Chill* might be able to rationalize and sanitize the sixties, but while *Woodstock* exists nobody can take it all away.

But to be there wasn't at all like watching this film or any film. Who were we, on that hillside? A lot of more than slightly delirious children, of various ages—I was a few months short of twenty-five, and I was older than most. I remember the shock of walking toward the lake and seeing three naked men walking casually down the road, unremarked by the crowd. And, at the lake, simply to sit and stare at the loveliness, the gentleness, of a lot of naked strangers looking truly innocent in that water. Yes, we'd gotten ourselves back to the Garden. The Army helicopters, bringing food and medical supplies, would buzz the lake and everybody would wave—everything was all right that day, even the Army. We seemed to sense that they were just kids like us. My friend took off his clothes and went in. I was too shy. I couldn't quite believe my eyes. I had the feeling that nobody could. Not at the lake, not while watching the music, and certainly not the musicians, who for us plebians were rather far-off, sheltered people. For *once* in American pop culture the show was not on the stage. What characterized the sixties often, and this weekend in particular, was that the show was in the audience, the show *was* the audience, and the music was inspiration, was accompaniment, was expression, but had no existence separate from that audience. These were *our* songs. They were just singing them. And they knew it. And they were proud of it. And we were too. And nobody could quite believe it really felt this way that day: oh my God I'm *not* here all alone.

This was the world we wanted. It had happened by mistake, because too many people had come to a concert, ten times more people than there were facilities for. And the leaders of the concert, who were no older than the rest of us, decided that instead of trying to control the situation—which was not possible, but could have been tried, with God knows what awful result—they would lose their million dollars and just try to take care of this migration of souls that had alighted in front of their stage. Nobody could have planned such a weekend—and every time someone's tried to plan "a Woodstock" since it's been hollow, or, at worst, it's been Altamont (put on by some of the same promoters). We all seemed to have come through a gap in our shared notions of the possible. Here was the dream come true. Here was the Promised Land, the New Age, the Other World. Nobody knew what to *do* with it, and it couldn't have gone on for another day, but here it had materialized, and there were many giddy expressions, as though to ask, Am I dreaming?

The answer, of course, was yes. We were dreaming. Together, in the same place, we were living the dream we'd dreamed. And what does one *do* with a dream but remember it? You may or may not interpret it, but interpretations fade and you remember the images, the feeling—some dreams stick with us for decades that way. You may not be able to live them, but to deny them would be to deny yourself. You keep their possibility within you, and try not to stray too far in your heart from the moment when dream reached toward reality and reality reached back to dream and taught you that the world is immense, truly, and the way we're doing things in this world is only one of the many ways we might be doing them. Once you know this, then you know that we're not just alive, we're the bearers of life. *Anything* can change.

Woodstock was all this, certainly. And it was just as certainly the beginning of the end. You can't film or record a smell, but the stench there was a part of its meaning as well. The overpowering odor of garbage in the heat in front of the stage. The songs and film tell you nothing of people sitting in, even sleeping in, the mud from the overflowing latrines, a mud rich in shit and piss. We were *that* powerless. Even in our dream. A decade was ending. It had taken all our energy to get to that hillside, and once there we had just enough left to say, "Wow," softly, in utter bewilderment that we'd made it, and listen to Grace Slick as the sun came up— "You are the crown of Creation," she sang, as we took a morning piss in our own mud. My friend and I trudged off through that mud for home, utterly exhausted, exhilarated and depressed at once, long before the next dawn when Jimi Hendrix would play his electric version of "The Star-Spangled Banner." That was the summer that we first put men on the moon, but soon the concert at Woodstock would seem a lot farther away than the moon ever had.

1980, L.A. There was a documentary playing called *The War at Home*. An intimate look at the movement to stop the war in Vietnam. I was smart enough to go alone but not intuitive enough to go when no one else I knew would be there. It was painful to watch that screen and see how young we were, how hard we tried, and how narrowly we thought. How so much enthusiasm and so little knowledge combined mainly to make a lot of noise. Useful noise, to be sure. Honorable noise, certainly. It is possible that, as a result, never again will the United States be able to embark upon such a questionable war without a serious cross-examination. An amazing effect, really, when you see in the film what you couldn't see at the time, being part of it all: which is, that these were *children*.

There are such high-handed critiques now about what they did and did not do, these children. Memory is devious, even when it doesn't dissolve into nostalgia, and one forgets one's own freshly minted, wide-open, nineteen-year-old face, and the faces of one's friends— the faces of most of those demonstrators. These children believed so hard and did what they could and nothing was ever the same afterwards, and that is quite a record for a lot of children led largely by children. How amazed they were, in their innocence, that simply pointing up to their elders that this war was an atrocity was not enough. How silly and spoiled and brave. How very much *for real* they were.

After the film the lobby was thick with friends and

acquaintances who didn't look like that anymore, and who weren't nearly so silly or for real, and many of them were inviting each other to a party at a well-known producer's place—a "reception" for the film, just like we'd all gotten married or something, and it was obvious that the conversation would be informed and intelligent, the faces cheery, the wine decent, there would be good food and the music wouldn't be too intrusive. It was three years before *The Big Chill,* but the film was very much alive in these faces.

Well, I got as far as the door of that polite party, and then was very rude to some good people whom I had no call to be rude to, and sulked, positively sulked, off into the night, yelling something over my shoulder that I hope nobody heard. But we had just seen it all over again, the napalm and the villagers it burned and the children who protested it and Nixon and Johnson and the cops and all of us together in the street, and it seemed to me then and it seems to me now that to have enthusiasm for such a party after seeing such things was to have enthusiasm for one's own resignation, for the distance one has achieved from the heart of what was once a great collective emotion. If that is what is meant by "maturity," you can keep it.

I'm looking for a maturity more alive, a maturity that's not afraid to be desperate, a maturity that isn't terrified of looking ridiculous. A maturity that's still willing to get dangerous if that's what it takes. I would like to have a noble object for this, but I don't. I'm not looking for peace of mind and admittedly wouldn't know what to do with it if I found any. It is just that, as Miguel de Unamuno put it, "we die of cold and not of darkness."

Fortunately it was only a few blocks from that reception to a little bar that doesn't exist anymore called the Taurus Tavern, which was too little, mixed black and white too thoroughly, and could get too rough for

any of the music critics of any of the L.A. papers to frequent, and where, on this Friday like all those Fridays,
A Band Called Sam would play rhythm and blues too
loud and too real for anyone to talk about what they did
or didn't do in the sixties, what happened or failed to
happen in the seventies, and what the eighties, the vor-
tex of the eighties, were up to. Sam Taylor was in his
forties, had played with Otis Redding and had been the
vocal coach for Sam and Dave, and he knew what he was
doing. Juke Logan, his harp-man, was wailing behind as
he yelled Wilson Pickett's old "ninety-nine and a half
won't do—got to have a hundred!"

The people crowded onto that very small dance floor
—seventy people could crowd the entire club, and there
were more than that this night—sweating, dancing together and alone, faces masked by poses and faces
naked, dancing slick or dancing awkward, and it could
have been a wedding or a wake, the first night of all or
the last, and this would be a good place to be. It can be a
beautiful thing to dance all night in an evil time.

I wasn't the only one who couldn't take that party.
Faces started showing up at the Taurus who'd been at
the movie, and then the party, and then couldn't go
home. And Sam was singing, "An' I won't stop tryin' till
I cre-ate dis-tur-bance, in your mind," and the dancers
gathered around this music like shivering people around
a fire.

As the band took a break one woman who'd seen the
movie said, "I was *in* it. I was the black-and-white historical footage." Which is probably why some of us had
gravitated to that sweaty juke joint. We did not like the
idea of being reduced to black-and-white historical footage. Nor would some of us ever swallow the nostalgic
evasions of *The Big Chill*. We knew where we'd been and
why we'd been there. We didn't know where we were
going—but who does? "Come and get your spirit/come
and get your spirit come and get your spirit," Sam Tay-

lor sang (his own tune) again and again into the dark that night, and we, as Buddy Holly once put it, raved on.

1985. Sometimes when Brendan, age eleven, is supposed to have gone to sleep, I pass by his slightly ajar door and hear his soft, out-of-tune singing in the dark. He has the earphones on and isn't aware of how loudly he's singing along. The first records he got himself after we gave him the stereo were the Beatles, Bob Dylan, and Jim Morrison. He listens to the oldies station a lot, especially late at night. He also has the names "Frankie Goes to Hollywood" and "David Bowie," among others, written boldly on the looseleaf binder he carries to school, and he watches his share of MTV. But when I hear his soft, off-key versions of "You Can't Always Get What You Want," "Here Comes the Sun," and "Subterranean Homesick Blues"; when I know that for him and for others like him these tunes are still very much alive after going on twenty years; when I know that for him they blend with the new music that I don't know as well, as he synthesizes all these meanings every day into something he can grow up with and grow into; then I don't think so much about the people of my generation who gave up trying to live out their best thoughts—I think of those who haven't, and won't, and I think of those who are coming up and the fires we've left them, both the inner fires and the fires they'll have to walk through. And whenever Brendan fights me about some damn thing, so fierce about whether or not a chore or a bedtime is fair, testing his ability to take us on, win or lose I'm always so very thankful for his fierceness. May it last, I pray. May he not be one of those who forgets.

"THE MOST
ESSENTIAL DOCUMENTS"

To remember. To re-member. To put the pieces back together. America is being forgotten. America must be remembered.

But can the pieces be put *back* together, or must we imagine them all over again, every generation, every day? Is our failure to *be* America literally a failure of the imagination? Because America was an act of imagination to begin with. There had been nothing like it; there was no model. Our revolutionaries were clearly "imagining things."

In the summer of 1815, former president John Adams, eighty years old, wrote to his friend, former president Thomas Jefferson, seventy-two years old:

> As to the history of the Revolution, my Ideas may be peculiar, perhaps singular. What do We Mean by the Revolution? The War? That was no part of the Revolution. It was only an Effect and Consequence of it.

The Revolution was in the minds of the People . . .

It had been thirty-nine years since the Declaration of Independence—roughly the time from the Second World War to now. Already they felt that their revolution was irrecoverable. A month before, Adams had written to Jefferson: "Who shall write a history of the American revolution? Who can write it? Who will ever be able to write it?

"The most essential documents, the debates and deliberations in Congress from 1774 to 1783 were all in secret, and are now lost forever. Mr. Dickinson printed a speech, which he said he made in Congress against the Declaration of Independence, but it appeared to me very different from that, which you, and I heard."

Ten days later Jefferson wrote back: "On the subject of the history of the American revolution, you ask 'Who shall write it? Who can write it? And who will ever be able to write it?' Nobody; except the external facts . . .

"Botta [who had written one of its first histories], as you observe, has put his own speculations and reasonings into the mouths of persons whom he names, but who, you and I know, never made such speeches."

I think of the enormous courage of John Adams, who had the courage to struggle for what he thought *should* be, *though he never believed, even as a young man, that the creation of this country would be valued by this country*. In 1787, ten years before he became its second president, he wrote to Jefferson: "Lessons my dear sir, are never wanting. Life and history are full . . . Moral Reflections, wise Maxims, religious Terrors, have little Effect upon Nations when they contradict a present Passion, Prejudice, Imagination, Enthusiasm, or Caprice . . . In short my dear Friend you and I have been indefatigable Labourers through our whole lives for a cause which will be thrown away in the next generation, upon the Vanity and Foppery of Persons of whom we do not know the Names perhaps."

To struggle for a nation which you believe beforehand is, because of the nature of humankind, already lost, yet to struggle because of the *beauty* of the nation which you hopelessly imagine—this is an artist's courage more than a leader's. Can you think of another leader who did not nurture the hope that at least some future generation would carry on the struggle and win?

Adams's is not the doctrine of a politician. It is the fire of a revolutionary—a man for whom politics is part poetics. We call them the Founding Fathers to make them safe. To forget them. "Fathers," in that usage, are not dangerous men. But a man who, like Adams, can harbor such disbelief yet fight tirelessly for his belief, is an incredibly dangerous man. What can you do to him? How can you frighten him?

This is a *political* legacy, this attitude that achieves its victories through despising victory, that fights not for gain but because it has imagined something beautiful.

Can this be remembered? Can this piece be put back? Is there the present possibility of a politics that is again a fundamental expression of minds rather than of interests vying for comforts? These are the questions that the politically active are now not asking, but living through. The only answer will be how they live their lives.

Revolutions occur "in the minds of the people." This may be why no fully industrialized nation has ever had a revolution. The major revolutions—in the United States, France, Mexico, Russia, China, and now all over the Third World—all have taken place in agrarian cultures, cultures where the mental processes cannot be outflanked and overwhelmed by technology and media. Ideas have tremendous force in agrarian cultures, once they catch on; whereas in North America or Europe ideas are now lost in the cacophony of media, and the most forceful elements for change are new technologies.

(It is interesting that Marxism only takes root in a society that is *imagining* having industry. Industrialized cultures see quickly that Marxism is too simplistic for a complex socio-economic structure, and either they reject it out of hand or water it down till it cannot be called Marxism except out of sentimentality.)

John Adams did not imagine any "ism," any more than did Zapata. In all their fifty years of correspondence, Adams and Jefferson have no catchword for the balance they sought between individual liberty and mutually beneficial law. They understood that a nation is re-created every day in the minds of the people, and so there are days when it is forcefully and brilliantly a nation, and there are days when it is hardly a nation at all.

Nor would they have criticized Nicaragua's Sandinistas for not holding free elections, for instance, so quickly after their revolution, since the new United States, with no enemies on its borders, no great nations sending money to bring it down, took much longer to hold its first free election. The American Revolution was over in 1781; Washington wasn't elected our first president until 1789, and he was not elected by the people in a free election but by the select, male-only Federal Constitutional Convention. Our Founding Fathers, then, would have shown more tolerance for the ebb and flow of a new nation's often violent struggles, and would have been appalled at our squeaky-clean, pompous image of our own early days. Adams recalled to Jefferson in 1813:

> *You certainly never felt the Terrorism, excited by Genet, in 1793, when ten thousand People in the Streets of Philadelphia, day after day, threatened to drag Washington out of his House [Philadelphia was then the nation's capital], and effect a Revolution in the Government, or compel it to declare war in*

favour of the French Revolution, and against England? The coolest and firmest minds, even among the Quakers in Philadelphia, have given their Opinions to me, that nothing but the Yellow Fever, which removed Dr. Hutchinson and Jonathan Dickenson Sargent from this World, could have saved the United States from the total Revolution of Government. I have no doubt You was [sic] fast asleep in philosophical Tranquility, when ten thousand People, and perhaps many more, were parading in the streets of Philadelphia, on the Evening of my Fast Day [April 25, 1799, President Adams had called for a fast day, that God "would withhold us from unreasonable discontent, from disunion, faction, sedition and insurrection," so critical was the state of the new union]; When even Governor Mifflin himself thought it his Duty to order a Patrol of Horse and Foot to preserve the peace; when Markett Street was as full as Men could stand by one another, and even before my Door; when some of my Domesticks in Phrenzy, determined to sacrifice their Lives in my defence [sic]; when all were ready to make a desperate Salley among the multitude, and others were with difficulty dragged back by the others; when I myself judged it prudent and necessary to order Chests of Arms from the War Office to be brought through bye Lanes and back Doors; determined to defend my House at the Expence [sic] of my Life, and the Lives of the few, very few Domesticks and Friends within it. What think you of Terrorism, Mr. Jefferson?

Yet this same President Adams pardoned one John Fries, sentenced to hang for leading an armed rebellion against the federal government's right to tax his land. These men were revolutionaries, not politicians. Having had no illusions about their own day, they surely would have had patience with the Sandinistas, with Allende, with Castro. But what would our politicians and pundits be saying if the same scenes that Adams described of his presidency and of George Washington's were taking place now in the Sandinista capital?

"Shall I tell you what America is?" wrote a reader, Mr. Ernest Kearny, in a letter to the *L.A. Weekly*. "It is an oath. A pledge to its own people and the people of all nations."

The Founding Fathers would have agreed. At the age of eighty, in 1823, three years before they both died on the afternoon of July 4, 1826, the fiftieth anniversary of the Declaration, Jefferson wrote to Adams:

> *The generation which commences a revolu-*
> *tion can rarely complete it. Habituated from*
> *their infancy to passive submission of body*
> *and mind to their kings and priests, they are*
> *not qualified, when called on, to think and*
> *provide for themselves and their experience,*
> *their ignorance and bigotry make them in-*
> *struments often, in the hands of the Bona-*
> *partes and Iturbides, to defeat their own*
> *rights and purposes. This is the present*
> *situation in Europe and Spanish America.*
> *But it is not desperate. The light which has*
> *been shed on mankind by the art of printing*
> *has eminently changed the condition of the*
> *world . . . It continues to spread . . . To attain*
> *all this, however, rivers of blood must yet*

flow, and years of desolation pass over. Yet the object is worth rivers of blood, and years of desolation, for what inheritance so valuable can man leave to his posterity?

Adams believed the idea alone worth the trouble; he didn't trust posterity. But Jefferson believed that "the idea of resistance to government is so valuable on certain occasions, that I wish it always to be kept alive. It will often be exercised when wrong, but better so than not to be exercised at all. I like a little rebellion now and then. It is like a storm in the Atmosphere."

But it's no good looking for these men in the past, and it's certainly no good to look for them in the White House. Yet if they are really our fathers, and we are really their children, it might still be possible to look for them in ourselves.

REPORT FROM EL DORADO

To go from a job you don't like to watching a screen on which others live more intensely than you . . . is American life, by and large.

This is our political ground. This is our artistic ground. This is what we've done with our immense resources. We have to stop calling it "entertainment" or "news" or "sports" and start calling it what it is: our most immediate environment.

This is a very, very different America from the America that built the industrial capacity to win the Second World War and to surge forward on the multiple momentums of that victory for thirty years. That was an America that worked at mostly menial tasks during the day (now we work at mostly clerical tasks) and had to look at each other at night.

I'm not suggesting a nostalgia for that time. It was repressive and bigoted to an extent that is largely forgotten today, to cite only two of its uglier aspects. But in that environment America meant *America:* the people and the land. The land was far bigger than what we'd done with the land.

This is no longer true. Now the environment of America is media. Not the land itself, but the image of the land. The focus is not on the people so much as it is on the interplay between people and screens. What we've done with the land is far more important now than the land—we're not even dealing with the land anymore, we're dealing with our manipulation and pollution of it.

And what we've done with the very concept of "image" is taking on far more importance for many of us than the actual sights and sounds of our lives.

For instance: Ronald Reagan stands on a cliff in Normandy to commemorate the day U.S. Army Rangers scaled those cliffs in the World War II invasion. Today's Rangers reenact the event while some of the original Rangers, in their sixties now, look on. Except that it is the wrong cliff. The cliff that was actually scaled is a bit further down the beach, but it's not as photogenic as this cliff, so this cliff has been chosen for everybody to emote over. Some of the old Rangers tell reporters that the historical cliff is over yonder, but the old Rangers are swept up (as well they might be) in the ceremonies, and nobody objects enough. This dislocation, this choice, this stance that the real cliff is not important, today's photograph is more important, is a media event. It insults the real event, and overpowers it. Multiplied thousands of times over thousands of outlets of every form and size, ensconced in textbooks as well as screenplays, in sales presentations as well as legislative packages, in religious revivals as well as performance-art pieces, this is the process that has displaced what used to be called "culture."

"I'm not even sure it's a culture anymore. It's like this careening hunger splattering out in all directions." Jeff Nightbyrd was trying to define "culture" in the wee hours at the Four Queens in Las Vegas. It was a conversation that had been going on since we'd become friends working on the *Austin Sun* in 1974, trying to get our bearings now that the sixties were *really* over. He'd spent that triple-time decade as an SDS organizer and editor of *Rat,* and I'd hit Austin after a few years of road-roving, commune-hopping, and intensive (often depressive) self-exploration—getting by, as the song said, with a little help from my friends, as a lot of us did then. This particular weekend Nightbyrd had come to Vegas from Austin for a computer convention, and I had taken off from my duties at the *L.A. Weekly* for some lessons in craps (at which Jeff is quite good) and to further our rap. The slot machines clattered around us in unison, almost comfortingly, the way the sound of a large shaky air-conditioner can be comforting in a cheap hotel room when you're trying to remember to forget. We were, after all, trying to fathom an old love: America.

There are worse places to indulge in this obsession than Las Vegas. It is the most American, the most audacious, of cities. Consuming unthinkable amounts of energy in the midst of an unlivable desert (Death Valley is not far away), its decor is based on various cheap-to-luxurious versions of a 1930s Busby Berkeley musical. Indeed, no studio backlot could ever be more of a set, teeming with extras, people who come from all over America, and all over the world, to see the topless, tasteless shows, the Johnny Carson guests on parade doing their utterly predictable routines, the dealers and crap-table croupiers who combine total boredom with ruthless efficiency and milk us dry—yet at least these tourists are risking something they genuinely value: money. It's a quiz show turned into a way of life, where you can get a good Italian dinner at dawn. Even the half-lit hour of the wolf doesn't faze Las Vegas. How could it, when the town has survived the flash of atom bombs tested just over the horizon?

The history books will tell you that, ironically

enough, the town was founded by Mormons in 1855. Even their purity of vision couldn't bear the intensity of this desert, and they abandoned the place after just two years. But they had left a human imprint, and a decade later the U.S. Army built a fort here. The settlement hung on, and the railroad came through in 1905. During the Second World War the Mafia started to build the city as we know it now. Religious zealots, the Army, and the Mafia—quite a triad of founding fathers.

Yet one could go back even further, some 400 years, when the first Europeans discovered the deserts of the American West—Spaniards who, as they slowly began to believe that there might be no end to these expansive wilds, became more and more certain that somewhere, somewhere to the north, lay El Dorado—a city of gold. Immeasurable wealth would be theirs, they believed, and eternal youth. What would they have thought if they had suddenly come upon modern Las Vegas, lying as it does in the midst of this bleached nowhere, glowing at night with a brilliance that would have frightened them? We have built our desert city to their measure— for they were gaudy and greedy, devout and vicious, jovial and frenzied, like this town. They had just wasted the entire Aztec civilization because their fantasies were so strong they couldn't see the ancient cultural marvels before their eyes. The Aztecs, awed and terrified, believed they were being murdered by gods; and in the midst of such strangeness, the Spaniards took on godlike powers even in their own eyes. As many Europeans would in America, they took liberties here they would never have taken within sight of their home cathedrals. Their hungers dominated them, and in their own eyes the New World seemed as inexhaustible as their appetites. So when Nightbyrd described our present culture as "a careening hunger splattering out in all directions," he was also, if unintentionally, speaking about our past. Fittingly, we were sitting in the midst of a city that had been fantasized by those seekers of El Dorado 400 years ago. In that sense, America had Las Vegas a century before it had Plymouth Rock. And our sensibility has been caught between the fantasies of the conquistadors and the obsessions of the Puritans ever since.

Yes, a fitting place to try to think about American culture.

"There are memories of culture," Nightbyrd was saying, "but the things that have given people strength have dissolved. And because they've dissolved, people are into distractions. And distractions aren't culture."

Are there even memories? The media have taken over our memories. That day Nightbyrd had been driving through the small towns that dot this desert, towns for which Vegas is only a dull glow to the southwest. In a bar in one of those towns, "like that little bar in *The Right Stuff*," he'd seen pictures of cowboys on the wall. "Except that they weren't cowboys. They were movie stars. Guys who grew up in Glendale [John Wayne] and Santa Monica [Robert Redford]." Surely this desert had its own heroes once, in the old gold-mining towns where a few people still hang on, towns like Goldfield and Tonopah. Remembering those actual heroes would be "culture." Needing pictures of movie stars for want of the real thing is only a nostalgia for culture.

Nostalgia is not memory. Memory is specific. One has a relationship to a memory, and it may be a difficult relationship, because a memory always makes a demand upon the present. But nostalgia is vague, a sentimental wash that obscures memory and acts as a narcotic to dull the importance of the present.

Media as we know it now thrives on nostalgia and is hostile to memory. In a television bio-pic, Helen Keller is impersonated by Mare Winningham. But the face of Helen Keller was marked by her enormous powers of concentration, while the face of Mare Winningham is merely cameo-pretty. A memory has been stolen. It takes a beauty in you to see the beauty in Helen Keller's face, while to cast the face of a Mare Winningham in the role is to suggest, powerfully, that one can come back from the depths unscathed. No small delusion is being sold here. Yet this is a minor instance in a worldwide, twenty-four-hour-a-day onslaught.

An onslaught that gathers momentum every twenty-four hours. Remember that what drew us to Las Vegas was a computer fair. One of these new computers does interesting things with photographs. You can put a photograph into the computer digitally. This means the photograph is in there without a negative or print, each element of the image stored separately. In the computer, you can change any element of the photograph you wish, replacing it or combining it with elements from other photographs. In other words, you can take composites of different photographs and put them into a new photograph of your own composition. Combine this with computer drawing, and you can touch up shadows that don't match. When it comes out of the computer the finished product bears no evidence of tampering with any negative. The possibilities for history books and news stories are infinite. Whole new histories can now be written. Events which never happened can be fully documented.

The neo-Nazis who are trying to convince people that the Holocaust never happened will be able to show the readers of their newsletter an Auschwitz of well-fed, happy people being watched over by kindly S.S. men while tending gardens. And they will be able to make the accusation that photographs of the *real* Auschwitz were created in a computer by manipulative Jews. The Soviet Union can rewrite Czechoslovakia and Afghanistan, the United States can rewrite Vietnam, and atomic weapons proponents can prove that the average resident of Hiroshima was unharmed by the blast. On a less sinister, but equally disruptive, level, the writers of business prospectuses and real-estate brochures can have a field day.

Needless to say, when any photograph can be processed this way then all photographs become suspect. It not only becomes easier to lie, it becomes far harder to tell the truth.

But why should this seem shocking when under the names of "entertainment" and "advertising" we've been filming history, and every facet of daily life, in just this way for nearly a century now? It shouldn't surprise us that the ethics of our entertainment have taken over, and that we are viewing reality itself as a form of entertainment. And, as entertainment, reality can be rewritten, transformed, played with, in any fashion.

These considerations place us squarely at the center of our world—and we have no choice, it's the only world there is anymore. *Electronic media has done for everyday reality what Einstein did for physics:* everything is shifting. Even the shifts are shifting. And a fact is not so crucial anymore, not so crucial as the process that turns a fact into an image. For we live now with images as much as facts, and the images seem to impart more life than facts *precisely because they are so capable of transmutation, of transcendence, able to transcend their sources and their uses.* And all the while the images goad us on, so that we become partly images ourselves, imitating the properties of images as we surround ourselves with images.

This is most blatant in our idea of "a vacation"—an idea only about 100 years old. To "vacation" is to enter an image. Las Vegas is only the most shrill embodiment of this phenomenon. People come here not so much to gamble (individual losses are comparatively light), nor for the glittery entertainment, but to step into an image, a daydream, a filmlike world where "everything" is promised. No matter that the Vegas definition of "every-

thing" is severely limited, what thrills tourists is the
sense of being surrounded in "real life" by the same images that they see on TV. But the same is true of the
Grand Canyon, or Yellowstone National Park, or Yo-
semite, or Death Valley, or virtually any of our "natural" attractions. What with all their roads, telephones,
bars, cable-TV motels, the visitors are carefully protected from having to *experience* the place. They view its
image, they camp out in its image, ski down or climb up
its image, take deep breaths of its image, let its image
give them a tan. Or, when they tour the cities, they ride
the quaint trolley cars of the city's image, they visit the
Latin Quarter of its image, they walk across the Brooklyn Bridge of its image—our recreation is a *re*-creation
of America into one big Disneyland.

And this is only one way we have stripped the very
face of America of any content, any reality, concentrating only on its power as image. We also elect images,
groom ourselves as images, make an image of our home,
our car, and now, with aerobics, of our very bodies. For
in the aerobics craze the flesh becomes a garment, susceptible to fashion. So it becomes less *our* flesh, though
the exercise may make it more serviceable. It becomes
"my" body, like "my" car, "my" house. What, within us,
is saying "my"? What is transforming body into image?
We shy away from asking. In this sense it can be said
that after the age of about twenty-five we no longer *have*
bodies anymore—we have possessions that are either
more or less young, which we are constantly trying to
transform and through which we try to breathe.

It's not that all this transmutation of realities into
un- or non- or supra-realities is "bad," but that it's unconscious, compulsive, reductive. We rarely make things
more than they were; we simplify them into less.
Though surely the process *could*—at least theoretically
—go both ways. Or so India's meditators and Zen's
monks say. But that would be to *increase* meaning, and

we seem bent on the elimination of meaning. We're Reagan's Rangers, climbing a cliff that *is* a real cliff, except it's not the cliff we say it is, so that the meaning of both cliffs—not to mention of our act of climbing—is reduced.

As I look out onto a glowing city that is more than 400 years old but was built only during the last forty years, as I watch it shine in blinking neon in a desert that has seen the flash of atom bombs, it becomes more and more plain to me that America is at war with meaning. America is form opposed to content. Not just form *instead* of content. Form opposed. Often violently. There are few things resented so much among us as the suggestion that what we do *means*. It *means* something to watch so much TV. It *means* something to be obsessed with sports. It *means* something to vacation by indulging in images. It means something, and therefore it has consequences. Other cultures have argued over their meanings. We tend to deny that there is any such thing, insisting instead that what you see is what you get and that's *it*. All we're doing is having a *good time,* all we're doing is making a buck, all we're doing is enjoying the spectacle, we insist. So that when we export American culture what we are really exporting is an attitude toward content. Media is the American war on content with all the stops out, with meaning in utter rout, frightened nuances dropping their weapons as they run.

"Media is the history that forgives," my friend Dave Johnson told me on a drive through that same desert a few months later. We love to take a weekend every now and again and just *drive*. Maybe it started with reading *On the Road* when we were kids, or watching a great old TV show called *Route 66* about two guys who drove from town to town working at odd jobs and having adventures with intense women who, when asked who they were, might say (as one did), "Suppose I said I was the Queen of Spain?" Or maybe it was all those rock 'n' roll songs about "the road"—the road, where we can blast our tape-decks as loud as we want, and watch the world go by without having to touch it, a trip through the greatest hologram there is, feeling like neither boys nor men but both and something more, embodiments of some ageless, restless principle of movement rooted deep in our prehistory. All of which is to say that we're just as stuck with the compulsion to enter the image as anybody, and that we love the luxuries of fossil fuel just as much as any other red-blooded, thickheaded Americans.

Those drives are our favorite time to talk, and, again, America is our oldest flame. We never tire of speaking of her, nor of our other old girlfriends. For miles and miles of desert I thought of what Dave had said.

"Media is the history that forgives." A lovely way to put it, and quite un-Western. We Westerners tend to think in sets of opposites: good/bad, right/wrong, me/you, past/present. These sets are often either antagonistic (East/West, commie/capitalist, Christian/heathen) or they set up a duality that instantly calls out to be bridged (man/woman). But Dave's comment sidesteps the dualities and suggests something more complex: a lyrical impulse is alive somewhere in all this media obfuscation. It is the impulse to redeem the past—in his word, to *forgive* history—by presenting it as we would have most liked it to be.

It is one thing to accuse the media of lying. They are, and they know it, and they know we know, and we know they know that we know, and nothing changes. It is another to recognize the rampant lying shallowness of our media as a massive united longing for ... innocence? For a sheltered childlike state in which we need not know about our world or our past. We are so desperate for this that we are willing to accept ignorance as a substitute for innocence. For there can be no doubt anymore that this society *knowingly* accepts its ignorance as innocence—we have seen so much in the last twenty years that now we know what we *don't* see. Whenever a TV show or a movie or a news broadcast leaves out crucial realities for the sake of sentimentality, we pretty much understand the nature of what's been left out and why.

But American media *forgives* the emptiness and injustice of our daily life by presenting our daily life as innocent. Society, in turn, forgives American media for lying because if we accept the lie as truth then we needn't *do* anything, we needn't change.

I like Dave's line of thought because it suggests a motive—literally, a motive force—for these rivers of glop that stream from the screens and loudspeakers of our era. Because, contrary to popular belief, profit is *not* the motive. That seems a rash statement to make in the vicinity of Las Vegas, but the profit motive merely begs the question: *why* is it profitable? Profit, in media, is simply a way of measuring attention. Why does what we call "media" attract so much attention?

The answer is that it is otherwise too crippling for individuals to bear the strain of accepting the unbalanced, unrewarding, uninspiring existence that is advertised as "normal daily life" for most people who have to earn a living every day.

Do those words seem too strong? Consider: to go to a job you don't value in itself but for its paycheck, while your kids go to a school that is less and less able to educate them; a large percentage of your pay is taken by the government for defenses that don't defend, welfare that doesn't aid, and the upkeep of a government that is impermeable to the influence of a single individual; while you are caught in a value system that judges you by what you own, in a society where it is taken for granted now that children can't communicate with their parents, that old people have to be shut away in homes, and that no neighborhood is *really* safe; while the highest medical costs in the world don't prevent us from having one of the worst health records in the West (for instance, New York has a far higher infant mortality rate than Hong Kong), and the air, water, and supermarket food are filled with God-knows-what; and to have, at the end of a busy yet uneventful life, little to show for enduring all this but a comfortable home if you've "done well" enough; yet to *know* all along that you're living in the freest, most powerful country in the world, though you haven't had time to exercise much freedom and don't personally have any power—this is to be living a life of slow attrition and maddening contradictions.

Add to this a social style that values cheerfulness more than any other attribute, and then it is not so strange or shocking that the average American family watches six to eight hours of network television a day. It is a cheap and sanctioned way to partake of this world without having actually to live in it.

Certainly they don't watch so much TV because they're bored—there's far too much tension in their lives to call them bored, and, in fact, many of the products advertised on their favorite programs feature drugs to calm them down. Nor is it because they're stupid—a people managing the most technically intricate daily life in history can hardly be written off as stupid; nor because they can't entertain themselves—they are not so different from the hundreds of generations of their forebears who entertained themselves very well as a matter of course. No, they are glued to the TV because one of the most fundamental messages of television is: "It's all right."

Every sitcom and drama says "It's all right." Those people on the tube go through the same—if highly stylized—frustrations, and are exposed to the same dangers as we are, yet they reappear magically every week (every day on the soap operas) ready for more, always hopeful, always cheery, never questioning the fundamental premise that this is the way a great culture behaves and that all the harassments are the temporary inconveniences of a beneficent society. It's going to get even *better,* but even now *it's all right.* The commercials, the Hollywood movies, the universal demand in every television drama or comedy that no character's hope can ever be exhausted, combine in a deafening chorus of: *It's all right.*

As a screenwriter I have been in many a film production meeting, and not once have I heard any producer or studio executive say, "We have to lie to the public." What I have heard, over and over, is, "They have to leave the theater feeling good." This, of course, easily (though not always) translates into lying—into simplifying emotions and events so that "it's all right." You may measure how deeply our people know "it" is *not* all right, not at all, by how much money they are willing to pay to be ceaselessly told that it is. The more they feel it's not, the more they need to be told it is—hence Mr. Reagan's popularity.

Works that don't say "It's all right" don't get much media attention or make much money.

The culture itself is in the infantile position of needing to be assured, every day, all day, that this way of life is good for you. Even the most disturbing news is dispensed in the most reassuring package. As world news has gotten more and more disturbing, the trend in broadcast journalism has been to get more and more flimflam, to take it less seriously, to keep up the front of "It's really quite all right." This creates an enormous tension between the medium and its messages, because everybody knows that what's on the news is *not* all right. That is why such big money is paid to a newscaster with a calm, authoritative air who, by his presence alone, seems to resolve the contradictions of his medium. Walter Cronkite was the most popular newscaster in broadcast history because his very presence implied: "As long as I'm on the air, you can be sure that, no matter what I'm telling you, *it's still all right.*"

Which is to say that the media has found it profitable to do the mothering of the mass psyche. But it's a weak mother. It cannot nurture. All it can do is say it's all right, tuck us in, and hope for the best.

Today most serious, creative people exhaust themselves in a sideline commentary on this state of affairs, a commentary that usually gets sucked up into the media and spewed back out in a format that says "It's all right. What this guy's saying is quite all right, what this woman's singing is all right, all right." This is what "gaining recognition" virtually always means now in America: your work gets turned inside out so that its meaning becomes "It's all right."

Of course, most of what exists *to make media of,* to make images of, is more and more disorder. Media keeps saying, "It's all right" while being fixated upon the violent, the chaotic, and the terrifying. So the production of media becomes more and more schizoid, with two messages simultaneously being broadcast: "It's all right. We're dying. It's all right. We're all dying." The other crucial message—"We're dying"—runs right alongside *It's all right.*

Murder is the crux of much media "drama." But it's murder presented harmlessly, with trivial causes cited. Rare is the attempt, in all our thousands of murder dramas, to delve below the surface. We take for granted now, almost as an immutable principle of dramatic unity, that significant numbers of us want to kill significant numbers of the rest of us. And what are all the murders in our media but a way of saying "We are being killed, we are killing, we are dying"? Only a people dying and in the midst of death would need to see so much of it in such sanitized form *in order to make death harmless.* This is the way we choose to share our death.

Delete the word "entertainment" and say instead, North Americans devote an enormous amount of time to the ritual of sharing death. If this were recognized as a ritual, and if the deaths were shared with a respect for the realities and the mysteries of death, this might be a very useful thing to do. But there is no respect for death in our death-dependent media, there is only the compulsion to display death. As for the consumers, they consume these deaths like sugar pills. Their ritual goes on far beneath any level on which they'd be prepared to admit the word "ritual." So we engage in a ritual we pretend isn't happening, hovering around deaths that we say aren't real.

It is no coincidence that this practice has thrived while the Pentagon uses the money of these death watchers to create weapons for death on a scale that is beyond the powers of human imagination—the very same human imagination that is stunting itself by watching ersatz deaths, as though intentionally crippling its capacity to envision the encroaching dangers. It is possible that the Pentagon's process could not go on without the dulling effects of this "entertainment."

When we're not watching our screens, we're listening to music. And, of course, North Americans listen to love songs at every possible opportunity, through every possible orifice of media. People under the strain of such dislocating unrealities need to hear "I love you, I love you," as often as they can. "I love you" or "I used to love you" or "I ought to love you" or "I need to love you" or "I want to love you." It is the fashion of pop-music critics to discount the words for the style, forgetting that most of the world's cultures have had songs about *everything*, songs about work, about the sky, about death, about the gods, about getting up in the morning, about animals, about children, about eating, about dreams—about everything, along with love. These were songs that everybody knew and sang. For a short time in the late sixties we moved toward such songs again, but that was a brief digression; since the First World War the music that most North Americans listen to has been a music of love lyrics that rarely go beyond adolescent yearnings. Either the song is steeped in the yearnings themselves, or it is saturated with a longing for the days when one could, shamelessly, feel like an adolescent. The beat has changed radically from decade to decade, but with brief exceptions that beat has carried the same pathetic load. (The beat, thankfully, has given us other gifts—we'll get to those later in this book.)

It can't be over-emphasized that these are entertainments of a people whose basic imperative is the need not to think about their environment. The depth of their need may be measured by the hysterical popularity of this entertainment; it is also the measure of how little good it does them.

Media is not experience. In its most common form, media substitutes a fantasy of experience or (in the case of news) an abbreviation of experience for the living fact. But in our culture the absorption of media has become a substitute for experience. We absorb media, we don't live it—there is a vast psychological difference, and it is a difference that is rarely brought up.

For example, in the 1940s, when one's environment was still one's *environment,* an experience to be lived instead of a media-saturation to be absorbed, teenagers like Elvis Presley and Jerry Lee Lewis didn't learn their music primarily from the radio. Beginning when they were small boys they sneaked over to the black juke joints of Louisiana and Mississippi and Tennessee, where they weren't supposed to go, and they listened and learned. When Lewis and Presley began recording, even though they were barely twenty they had tremendous authority because they had experience—a raw experience of crossing foreign boundaries, of streets and sounds and peoples, of the night-to-night learning of ways that could not be taught at home.

This is very different from young musicians now who learn from a product, not a living ground. Their music doesn't get to them till it's been sifted through elaborate corporate networks of production and distribution. It doesn't smack of the raw world that exists before "product" can even be thought of.

The young know this, of course. They sense the difference intensely, and often react to it violently. So white kids from suburban media culture invented slam dancing (jumping up and down and slamming into each other) while black kids from the South Bronx, who have to deal with realities far more urgent than media, were elaborating the astounding graces of break dancing.

Slam dancing was a deadend. Break dancing, coming from a living ground, goes out through media but becomes ultimately transformed into another living ground—the kids in the elementary school down the street in Santa Monica break dance. Which is to say, a grace has been added to their lives. A possibility of grace. With the vitality that comes from having originated from a living ground. The media here is taking its proper role as a channel, not as a world in itself. It's possible that these kids are being affected more in their bodies and their daily lives by the South Bronx subculture than by high-gloss films like *Gremlins* or *Indiana Jones and The Temple of Doom*. Even through all this static, life can speak to life.

Of course, break dancing inevitably gets hyped, and hence devalued, by the entertainment industry, the way Elvis Presley ended up singing "Viva Las Vegas" as that town's most glamorous headliner. He went from being the numinous son of a living ground to being the charismatic product of a media empire—the paradigm of media's power to transform the transformers. The town veritably glows in the dark with the strength of media's mystique.

We do not yet know what life *is* in a media environment. We have not yet evolved a contemporary culture that can supply that definition—or rather, supply the constellation of concepts in which that definition would live and grow. These seem such simple statements, but they are at the crux of the American dilemma now. An important aspect of this dilemma is that we've barely begun a body of thought and art which is focused on what is really *alive* in the ground of a media-saturated daily life. For culture always proceeds from two poles: one is the people of the land and the street; the other is the thinker. You see this most starkly in revolutions: the groundswell on the one hand, the thinker (the Jefferson, for instance) on the other. Or religiously, the groundswell of belief that is articulated by a Michelangelo or a Dante. The two poles can exist without each other but they cannot be effective without each other.

Unless a body of thought connects with a living ground, there is no possibility that this era will discover itself within its cacophony and create, one day, a post-A.D. culture. It is ours to attempt the thought and seek the ground—for all of us exist between those poles. We are not only dying. We are living. And we are struggling to share our lives, which is all, finally, that "culture" means.

HEAR THAT
LONG SNAKE MOAN

But don't hunt for dissonance;
because, in the end, there is no
  dissonance.
When the sound is heard people dance.
                              —Antonio Machado,
                          translated by Robert Bly

T*he Voodoo ceremonies of Haiti are danced*
around a centerpost, a kind of maypole through which the
gods pass from where they dwell into the ceremony. This
essay is the centerpost of this book. It is nothing less than
a history of my country. Of course, a country has an amaz-
ing number of interlocking histories. This is a history of its
music, its dancing—and yet not even those, but the longing
they expressed. As such, with this enormous subject, it is
the longest chapter in the book. A scholarly work, putting
together facts which, to my knowledge, have not yet been
seen as a coherent whole; yet, while we must concentrate
on facts and sources and such, this is as much a meditation
as an essay on history. A meditation on the music and a
meditation within the music.

   Every true work of culture is a work of resurrection, a
work of remembrance that creates the remembered mo-
ment anew and blends it with the present moment to cre-
ate the possibilities of the future. How does American
music do this? For only when we see clearly the meaning

*that this music incorporated can we understand both the
history of this music and the history that this music
made.*

"Rock 'n' roll" is a word from the depths. As a word,
there is no modern word that can compare to it. It's as
resonant as a Chaucer word. First, each of its parts is
both a verb and a noun. "Rock," the noun *(Rock the
noun!)*, is a most basic object. Hard. "Upon this rock I
will build my church," said Jesus. An object-word that
defies scale—it can fit into your hand, a rock, or it could
be the whole planet. While as a verb, it leaps from the
sturdiness of its noun-definition into movement, back
and forth, oscillating, going from yin to yang and back
again, rocking.

"Roll" is sweet, as a noun. Lush. Soft. Eschewing
every traditional Anglo-Saxon word for the female organ, recently freed New Orleans slaves were calling the
cunt a "jelly roll" over 100 years ago. So juicy did they
find the expression that it came to mean cock as well as
cunt, both genders singing about "my jelly roll." The
first great jazz composer called himself Jelly Roll Morton. Then there's "roll of fat," "roll of bills"—that kind of
roll. And as a verb *(Roll the verb!)*, it can move and it
can move and it might never stop, end over end over
infinity. Oceans roll.

Putting the two together, "rock 'n' roll" was a term
from the juke joints of the South, long in use by the forties, when a music started being heard that had no
name, wasn't jazz and wasn't simply blues and wasn't
Cajun, but had all those elements and could not be ignored. In those juke joints "rock 'n' roll" hadn't meant
the name of a music, it meant "to fuck." "Rock," by itself, had pretty much meant that, in those circles, since
the twenties at least. "Rock 'n' roll" was a juicy elabora-
tion on the old usage. When, finally, in the mid-fifties,
the songs started being played by white people and aired

on the radio—"Rock Around the Clock," "Good Rockin'
Tonight," "Reelin' And A-Rockin' "—the meaning hadn't
changed. The word was so prevalent that the music began to be called "rock 'n' roll" by disc jockeys who either
didn't know what they were saying or were too sly to
admit what they knew. The term stuck.

But it had a meaning with yet another root. For
since roughly the turn of the century, and possibly much
longer, in the singing churches of the blacks, when the
songs were yelled and sung and the hands were clapped
and the sweat was pouring and people were testifying,
fainting, speaking in tongues, being at least transported
and often saved, which meant to be overwhelmed by the
Holy Ghost—that was called "rockin' the church." "They
made the church rock." Upon *that* rock their church was
built, more than on the stone of Peter. And the screams
of rock that go right through you—high pitched screams
that aren't joy and aren't agony but sound like both together, and sometimes like the human equivalent of mi-
crophone feedback, screams that yet are beautiful in
their raw and naked and utterly committed flight out of
the throat; the screams of Little Richard and Janis Joplin and Aretha Franklin and James Brown and Bruce
Springsteen—those screams came straight out of those
churches. You can hear them on virtually any recording
of black church music—either field recordings from the
little shacklike rural churches, or more sophisticated
gospel recordings by people who sing the music as
professionals. Such a scream. What can we call it but a
holy scream? Unlike anything in Western music before
it.

We will try to enter that scream, insofar as an essay's prose can, and to enter the scream is, first, to contemplate Africa. To be precise, the west coast of Africa.

That American music is rooted in Africa is a cliché,
and clichés are useless. But to trace that root is a revelation. It's a root that goes so deep that some of our most

common terms—terms often associated with the music—
are from African languages that haven't been spoken on
this continent conversationally in close to two centuries.
Robert Farris Thompson, the art and music historian, has
found that "funky" is from the Ki-Kongo *lu-fuki,* meaning "positive sweat." Which is virtually what it means,
in a metaphoric sense, in American language today. He
notes that now the Bakongo people use the American
"funky" and their own *lu-fuki* interchangeably "to
praise persons for the integrity of their art." It's a word
that's been around America for a long time. Song titles
place it in New Orleans circa 1900, and it was apparently well established by then. *Which means this is not
slang. This is a word in the American language.* Its roots
and its longevity prove that, whether or not the word
has found its way into our dictionaries and our middle-
class usage.

Mojo, a word found in many a rock and blues tune,
is Ki-Kongo for "soul." In North America for at least a
century it has meant an object that's been invested with
spirit power, soul power, and has the capacity to cure or
heal or influence. "I got my mojo workin'," one song
says. When my family moved not long ago, one of the
movers, a black carrying a packing box of mine labeled
"Voodoo," looked at me humorously and took his "mojo
stone" out of his pocket to show me. When I asked to
hold it, he wouldn't let me.

Again, this isn't jive-talk or a fad of speech. Its usage is too firmly rooted and too constant. This is our
language.

Our "boogie" comes from the Ki-Kongon *mbugi,*
meaning, according to Thompson, "devilishly good."
Juke, as in our jukebox and juke joint (which often did
not have juke-boxes) is the Mande-kan word for "bad,"
for among righteous blacks as well as righteous whites,
this was bad music played by bad people in bad places.

Robert Farris Thompson thinks that "jazz" and

"jism" likely derive from the Ki-Kongo *dinza*, which means "to ejaculate." And the use of the concept "cool" among the Yoruba people of Africa is precisely the same as its use as popularized by jazz musicians in New York forty years ago—another usage that's remained constant with us. Said one Yoruba informant to Thompson, "Coolness is the correct way you represent yourself to a human being."

In his remarkable book *Flash of the Spirit* Thompson writes:

> *Like character, coolness ought to be internalized as a governing principle for a person to merit the high praise, "His heart is cool"* (okan e tutu). *In becoming sophisticated, a Yoruba adept learns to differentiate between forms of spiritual coolness ... So heavily charged is this concept with ideas of beauty and correctness that a fine carnelian bead or a passage of exciting drumming may be praised as "cool."*
>
> *Coolness, then, is a part of character ... To the degree that we live generously and discreetly, exhibiting grace under pressure, our appearance and our acts gradually assume virtual royal power. As we become noble, fully realizing the spark of creative goodness God endowed us with ... we find the confidence to cope with all kinds of situations. This is* ashe. *This is character. This is mystic coolness. All one. Paradise is regained, for Yoruba art returns the idea of heaven to mankind wherever the ancient ideal attitudes are genuinely manifested.*

Coolness doesn't mean coldness. Cool art is passionate art. In American culture, Miles Davis has been the exemplar of this aesthetic. When in 1949 and 1950 he was making the recordings—with, it should be noted, white musicians like Gerry Mulligan, Lee Konitz, Gunther Schuller and Gil Evans, as well as blacks like J. J. Johnson, John Lewis, Kenny Clarke and Max Roach—Davis would call those sessions "birth of the cool." But those sessions might better have been called "rebirth of the cool." They were, in music, a restatement of this African philosophy in American terms. That has been the life of all Miles Davis's music, and he himself has been absolutely sure of this.

Sidney Bechet, the great New Orleans reed player, feeling these linkages instinctively, called his music "the remembering song. There's so much to remember," he said, speaking of "the long song that started back there"—back in the South, and farther back still, in Africa.

To re-member. To put back together.

"Back there" are the people of Kongo, Dahomey, and Yorubaland. These were not jungle bunnies living, insensate, under an eternal sun. They were at once tribal and urban. It is hard, after so many bad movies and so many encrusted lies, to think of them as urban, and it is hard for a Western mind to conceive of "tribal" and "urban" together; yet as late as the mid-nineteenth century the Yoruba city of Abeokuta ran six miles along the bank of the Ogun River and had a population estimated at 200,000. Its craft industries thrived—ironwork, carpentry, tailoring, farming, tool-making, textiles. And this urban culture had been thriving for centuries, a city probably older than, say, New York is now.

Here, intact, a little more than a century ago, was a mature culture which had chosen not to go the way of monotheism and the father gods, but had, like India, kept its polytheistic pantheon rooted in the Great Mother religions—or rather, in the religious impulse we now identify with the Great Mother. They shared with the Hopi, with the ancient Irish and Welsh and all the Druid peoples, as well as with the Chinese and the Egyptians, the mother symbol of the serpent—as Thompson puts it, "ancient Yoruba image of coolness, peace and power." And they shared with pre-Christianist Europe—the so-called pagan religions—the conviction that religious worship is a *bodily* celebration, a dance of the entire community; or, as it would have been called in Europe when such belief had been driven underground, a "sabbat." The mind-body split that governs European thought seems never to have entered African religion, African consciousness—at least not until imported there by missionaries. To meditate was to dance.

Hence in this culture the drum is so sacred an instrument that some are built only for display. They are too holy to touch. "An instrument of significant silence, not reverberation," is Thompson's phrase. It's as though such a drum is there to say that within the astonishingly complex rhythms of Africa—rhythms which Western musical notation is too crude, rhythmically, to express—within the multitoned din is a core of quietude, of calm, the focused silence of the Master, the silence out of which revelation rises. Sometimes such a drum is six feet high.

This is the drum within. It exists in all people. As quiet a man as Thoreau heard it and spoke of it. What else was the "different drummer" that allowed him to know that violence can be met with peace, and that "the sun is but a morning star"?

"Westerners always stay in temperate zones when they're looking for philosophy," Thompson said in an interview in *Rolling Stone*. "Jews become Buddhists, Methodists become Bahais; they never go south." What would they find if they did? What is the metaphysical goal of African thought?

Africans don't conceive of the other world—the world of the spirit, the divine—as existing above this one, or below it, or even alongside it. Neither heaven nor hell, nor Olympus or Hades, nor the Australian Dreamtime. For the African, the human world and the spirit world *intersect*. Their sign for this is the cross, but it has nothing to do with the Christianist cross, which impales a man in helpless agony upon the intersection. That is what the West feels. In Africa, the cross is of two roads intersecting to flow into each other, to nourish each other. The earthly and the spirit worlds meet at right angles, and everything that is most important happens at the spot where they meet, which is neither solely of one world nor the other.

The metaphysical goal of the African way is to *experience* the intense meeting of both worlds at the crossroads. Writes Thompson, "Ritual contact with divinity underscores the religious aspirations of the Yoruba. To become possessed by the spirit of the Yoruba deity, which is *a formal goal* of the religion, is to 'make the god,' to capture numinous flowing force *within one's body*." (Italics mine.)

Spurred by the holy drums, deep in the meditation of the dance, one is literally entered by a god or a goddess. Goddesses may enter men, and gods may enter women. Westerners call this "possession." That's too crude a concept for this, though good writers describing the phenomenon have been forced to use it; we have no other word or concept that comes close. But instead of possession, it seems more accurate to think of "a flowing through." The one flows through the other. They flow through each other. As Maya Deren put it in her study of Haitian Voodoo, *Divine Horsemen: The Living Gods of Haiti*: "*The loa [spirit], then, partakes of the head that bears it. The principle is modified by the person.*" (Deren's italics.) The body, literally, becomes the crossroads. Human and divine are united within it—and it can happen to anyone.

What a frightening, utterly terrifying concept to our

Western minds. Far from inflating the ego, the experience demolishes it while the state lasts. People who've been in this state commonly can't remember what they've said or done, and part of the function of the ceremony is to have witnesses who will later tell them what the god said through them. In the West we are so frightened of such states that we assume, when we see them in isolated cases, that they are symptoms of psychosis, if we are charitable; if we are not, we assume—as the first Westerners to see such things assumed—that this is possession by the Devil, and that anything, anything at all, is justified in blotting it out. It is no wonder we tend not to "go south" for our philosophy.

In Abomey, Africa, these deities that speak through humans are called *vodun*. The word means "mysteries." From their *vodun* comes our "Voodoo." And it is to Voodoo that we must look for the roots of our music.

To get to Voodoo conceptually we must, as the Africans actually did, go through slavery. The fact of slavery is something else that is not race-specific. Africa practiced slavery long before the whites came. The whites did not bring a strange idea. And several strong African tribes grew rich by enslaving their neighbors and selling them to whites. (Later, in the New World, it was not uncommon for "free people of color" to own slaves.) The Atlantic slave trade could not have existed without the complicity of African profiteers.

This doesn't lift the onus of slavery from Christianist whites. But it gives us some idea of the depths, the complexities, of a slave's agony. Where could one find one's being? Sold by one's kind to another kind. Taken under unspeakable conditions in a vehicle, and across an expanse, as inescapable to them as though a UFO were to take one of us to another galaxy. And then to see, in the eyes of your captors, not only brutality and fear but the linked impulses of revulsion and attraction—revulsion freely expressed and attraction twisted into rape and murder. And this went on for 300 years. How could one feel one's being?

We can measure the strength of the metaphysics of Africa—we can gauge the depth of its relevance to the human condition everywhere—by the bare fact that it survived through this centuries-long ordeal. "Lord, you made the night too long," Louis Armstrong once sang. He expressed his feeling through a music that had come through that night. The slaves kept their mysteries, their *vodun,* and their mysteries kept them.

Their effort may not be easily understood by a generation whose arts are more and more dependent upon the generosity of corporate foundations, universities, and government grants. The anthropologist Alfred Métraux described it like this in his classic *Voodoo in Haiti:*

> *The degree of [the African's] attachment to his gods may be measured by the amount of energy he spent in honouring them—and this at the risk of the terrible punishment meted out to those who took part in pagan ceremonies in which the colonists saw nothing but sorcery ... The overexertion was so crushing that the life of a Negro sold to a plantation in Saint-Domingue was reckoned at never more than ten years. We can but admire the devotion of those slaves who sacrificed their rest and their sleep to resurrect the religions of their tribes—this under the very eyes of the Whites, and in the most precarious conditions. Think what energy, what courage it took to enable the songs and rites due to each god to be handed down across the generations!*

In the West Indies these practices survived. In

North America they largely didn't. Except in New Orleans, slaves were not allowed to gather in groups, even for entertainment. Again except in New Orleans, drums were forbidden. In place of drumming, North American slaves developed what we now know as tap dancing, but the loss of the drum meant the loss of their ceremonies. Their Africa survived in silence, without form, waiting for the evolution of new forms to revive it. For the survival of Africa in African forms we have to look to the West Indies. There, we have reliable accounts dating from the late 1700s until the present describing ceremonies in which African metaphysics not only survived but thrived.

The stately impression we are given of the depth of African life is nothing like the vibes we get from the word "voodoo." Voodoo is the African aesthetic shattered and then desperately put back together. More than simply "put back together," it has been recreated to serve its people under the shattering impact of slavery and poverty. Voodoo is not so much Africa *in* the New World as it is Africa meeting the New World, absorbing it and being absorbed by it, and *re-forming* the ancient metaphysics according to what it now had to face.

How many metaphysics, ever, have been tested under such fire?

A vast synthesis had to occur. Tribes, thrown together, had to sift through what they had most in common and discard what had previously kept them apart. People who were separated by class and caste within the tribal structures had to come together on new terms. Catholicism had to be dealt with. From the late 1700s to this day Haitian Voodoos profess themselves to be good Catholics, and Catholic prayers have become an integral part of Voodo ceremony—and had obviously been so for a long while when the fact was finally noted by white observers around 1820. Catholicism was used to saint worship, and had indeed fostered saint worship as an accommodation to pagan converts, so Voodoo presented nothing new. Africans, for their part, loved Catholic iconography. They felt they were seeing pictures of their gods. Saint Patrick holding a scepter and commanding snakes was obviously, as far as they were concerned, a shaman—a *hungan*—with a power-stick (in the popular print, the saint's scepter looks much like the ceremonial staff passed from speaker to speaker in some tribal councils as symbol of the right and authority to speak); he was communing with serpents. This became a favorite depiction of Damballah-wedo, the great serpent spirit. In Saint James on his horse, wielding his sword, they saw their warrior spirit Ogu. Writes Thompson, "Everywhere in *vodun* art, one universe abuts another."

But the religion keeps the same goal. The *hungan* may be healer, personal adviser, and political broker, but his—or, for a *mambo,* hers, for women are as numerous and powerful as men in this religion—most important function is to organize and preside over the ceremonies in which the *loa,* the gods, "ride" the body of the worshiper. The ecstasy *and* morality of *vodun* intersect in this phenomenon. The god is seen as the rider, the person is seen as the horse, and they come together in the dance. When the god speaks through the person *about* that person, almost every sentence is prefaced with the phrase "Tell my horse..."—because the "horse" will have no memory of the "ride" when it is over, and will have to learn of it from others. The morality implicit in this is stated best in Maya Deren's favorite Haitian proverb: great gods cannot ride little horses.

"There's a whole language of possession," Thompson says, "a different expression and stance for each god." All the accounts are clear that a god is instantly recognizable by its movements, and the movements are different for each. So if the ceremony is to honor Ghede, their equivalent of Hermes, perhaps Erzulie, their Aphrodite, shows up uninvited. But she is recognizable whether she

rides a man or a woman because of her distinctive movements and behavior. This suggests a psychic suppleness
that has to be staggering to any Westerner. Staggering,
and frightening, if we are honest with ourselves. We
may speak of a new model of the psyche, we may even be
learning to experience life in a way that is more true to
the way our many-faced psyches are structured—which
is to say, the way they were created to live—but here are
people who can *dance* it!

Here are people who can, to use Jungian terminol-
ogy, *embody* an archetype—any single Voodoo worshiper
may embody many during a lifetime of ceremonies. They
will dance it, speak it, make love through it, manifest it
in every possible way, entering and leaving the experience *without psychosis,* without "mind-expanding"
drugs, *and* while having the support and help of their
community, for all of this is integral with their daily
lives.

Can there be much doubt that this is a metaphysical
achievement as great as, say, the building of Chartres or
the writing of the Bhagavad-Gita? It's no wonder that
they risked so much to keep their metaphysics alive.
These people built their cathedrals and wrote their
scripture within their bodies, by means of a system that
could be passed from one generation to the next. That
system was rhythm.

In Haitian Voodoo as in Africa the drum is holy.
The drummer is seen merely as the servant of the drum
—he has no influence within the hierarchy of the religion, but through his drum he has great influence on the
ceremony. Each *loa* prefers a fundamentally different
rhythm, and the drummer knows them all and all their
variations. He can often invoke possession by what he
plays, though a drummer would never play a rhythm
that would go contrary to the ceremony's structure as set
by the *hungan* or *mambo*. There are drums which are
ceremonially fed the night before a gathering, and then

"put to bed" to bolster their strength. And here, too, are the drums of silence.

The drumming and dancing together form an entity from which, in Métraux's words (and my italics), "emanates a power *that affects the supernatural world* ... If the music and dancing please the spirits to such an extent that they are affected, even against their will, then it is because *they themselves are dancers* who allow themselves to be carried away by the supernatural power of rhythm."

To dance is to meditate because the universe dances. And, because the universe dances, "he who does not dance does not know what happens."

This is, literally, the body and soul of Voodoo, but it is not what Westerners think of when they think of Voodoo. They think of drums, perhaps, but also of potions, spells, sorcery and zombies. Much of what's lumped together by Westerners that way are forms of healing and forms of prayer. Some of it is sorcery in the classic sense, invoking the supernatural for the control of others. I mention these only to note that Voodoo, like Judeo-Christianism, has its nether side, but it defines that nether area differently. For Judeo-Christianism the nether side *is* the body. The Fall came about through the body. The apple was *eaten*. The Fall *became* the body. The resulting mind-body split pervades everything. Even when Westerners go East for philosophy, to India especially, they often seek techniques for controlling and pacifying the body, which still, to their "enlightened" minds, is evil meat. Kundalini especially turns sex (body energy) into mind (spirit energy).

The nether side of Voodoo is completely different. Its witchy potions, amulets and evil spells *are* for interfering with and controlling the body, but the *implication* is that the body's progress is natural, even, as in the dance, holy, while manipulation is not. Manipulation is unclean. And to create a zombie (a corpse brought back to life) is the ultimate evil magic, because a body then is not allowed to go to its rest and join the *loa,* perhaps to become a *loa* itself.

I mention these to emphasize that even in its perverse forms—and every religion has its perverse forms—Voodoo consistently emphasizes that the holy and the earthly *are supposed to* meld in the body itself, and that to split the mind from the body is to do evil.

Voodoo is fundamentally African, yet there is more than Africa in Voodoo. Métraux mentions Masonic elements, and he states that the Voodoos "have kept alive beliefs and rituals inherited from the ancient religions of the classical East and the Aegean world," but he doesn't elaborate. The mythologist Joseph Campbell, who edited Deren's book *Divine Horsemen,* says in his foreword that the "day-to-day epiphanies of Voudoun" are what the Greeks called being "full of the God," and that this is fundamentally the same experience "as precipitated much of the mythology preserved in Greek and Roman documents ..." He also believed that it's possible "to recognize the well-preserved lineaments in Haitian Voodoo of an esoteric philosophy of the Gnostic-Hermetic-Kabbalistic order."

I don't mean to get so academic, but remember, we're on the trail of the metaphysics of American music. It's a very winding trail, it goes through jungles, and there are places where it's completely overgrown. The major studies don't mention that Africans were not the only slaves in the West Indies; they were not even the only slaves who had a non-Christian—usually called, in unconsciously slanted language, "pre-Christian"—cosmology. In the 1650s, after Oliver Cromwell had conquered Ireland in a series of massacres, he left his brother, Henry, as the island's governor. In the next decade Henry sold thousands of Irish people, mostly women and children, as slaves to the West Indies. Estimates range between 30,000 and 80,000. The higher number seems quite likely, in the light of a letter Henry Cromwell wrote to a slaver, saying "it is not in the least doubted you may have such number of them as you think fitt . . . I desire to express as much zeal in this design as you could wish." This Henry of the Uprighte Harte, as he called himself, said in another letter to a slaver who wanted only girls, "I think it might be of like advantage to your affaires there, and to ours heer, if you should thinke fitt to sende 1500 or 2000 young boys of from twelve to fourteen years of age, to the place aforementioned. We could well spare them . . ."

The Irish slaves, most of them women, were mated with the Africans. There is "a tradition"—as historians sometimes call something which they have good reason to believe but can't prove—that up to the early nineteenth century there were blacks on some of the islands who spoke Gaelic. In any case, the West Indian accent becomes much more comprehensible when the Irish slaves are taken into account. If you don't know anyone from there, listen to the language in a film like *The Harder They Come*. The Irish tinge is unmistakable.

Why were these people sold into slavery? Henry gives us clues: "Concerninge the young women, although we must use force takeinge them up, yet it beinge so much to their owne goode . . ." And in another letter, the one in which he suggests some men be taken too: "who knows but that it may be the meanes to make them Englishmen, I mean rather Christians." In other words, Henry was trying to sell off as many pagans as he could. This was at the height of the English witch-craze, which was a pogrom against those who still adhered to the Celtic religions. Ireland was the stronghold for the old beliefs. This, better than anything else, explains the mercilessness of Cromwell's massacres there. How widespread could such beliefs have been? I know a woman whose Irish grandmother, in the 1950s, still referred to

Christianism as "the new religion," and taught her granddaughter what she could remember of the old Celtic rites. Jeanne Moreau's film *L'Adolescente* tells of a similar experience she had with her grandmother in rural France in the late 1930s. Such stories speak of traditions that had strength through the nineteenth century in Europe. In Cromwell's time "sabbats" are well-documented throughout the continent, and in Ireland the old ways were more a way of life than anywhere else.

And so we find, in West Indian Voodoo, a centerpost, a gaily painted pole very like the maypole that survives in Europe from Celtic pagan celebration, at the center of every ceremony. You see it plainly in Maya Deren's 1949 footage, made into a documentary in the 1950s, titled, as is her book, *Divine Horsemen*. The gods are said to enter through the centerpost, and the dances for most ceremonies revolve around the centerpost. We don't find this in the accounts from Africa. It speaks of a definite Irish-pagan influence. Virtually every account of Voodoo notes, at some point, how similar are its sorcery practices to the practices of European witchcraft, but no one has, to my knowledge, mentioned the connection with the Irish slaves.

We will never have evidence, but nevertheless we have a good case: practicing pagans from Ireland infused their beliefs with the Africans, mingling in Voodoo two great streams of non-Christianist metaphysics. The snake, after all, was a holy symbol to both—Saint Patrick driving the snakes out of Ireland, and the classic statue of the Virgin Mary with her bare foot crushing a snake, were political cartoons in the sense that they symbolized the Catholic dominion over Celtic paganism. In their beliefs and symbology the pagan Irish were closer to Africa than to Puritan England. This is part of our buried history, and as we bring it out into the light it will become more important.

All of them—the many, many Africans who created Voodoo and the, let's say, 40,000 Irish who gave to Voodoo some of their flourishes and sorcery—would have their revenge. Jazz and rock 'n' roll would evolve from Voodoo, carrying within them the metaphysical antidote that would aid many a twentieth century Westerner from both the ravages of the mind-body split codified by Christianism, and the onslaught of technology. The twentieth century would dance as no other had, and, through that dance, secrets would be passed. First North America, and then the whole world, would—like the old blues says—"hear that long snake moan."

The questions of how Haitian Voodoo came to the continental United States, and the question of why jazz originated in New Orleans, are in fact parts of the same question. These questions haven't been joined before because the people who wrote extensively about Voodoo haven't known much about American music, and the people—mostly jazz critics—who've documented the history of American music, while establishing the beginning of the music in New Orleans, haven't considered *why* the music should have begun there rather than elsewhere. They've celebrated the facts without trying to interpret them.

New Orleans was unique in the South in more ways than one. It was the largest city and an important port through which the whole world passed. Until the Louisiana Purchase it was a Spanish and French city with a large population of "free people of color" (33 percent of its population in 1788, 25 percent in 1810). So it was the only major city in the United States that was not Anglo-Saxon and not Protestant, and not even all white. Here there was the same brand of Catholicism that had lived easily with African metaphysics in the West Indies. And, as I've said, believers in Voodoo usually proclaim themselves to be good Catholics.

A fascinating aside: while Catholicism and Voodoo blend, Protestantism and Voodoo are always at odds. A Haitian saying goes, "If you want the *loa* to leave you alone—become a Protestant." Métraux observed that some Voodoos become Protestants not out of faith but because "they felt themselves to be the target of angry *loa* and saw in Protestantism a refuge. Hence Protestantism beckons as though it were a shelter, or more precisely a magic circle, where people cannot be got at by *loa* and demons." In Protestantism we have the mind-body split at its most virulent, and anything which threatens the single-"I," egocentric view of the psyche is looked on with horror. A poverty of religious art. A Puritan morality trying to fulfill the function of spirituality. An equation of goodness with denial. It is no wonder Voodoo is beyond their toleration.

To return to New Orleans: finally, it was the only place in the United States where slaves were allowed to gather among themselves for their "entertainments," as they were called, and, most importantly, to play drums: therefore, it was the only place where slaves were allowed to form a culture of their own.

Yet white people in Louisiana knew and felt threatened by Voodoo. In 1782 Governor Galvez banned the buying of any blacks from Martinique because Voodoo was so strong there that they "would make the lives of the citizens unsafe." Ten years later blacks from Santo Domingo and Haiti were also banned. Whites had reason to be afraid. Haiti was at the beginning of the slave revolution that would make it the second republic of the New World and the location of the first successful black independence movement. Haitian historians fix the beginning of the revolution at a Voodoo ceremony on August 14, 1791, and believe Voodoo to be responsible for giving the slaves the unity that made their victory possible.

The Louisiana ban was lifted in 1803, though the

Haitian turmoil was at its height (independence would be proclaimed there in 1804). War continued in Haiti for some time, however, and many West Indians, including free blacks, emigrated to New Orleans because of the conflict. Robert Tallant, in his *Voodoo in New Orleans*, cites this as "the beginning of organized Voodoo" there, though the word "organized" may be too much of a word for what happened.

Every history of jazz goes back to the slave celebrations in a field that came to be called Congo Square in what was then the center of New Orleans. (Interestingly, the Oumas Indians once used the field for their corn feasts and considered it holy ground.) On Sundays, slaves from all over the city arrived, watched over by white police and an encircling throng of white spectators. The festivities were described in writing by fascinated and shocked spectators again and again. One of the best is from Henry Edward Durell, written in 1853, the heyday of the Congo Square dances:

> *Let a stranger to New Orleans visit of an afternoon of one of its holy days, the public squares in the lower portion of the city, and he will find them filled with its African population, tricked out with every variety of show costume, joyous, wild, and in the full exercise of a real saturnalia ...*
>
> *Upon entering the square the visitor finds the multitude packed in groups of close, narrow circles, of a central area of only a few feet; and there in the center of each circle sits the musician, astride a barrel, strong-headed, which he beats with two sticks, to a strange measure incessantly, like mad, for hours together, while the perspiration literally rolls in streams and wets the ground; and there, too, labor the dancers male and*

female, under an inspiration of possession,
which takes from their limbs all sense of
weariness, and gives to them a rapidity and a
duration of motion that will hardly be found
elsewhere outside of mere machinery. The
head rests upon the breast, or is thrown back
upon the shoulders, the eyes closed, or glar-
ing, while the arms, amid cries, and shouts,
and sharp ejaculations, float upon the air, or
keep time, with the hands patting upon the
thighs, to a music which is seemingly eternal.

Keep in mind that Métraux observed in Haiti a century later: "The classic distinction between dances sacred
and profane is not always very clear . . . at certain public
jollifications dances are done which differ little or not at
all from ritual dances."

This seems especially true of the Congo Square
dances when you learn why Congo Square happened in
the first place. The dances were an attempt by the city
government to deal with the increase in Voodoo that had
resulted from the recent Haitian immigration. It was
feared that Voodoo meetings were being held to work
sorcery against whites, and perhaps to plot revolution,
so in 1817 the Municipal Council forbade slaves to con-
gregate for any reason, including dancing, except in designated places on Sundays. Congo Square was the major
place.

This is the way of things. It was precisely by trying
to stop Voodoo that, for the first time in the New World,
African music and dancing was presented both for Africans and whites as an end in itself, a form on its own.
Here was the metaphysics of Africa set loose from the
forms of Africa. For this form of *performance* wasn't
African. In the ceremonies of Voodoo there is no audience. Some may dance and some may watch, but those
roles may change several times in a ceremony, and all

are participants. In Congo Square, African music was put into a Western form of presentation. From 1817 until the early 1870s, these dances went on with few interruptions, the dance and the music focused on for their own sake by both participants and spectators. It is likely that this was the first time blacks became aware of the music *as music* instead of strictly as a part of ceremony. Which means that in Congo Square, African metaphysics first became subsumed in the music. A secret within the music instead of the object of the music. A possibility embodied by the music, instead of the music existing strictly as this metaphysics's *technique*. On the one hand, something marvelous was lost. On the other, only by separating the music from the religion could either the musics or the metaphysics within it leave their origins and deeply influence a wider sphere.

In his foreword to Maya Deren's book, Joseph Campbell quotes Ananda K. Coomaraswamy as saying, "The content of folklore is metaphysical . . . *So long as the material of folklore is transmitted, so long is the ground available on which the superstructure of full initiatory understanding can be built.*" (Coomaraswamy's italics.) In African culture, what they are calling folklore is at least as much musical as verbal. One day the music would carry initiations to people who would only vaguely sense they were being initiated, but who would feel compelled to join the dance. As happens with initiations, their dance would change their lives.

It is time to speak of Marie Laveau. I hesitate to, the way one would hesitate to tell an adopted child who his real mother is. In New Orleans she is a legend, but stories are told of her—conversationally and in print—without any attempt to assess her significance. If you go to her tomb in the oldest cemetery of the city—St. Louis Cemetery #1, right near were Storyville used to stand, and a brief walk from the old site of Congo Square—you will see fresh offerings and old ones, tidbits that are the remains of Voodoo charms, and chalked *X*'s people have made to help their prayers find Marie. I suspected some tourist-conscious caretaker of doing it until I saw people —not tourists—leave plastic flowers. As for me, I left a note of thanks, for the more I consider the achievements of Marie Laveau, the more I feel her to be one of the most important Americans of the nineteenth century.

Yet what we know of her is piecemeal, though her name still resonates in New Orleans a century after her death. Marie Laveau was what we once would have called a witch and now might call a shaman. In Haiti she would have been called a *mambo* and in New Orleans she was called a queen. She was racially a mixture of black, Indian, and white. Her father was said to be a wealthy white planter, and her marriage certificate says she was illegitimate. A free woman of color—virtually all the New Orleans "doctors" (hungans) and queens were free blacks—both her first husband Jacques Paris and her second, de Glapion (whom she never officially married, but lived with for decades and to whom she bore, it is said, at least fifteen children!) came from Haiti. The first official record of her is of her first marriage in 1819. The marriage contract called her "a native of New Orleans," but the innovations she would bring to Voodoo were Haitian. By 1830 she was considered to be the queen of all the New Orleans Voodoos.

The dances on Congo Square hadn't stopped or even distracted the practice of Voodoo. Out on Bayou St. John and Lake Pontchartrain huge ceremonies occurred regularly. They would continue till nearly the end of the nineteenth century. When Marie Laveau became queen —overpowering, and, it is said, sometimes causing the death of other queens who wouldn't become subordinate to her—she presided both at Congo Square dances and at the lake ceremonies, as well as at the many smaller gatherings that were held for initiates alone. She is said to have given New Orleans Voodoo the Haitian stamp of

Catholicism, and to have maintained throughout her long reign—she died in 1881—that her people were Catholics and that she offered Voodoo to God.

White New Orleans knew her as a powerful woman. In her early years she was a hairdresser to New Orleans's elite, and she is said to have developed an intelligence network of hairdressers, servants, and slaves to ferret out the most embarrassing secrets of the white rich and to use them for blackmail. This seems to have made her invulnerable to the law. Over the years she was in court many times, on various charges and in various suits, and never lost a case. Neither her ceremonies nor her house (or houses) of prostitution were ever raided, at least so far as court records show. And she could come and go at will visiting the prisons (which she apparently did strictly as a lay Catholic, spending a great deal of time with prisoners who had been sentenced to death, bringing food, building altars, and praying with them). She opened the huge ceremonies on Lake Pontchartrain and Bayou St. John to whites and went so far as to invite the press at times. (From the beginning of the nineteenth century, whites—especially women— were heavily involved in Voodoo, especially the more orgiastic practices, and it was common, in the raids, for half the people arrested to be whites. This no doubt contributed to the southern saying that "there ain't no white people in New Orleans," and Bessie Smith's line to the effect that New Orleans is a right fine place, "whatever the folks do, the white folk do it too.") In 1850 the *Daily Picayune* referred to Marie Laveau in an article as "the head of the Voudou women," and she was still presiding over the more important lakeside ceremonies in 1869, when the *New Orleans Times* gave the last description of her doing so.

One of Robert Tallant's informants, an old man speaking around 1940, remembered what his grandfather told him when he was a boy: "Marie Laveau had a dance she did all by herself. She would wrap that snake around her shoulders and she'd shake and twist herself like she was a snake. Her feet would never move. She had another dance she did wit' a fish. She'd hold a big redfish behind her head and do her snake dance. My grandfather said that was something to see." This is virtually the same dance that Moreau de Saint-Mary described at the end of Haiti's colonial period: the *mambo* stands on a box in which the snake lies "and is penetrated by the god; she writhes; her whole body is convulsed and the oracle speaks from her mouth." (The snake in the box is also described in many accounts of the nineteenth-century New Orleans ceremonies.)

If we put it all together we see a black woman strong enough to have real authority in a time when neither blacks nor women had any, in the South right through the Civil War and Reconstruction. We see a woman who was a shaman, and therefore, to have any reputation, had to be a healer as well as a hexer. A woman through whom gods and goddesses—or, if you prefer, archetypes—spoke and who could induce this state in others. A woman who felt deeply enough about her theology to enforce its particular tenets—Voodoo-Catholicism—on her people. A woman who was hustler enough to make money through the gullibility of whites (and blacks, too, no doubt), tough enough to make more through prostitution, and cunning enough to protect herself and her religion from white law. And this money was not spent on herself: she lived most of her life in a small cottage on St. Anne Street in the Latin Quarter, with her virtual tribe of children and grandchildren, and had all the expenses of being a *mambo*—in Haiti it's the shaman's responsibility to provide the means for the ceremonies. It must have taken a steady flow of money just to keep up her work. *And* she was a dancer—by all accounts an incredible one, even among a society of incredible dancers. How many other figures have we in our history with such a range, with such long-lasting authority, and whose power—political, social, and spiritual—had nothing to back it up but her own intensity?

It is clear, both from the facts as we have them and from the power of her legend, that Marie Laveau centered and anchored what might otherwise have been continually more scattered and dissipating practices, especially with the shocks of the Civil War and Reconstruction—practices which, significantly, were ended on a large scale very soon after her death. Her centering effect can't be underestimated. What elsewhere in the South was a people who had to disguise its expression and conceal its spirit became in her reign a true culture, a culture that felt its identity deeply *as a culture*. And only out of such intensely felt culture could a creation like jazz be born.

Our accounts of Voodoo in New Orleans at that time are by whites who could not see past its strangeness and sensuality, but there's no reason to suppose it was any less a vehicle for African metaphysics than Haiti's, especially in the light of the astonishing musical flowering that soon came out of those people. Marie Laveau did not "create" this cultural moment—such things are not created by one person—but it's fair to assume that a person of her range was aware of what was at stake. She saw a role to be played in that world and she played it to the hilt, helping to coalesce a scattered and oppressed people into a culture. Out of that intensely localized culture would come a music that would leave its mark on the whole world, a music born out of what music historian Alan Lomax calls "a moment of cultural ecstasy." The shaman Marie Laveau is—along with the Indian medicine men, the Puritan preachers, the Mormon prophets, and our greatest revivalists—one of the major religious figures in American history.

The last account we have of her was an article published in 1886 by George W. Cable, a journalist con-

sidered in the South of that day second only to Mark
Twain:

> *I once saw, in extreme old age, the famed
> Marie Laveau. Her dwelling was in the quad-
> roon quarter of New Orleans, but a step or
> two from Congo Square . . . In the center of a
> small room whose ancient cypress floor was
> worn with scrubbing, sprinkled with crumbs
> of soft brick—a Creole affectation of superior
> cleanliness—sat, quaking with feebleness in
> an ill-looking old rocking chair, her body
> bowed, her wild, gray witch's tresses hanging
> about her shriveled, yellow neck, the queen of
> the Voodoos. Three generations of her chil-
> dren were within the faint beckon of her help-
> less, wagging wrist and fingers. They said
> she was over a hundred years old, and there
> was nothing to cast doubt upon the statement.
> She had shrunken away from her skin; it was
> like a turtle's. Yet withal one could hardly
> help but see that the face, now so withered,
> had once been handsome and commanding.
> There was still a faint shadow of departed
> beauty in the forehead, the spark of an old
> fire in the sunken, glistening eyes, and a ves-
> tige of imperiousness in the fine, slightly
> aquiline nose, and even about her silent,
> woebegone mouth . . . Her daughter was also
> present, a woman of some seventy years, and
> a most striking and majestic figure. In fea-
> tures, stature and bearing she was regal. One
> had but to look at her, and impute her bril-
> liances—too untamable and severe to be
> called charms and graces—to her mother,
> and remember what New Orleans was long
> years ago, to understand how the name of*

Marie Laveau should have driven itself inextricably into the traditions of the town and the times.

On June 16, 1881, New Orleans's newspapers announced that Marie Laveau was dead. They printed long, nostalgic articles about her. The *Times Democrat* wrote, "Much evil dies with her, but should we not add, a little poetry as well?" By "evil" they meant everything associated with the drum. But the "evil" they spoke of was just beginning.

American music starts here. At least, American music as we've known it. Within ten years of Marie Laveau's death the brass bands of New Orleans would be playing sounds no one had ever heard before. How important was Voodoo, the African metaphysical system, in that time and place? There are contemporary accounts of thousands of Voodoo celebrations on Lake Pontchartrain as late as 1875, and in 1895 they were written of as the quite recent past. All the men who were first playing jazz in the 1880s and 1890s would likely have known them firsthand, and most of them would be old enough to remember the dances of Congo Square as children (the dances were stopped in 1875 when New Orleans enacted its first Jim Crow laws, forbidding blacks to gather in a public park). In the redlight neighborhood known by musicians as "the District," and in legend as Storyville, Voodoo was, as one recorder has it, "the true religion." Al Rose, in *Storyville,* writes that "an association of Storyville madames, which met regularly, agreed to refuse to use the services of Lala and other [Voodoo] practitioners on each other." The favorite queen of the madames was Eulalie Echo. They were always requesting her services for cures and hexes. Her real name was Laura Hunter, and she raised Jelly Roll Morton. She was his godmother.

What was the strength of these forms? How seriously were they taken at that late date?

· They show both a conscious and an unconscious survival of the old ways. The best example of their conscious survival are the "Indians" of New Orleans, "gangs" of black men who dress head to foot in elaborate costumes of bright feathers, with huge headdresses, a true spectacle as they sing their songs in the parades of Mardi Gras. They give us some fascinating clues.

In 1938, Alan Lomax sat Jelly Roll Morton down at a piano in the Library of Congress and for five weeks recorded a verbal and musical autobiography. Morton described the Indians as he saw them in the New Orleans of his youth. He was born in 1885, and he remembers them from his earliest boyhood. In 1938 Morton hadn't lived in New Orleans, or even been there, for more than twenty years, but he sings the refrains of the black Indians—so-called nonsense words that have no literal meaning in any language spoken in New Orleans or anywhere else.

In the mid-1970s, one of these "tribes," the Wild Tchoupitoulas, recorded an album produced by the superb New Orleans rhythm-and-blues artist Allen Tossaint and coproduced, with background rhythm and vocals, by another living repository of New Orleans music, the Neville Brothers. Some of the tunes are credited to the Nevilles, some to "Big Chief" George Landry, then leader of the Wild Tchoupitoulas; but incorporated into these compositions as introductions and refrains are *precisely the same melodies, and precisely the same "nonsense" syllables,* that Jelly Roll Morton recorded forty years before, remembered from his boyhood nearly fifty years before that. When you remember that the black Indians were well established by the time Norton was born, you're looking at precise musical preservation, in spite of the onslaught of media, for well over a century.

In Maya Deren's 1949 documentary, you see Haitians on parade in exactly the same costumes; you see them in Brazil's celebrations too. Deren's footage of Haitian ceremonies show them opening with two flag-bearers flanking a sword-bearer, corresponding exactly to the "flag-boys" and "knife-boys" of the black Indians in their ritual place as they parade. The authentic Voodoo ceremony filmed in Marcel Camus's *Black Orpheus* (1958) in Rio de Janeiro, shows the *hungun* in Indian headdress and with a ceremonial bow hung around his shoulder. In Haiti and Brazil the connection with Voodoo is clear and strong; in New Orleans, nobody's saying. The point is that *forms* which were certainly begun before the Civil War, and perhaps in Haiti much earlier, and clearly connected with Voodoo, have remained constant and vital in New Orleans until today. And spirit always adheres to forms. *That is why forms survive.* Because even when specifics are forgotten, a form can retain the aura of what originated it and so pass on not the doctrine but the sense of life.

A far less conscious but far more important survival of African metaphysics in North America manifests itself in the black Sanctified and Holiness churches—where even today in the services, the women wear white dresses, with white kerchieflike headpieces, that are identical to what the Haitian Voodoo women wear in ceremonies photographed by Maya Deren. But the relationship of black churches to Africa goes far deeper than that. As James Baldwin puts it in *The Devil Finds Work,* "The blacks did not so much use Christian symbols as recognize them—recognize them for what they were before Christians came along—and, thus, reinvest these symbols with their original energy."

Even free blacks were not allowed to have their own churches, even Christianist churches, in North America until the 1840s. The movement grew in the 1850s, and after the Civil War it was everywhere. But 300 years is a long time to worship Jesus with African forms, and the style of the black church was instantly recognizable as African. Jefferson Hamilton of New England described one of the earliest churches in Louisiana in April of 1840: "The meeting commences with singing, through the whole congregation; loud and louder still were the devotions—and oh! what music, what devotion, what streaming eyes, and throbbing hearts; my blood ran quick in my veins, and quicker still ... It seems as though the roof would rise from the walls, and some of them would go up, soul and body both."

Soul and body both. From the first, there was no mind-body split in the *practice* of African Christianism, though the doctrine was just as fundamentalist, just as Puritan. The *style* of southern fundamentalism, as we know it today, white and black, came straight out of the African churches. Watch Jimmy Swaggart preach on television, and then see Ousmane Sembene's Senegalese film *Ceddo,* and you see that the style of address and retort that most fundamentalist preachers use is the formal style of an African tribal meeting. There's literally no difference but that in the tribal setting, as presented by Sembene, the Africans are more formal and have more decorum.

This is the bind the South has been in for at least a century and a half. A religion of denial worshiped with a religious *practice* that is anything but denial—the church sending out two contradictory signals at the same time, one to the body and one to the mind. So it should be no surprise that rhythm and blues and rock 'n' roll leaped from the South. Little Richard, Elvis Presley, Jerry Lee Lewis, Chuck Berry, Janis Joplin, all would rise out of places within half a day's drive of New Orleans, and they would sing their music with holy fury, with bodily abandon, that simply had never been seen before in Western performance. Little Richard would end up as a Pentecostal preacher doing *his same act* to a Christianist liturgy—in a quieter vein, later, so would

soul singer Al Green. Elvis Presley would contritely
record the spirituals of his youth. Jerry Lee Lewis, who
was a preacher for a short time in his youth, would be
convinced that he was possessed by the Devil but would
play anyway—"I'm draggin' the audience t'Hell with
me," he would say. Virtually all the most influential
black singers would begin (and this is still so) in church:
Aretha Franklin, Sam Cooke, Marvin Gaye, and on and
on, the list too long to write here. A doctrine that denied
the body, preached by a practice that excited the body,
would eventually drive the body into fulfilling itself
elsewhere. Above all denials, the worshiper would long
for the body-mind unity felt when the church was "rocking." In those churches the African metaphysic and the
Western metaphysic would blend, clash, feed and battle
each other, in each and every soul. It is no wonder there
is such weeping in a fundamentalist service.

The style of a Jimmy Swaggart (who, by the way, is
Jerry Lee Lewis's first cousin) would contradict every
word he preached, and both he and his listeners would
be ensnared in that contradiction, and this would be the
source of the terrible tension that drives their un-
checked paranoias.

W. E. B. DuBois described black Christianist religion as a meeting of three elements: "The Preacher, the
Music, and the Frenzy." It is in the frenzy that, with
both black and white fundamentalists, we find African
Voodoo absolutely intact, with merely the symbols
changed. The object of the Voodoo ceremony is possession by the god. Possession by the Holy Ghost is as much
"a formal goal of the religion" in Holiness and Pentecostal churches as possession is in Voodoo. Writes Paul Oliver in his *Songsters and Saints:* "Placing himself in the
hands of God, the supplicant sought possession by the
Holy Spirit ... Glossolalia, or uttering unintelligible
syllables believed to be the language of the Holy Ghost,
was evidence to many that the speaker was possessed by
the Holy Spirit ... and this was an essential part of the

process of sanctification. People possessed of the Spirit in church might 'fall out' in a trance and might even require to be forcibly held down or controlled until they came around."

Métraux observed the relationship, too, saying that "a pentecostal preacher describing his feelings when 'the spirit was upon him,' listed to me exactly the same symptoms as those which I heard from the mouths of people who had been possessed by the *loa* . . . Undeniably the ecstasy which breaks out during the ceremonies of certain Protestant sects in the South of the United States reflects a survival, if not of the rites, then at least of religious behavior."

The wild movements of the "horse" mounted by the godly "rider"; the wild speech, including speaking in tongues, which on Haiti is sometimes referred to as "talking with Africa"; the unpredictability of the possession, how, excited by the music, the frenzy can strike people who don't want it and don't believe in it—you find all of these central Voodoo phenomena in most black and white fundamentalist churches. Maya Deren tells of first resisting and then being overpowered by a god during a ceremony she was observing; James Baldwin, in *Go Tell It on the Mountain,* describes suddenly being possessed against his will by the Holy Ghost. Maya Deren described the climax of her involuntary-possession experience as "a white darkness"; Baldwin, after an infinitely more detailed and subtle passage, says, "the darkness, for a moment only, was filled with a light I could not bear." It should be no surprise that Baldwin's Christianist sense of the experience separates the light and dark at the climax, while Deren's Voodoo sense of the same experience blends both into "a white darkness."

So. We are in New Orleans, circa 1890. We know the depth and range of the African metaphysic as it is alive in the black culture of that moment. The twentieth century is already taking hold. Congo Square has been empty for fifteen years, to become a quiet park and then, in our day, a sports auditorium. (That Indian holy ground seems destined to be the place where people release themselves in abandon.) Bayou St. John and Lake Pontchartrain have seen the last time that thousands would gather in a Voodoo celebration. What observers would describe as genuinely African drumming and dancing would continue in New Orleans into the first part of the twentieth century, but it would no longer be focal to the life there. The African metaphysic was about to blend with black-American needs, European instruments, and Euro-American musical forms to create the first great wave of American music.

The brass band was already an American tradition when Sousa's marches swept the country in the 1890s. In New Orleans, the brass band blended with another living African tradition, vivid in Voodoo: ancestor worship. Not to hire musicians, not to sing, not to feast at a death, would have been sacrilegious. The liturgy was Christianist now, but the impulse for the ceremony was African—or, to use another word, pagan. For it is no accident that what most closely resembles an old New Orleans funeral is an Irish wake—these are the two modern cultures that are most in touch with their non-Christian roots.

The more socially acceptable, light-complexioned, and financially well-off Creole musicians—many of whom came from free people of color and not from slaves —tended to play their instruments "correctly," to read music, and to play for white functions. The darker, poorer, slave-rooted Negroes—as they were called at the time, distinguishing them from Creoles—played a very different music, closer both to Africa and to the blues. These were the people who came directly out of the Congo Square dances and the Lake Pontchartrain celebrations, and they played their Western instruments with the simultaneity, interchange, and percussive force of African music. They looked to their instruments for a different sound entirely, and got it. They played a lot of blues—which was the sound Africans had created when, in the United States, they had been deprived of their drums, forbidden to sing their tribal songs, and usually even forbidden, during slavery, to have their own Christianist churches. The blues was everything African that had been lost, distilled into a sound where it could be found again. And the blues was the losing and the finding, as well. One man could play the blues. So it was a form that allowed one man to preserve, add to, and pass on what in its native form had taken a tribe. Its beat was so implicit that the African, for the first time, didn't need a drum. The holy drum, the drum that is always silent, lived in the blues. One man with a guitar could play the blues and his entire tradition would be alive in his playing. Louis de Lisle "Big Eye" Nelson, considered the first man in New Orleans to play a "hot" clarinet, told Alan Lomax from his final sickbed in the 1940s, "The blues? Ain't no first blues. The blues always been. Blues is what cause the fellows to start jazzing."

Everyone there at the time said that the first man to play what came to be called "jazz" was the cornet player Buddy Bolden, sometime in the early 1890s. And what he usually played was the blues.

Here was the African metaphysic distilled by American circumstances into an extraordinarily supple form and played on European instruments with African simultaneity in an American-marching-band lineup. Here was the fruit of the hundred years' cohesion of New Orleans black culture—the sense of shared heritage, the sense of identity, fostered and exemplified by Marie Laveau. Here was a metaphysics finding, for the first time, an authentically American voice. What had been played at Congo Square was African music. What was played by Sousa and the popular songsters of the time was still a music derivative of Europe—especially of English music halls and Scotch-Irish airs. What Buddy Bolden started to play was American music. Within thirty years its impact would make an American tune instantly distinguishable from a European tune, no matter how strait-laced the music. And it would be a music, in all its forms, that would reject Puritan America. Even at its mildest it would have a beat, and in that beat would be everything that denied the split between the mind and the body.

In rural blues, all this had been and would be implicit in the tense containment of the form. In Buddy Bolden's music, the implicit would instantly become explicit.

Buddy Bolden. "On those old, slow blues," trombonist Bill Matthews remembered, "that boy could make the women jump out the window. On those old slow, low-down blues, he had a moan in his cornet that went all through you, just like you were in church or something." Words are as close as we'll get to how Buddy Bolden sounded—no black jazz band recorded till 1920, and none recorded extensively till 1923; a precious quarter century lost—but it's significant that people talking about this very secular music very often reach for sacred images. "Like you were in church or something."

"His playing had one indispensable feature, 'the trance.' He had the ability," wrote Harnett Kane in 1949 from descriptions of people who'd been there, "to immerse himself into the music until nothing mattered but himself and the cornet in fast communication."

Eighty years after Bolden, the jazz pianist and composer Cecil Taylor would use the same word that Kane's informants had used. "Most people don't have any idea what improvisation is . . . It means the magical lifting of one's spirits to a state of trance . . . It means experiencing oneself as another kind of living organism, much in the way of a plant, a tree—the growth, you see, that's what it is . . . it's not to do with 'energy.' It has to do with religious forces."

Another musician-composer, Sun Ra: "I wanna . . . put them in a sort of dream state between myth and reality. I'm dealing with myth, magic, things of great value."

And Cecil Taylor once more: "Part of what this music is about is not to be delineated exactly. It's about magic, and capturing spirits."

Thus here are the terms of Voodoo made explicit as the aesthetic of an art.

As for Buddy Bolden, we only know for sure one thing he ever said. Many have quoted it, but the New Orleans trombonist Kid Ory put it best when he remembered: "I used to hear Bolden play every chance I got. I'd go out to the [place] where he was [to be] playing, and there wouldn't be a soul around. Then, when it was time to start the dance, he'd say, 'Let's call the children home.' And he'd put his horn out the window and blow, and everyone would come running."

Let's call the children home.

That's what this music is for.

The music was nurtured and grew from Voodoo, but as soon as it was itself and no longer strictly African it kept Voodoo's metaphysic wordless within it and jettisoned the trappings. The overt practice of Voodoo faded at the very moment the music was born, as though it had done its job here. Voodoo imagery would live in the lyrics and song titles through all the music's forms—jazz, blues, rhythm and blues, rock 'n' roll and even some gospel—until the present, and many of the mojos sung about were real indeed. There is a lot of Voodoo practiced in the United States even now, particularly in New York, but it is furtive, scattered.

On a deeper level of consciousness, the archetypal snake, Damballah, would be sung of constantly and take many meanings. "I got a great long snake crawlin' around my room" is something Blind Lemon Jefferson, the first great rural blues singer to record, would sing in the 1920s; Joe Ely would rock the same line in the 1980s, and in both cases the image would overpower the song and the singers would have to wail a mystery that included sex but was more than sex. Willie Dixon would write Voodoo lyrics that Muddy Waters would make famous; the old blues singer, Victoria Spivey, when she formed her own small record label in the 1960s, would use for her logo a woman dancing with a snake. In the late 1970s Irma Thomas, the New Orleans singer, would record a tune called "Princess Lala"—based on Lala, a famous Voodoo queen in the New Orleans of the 1930s and 1940s—with by all accounts a fairly accurate Voodoo practice described in the lyric. And there would be Voodoo rumors all along: that Buddy Bolden's eventual insanity was a hex (though a man through whom so much numinous force was pouring might well break under the pressure after a few years); that Robert Johnson, the great blues player of the 1930s whose style and rhythms were a direct source for rock 'n' roll, sold his soul to the Devil to play and sing like he did, and that he was done in by Voodoo; and the mourners at Jelly Roll Morton's grave would say that his godmother, Eulalie Echo, a queen of Storyville, had sold his soul for her power when she was young and ruined his chance for happiness (though he had plenty of soul to play with—nobody ever played with more—for forty years). These are serious people saying these things, and it would be unwise to discount them out of hand. If you *think* your soul's been sold to the Devil, that could profoundly change your life, whether or not "soul" or "Devil" or a process of exchange exist. But we are interested here in

how the metaphysics lived on in the music, not the practices, now, by what evidence there is, mostly degener-
ated from transcendence to sorcery. These Voodoo nuances linger as a kind of coda to the direct influence of
indigenous African religion on American culture. From
here, the African metaphysic will be felt all in the music, all in the body, its direct lineage to Africa a thing of
the past.

The histories of jazz and rock 'n' roll are usually considered separately, yet when taken together they tell a
very different story. It is the story of how the American
sense of the body changed and deepened in the twentieth
century—how Americans began the slow, painful process, still barely started now, of transcending the mind-
body split they'd inherited from European culture.

Much of what would be unique to the twentieth century appeared in its first few years. Around 1895 Buddy
Bolden played the first jazz. In 1899 Freud published
The Interpretation of Dreams and Scott Joplin wrote
"Maple Leaf Rag." In 1901 Marconi received radio signals from across the Atlantic. In 1903 the first feature
film was shown in New York; Detroit had become the
center for the automobile invention that had grown
through the 1890s; the Wright Brothers took their first
flight; and Marie and Pierre Curie were awarded the
Nobel Prize for their work with radium, and their theories of radioactivity. In 1905 Einstein published his
special theory of relativity. And Edison's electric light
had been around for twenty years, though it would be
another twenty before it began to be applied on a large
scale. A tremendous energy was felt in the air, especially in the United States. No culture had ever been
assaulted by such radical changes in so short a period,
not before or since (for all the changes since have simply
been extensions of these). Freud, Marconi, Edison, the

Curies, and Einstein were demolishing the mechanical, linear outlook that had been Western thought for 500 years.

Henry Adams felt this with more clarity than anyone else of his time. Writing in 1906 in *The Education of Henry Adams* he said, "Evidently the new American would need to think in contradictions, and instead of Kant's famous four antinomies, the new universe would know no law that could not be proved by its anti-law."

Most people felt the changes inarticulately but no less profoundly. The very *air* of daily life was changing. This was not the pastoral time our conservatives would like to imagine it was. Children by the thousands were being worked mercilessly as virtual slave labor. Six- and seven-day work weeks, twelve-hour days, no benefits, and nominal pay were taken for granted by most people —a situation kept constant by a continual flow of desperate immigrants who needed any work they could get. The white middle class was rising on their backs, and each immigrant wave strove to rise on the backs of the wave that followed it. When we look at the silent films of that time, especially the documentary footage, the flickering fast-speed gestures of the people seem peculiarly appropriate. They felt that their world was speeding up under them like a treadmill going out of control, and they raced in jerky awkward strides to keep up. Adams's description of New York in 1905 is only one of many of its kind by travelers in that America: "The outline of the city became frantic in its effort to explain something that defied meaning. Power seemed to have outgrown its servitude and exerted its freedom. The cylinder had exploded, and thrown great masses of stone and steam against the sky. The city had the air of movement and hysteria, and the citizens were crying, in every accent of anger and alarm, that the new forces must at any cost be brought under control. Prosperity never before imagined, speed never reached by anything but a meteor, had made the world irritable, nervous, querulous, unreasonable and afraid."

The description serves our year as well as his, but that just underscores how frightening it must have been to a world not yet used to being so frightened. We have a pretty good idea why we're afraid, by now. Their fear was much more instinctive, much less clear, and so it must have been even more disorienting in many ways than ours. Seen this way, it becomes less surprising that, only nine years after Adams's description, the world, unable to stand it anymore, exploded into the worst conflagration it had ever known—a slaughter so out of proportion to its rather trivial causes that it staggers the senses. Frightened people slaying frightened people in a mad fever to release the tension, and we have been doing it ever since, in a century that seems to begin and end every day.

For most people of the time, most Western music—highbrow and lowbrow—could neither express nor release that tension. Even the greatest Western music, on the order of Bach and Mozart and Beethoven, was spiritual rather than physical. The mind-body split that defined Western culture was in its music as well. When you felt transported by Mozart or Brahms, it wasn't your body that was transported. The sensation often described is a body yearning to follow where its spirit has gone—the sense of a body being tugged upward, rising a little where you sit. And you almost always sit. And, for the most part, you sit comparatively still. The music doesn't change your body.

The classical dance that grew from this music had a stiff, straight back and moved in almost geometrical lines. The folk dances of the West were also physically contained, with linear gestures. The feet might move with wonderful flurries and intricate precision, but the hips and the spine were kept rigid. That way, the energy that lived in the hips and the loins would proceed through proper channels—and those channels were defined well outside the dance. Western movement and music were as linear as its thought.

In 1899, Scott Joplin's "Maple Leaf Rag" swept the United States. Joplin was working out of the "sporting houses" in Sedalia and St. Louis, Missouri, and his rag was influenced by the blues, by Sousa marches, by European music, and by the sounds from New Orleans. Hectic but well-formed, it contained both the frantic air of the new and the poise of the old, as most good ragtime did during the next twenty years of the form's popularity. Joplin's piece perfectly suited both the instincts and the hesitations of his time. Respectable orchestras like John Philip Sousa's could record rags and remain respectable. The dances ragtime inspired were wilder than most dances had been but still had decorum. The twentieth century could be admitted without necessarily being joined. The great beauty of Joplin's music is how his sadness flows over the beat. A grief lives in his sounds: never defiant, like the blues; almost defeated, but profound. In the slower pieces it is, for me, very like the tone of Henry Adams's prose.

Music that had been listened to for generations was overwhelmed by Joplin's, because people needed a music that was both satisfying in itself and a way of experiencing their time—especially as even the best verbal ways had been outstripped. There was very little of the African metaphysic in Joplin's music, at least as compared to New Orleans jazz, but it cultivated the public's receptivity to that metaphysic.

That metaphysic continued "underground," as far as mainstream culture was concerned, until 1917, when some Italian-Americans from New Orleans calling themselves the Original Dixieland Jass Band, and claiming to have invented the music themselves, recorded "Livery Stable Blues" and "The Original Dixieland One-Step." The world had gone mad, madder than anyone had ever thought it could, and ragtime was too mannerly to handle it. The ODJB's records were wild. They're still wild. With none of the musicianship, depth, or suppleness of the black New Orleans players who would have to wait another six years to record, the ODJB yet had a sound that pulled out all the stops. Every instrument is playing at once, full speed ahead, over a pounding drum. It's a giddy music, barely under control, and there's no way to dance to it but to wiggle your legs and flail your arms. Decorum is no longer important and no longer possible.

Their records sold in the millions, in numbers that would have made them superhits even in today's vastly larger market. The numbers were unheard-of then. Nearly everyone who owned a Victrola must have owned an ODJB record. What a desperate way for a still-Victorian people to behave. What a need gaped under their giddiness. In the war, bodies were being fed into a bloody maw. In the living rooms back home, bodies were being coaxed to imitate the world's hysteria. In that imitation must have been some solace. The body, long forgotten, was chasing wildly after the mind.

By 1918 black bands, mostly migrated from New Orleans after the closing of Storyville the previous year, were playing in the influential night spots of Chicago and New York. From 1923, they recorded. We take for granted now that this was called the "jazz age"—a word most Americans hadn't heard before 1917. The image of upper-crust college students in raccoon coats dancing the Charleston to a Dixieland band is a cliché for us. We take for granted that Al Jolson, the first great American pop star, sang in black face, in black style, and danced with black moves. We take for granted that black tap dancing, as soon as it was widely seen, became *the* dance form of American show business. Minstrel shows in blackface had been a staple of American culture for a long time, but they had not saturated the culture. But now, here was this thing called jazz, and people seemed to need it.

Within six years of the ODJB's first recordings, and a little more than twenty years after Joplin's first published rag, American popular culture had gone black— in its music, in its dance, in its fashions, in its language, in virtually everything but its imagery which, except for blackface, remained whiter than ever. On the screen, blacks were ridiculed and worse. Offscreen, they were (and are) slavishly imitated. It's no coincidence that the same years saw the fierce resurrection of the Ku Klux Klan, inspired by D. W. Griffith's 1915 film *The Birth of a Nation,* and that in 1919 northern cities saw their first race riots (described powerfully in James T. Farrell's novel *Studs Lonigan).* America was at war with itself as it had not been since 1865. What the body heard and felt was good, and the nation couldn't get enough of it. But Euro-American thought and values couldn't handle it, much less honor it. In social terms whites projected the mind-body split onto the whole country.

Whites were the mind, blacks were the body. Blacks were supposed to be incredibly potent, incredibly sexy, incredibly tough, and they had the infamous "natural sense of rhythm"—everything whites wanted and missed in their bodies was projected onto blacks. Christianism had always despised the body, and so most of its people despised blacks.

On the one hand, these are crude generalities. On the other hand, the realities they express are no less crude. James Baldwin puts it this way: "The root of the white man's hatred is terror, a bottomless and nameless terror, which focuses on the black, surfacing, and concentrating on this dead figure, an entity which lives only in his mind." Bottomless, yes, but perhaps not so nameless. It is the Christianist terror of having a body at all. The terror of that body's Original Sin, the terror of that body's death, the revulsion at that body's needs and functions, and the terror that one's very soul will be judged by how much control one was able to exert upon this filthy and insistent body. It is a terror expressed in every facet of Western life, a terror compacted into a tension beyond endurance, a tension that gave Western man the need to control every body he found—and he thanked his furious God that he found black bodies, because they were the screen on which he could project everything he feared and hated about his own. This is what made slavery so *appealing*. All that buying of bodies, coveting of bodies, putting bodies up on the block, comparing them, assessing them, owning them—here at last the body could be both reviled and controlled.

Of course, all of this had been around before the jazz age. But the heightened virulence of racism during this time has to be seen as a reaction to the sudden leap of black culture into such a central place in American life, becoming and remaining its dominant musical expression. This event brought to surface all our most dread diseases, all our most feared contradictions.

This was the first necessary step in a process of healing that has been taking place at the deepest levels of our culture ever since, and that continues its difficult way even as we speak. It is the great strength of this music that it has been able both to reveal the disease and to further its healing. And the disease, again and again, whether manifesting itself as racism or as an armaments race, is the Western divorce of consciousness from flesh. "In the beginning was the Word," "I think therefore I am." The Second Coming will appear and the whore of Babylon (the body) will be dismembered by God. Every day even the most inarticulate among us live this out. And every day the very same people seek not to live it out, or why would so many fixate on a music, surround themselves with a music, in which lives a metaphysic that sees the body as *embodied*, as empowered, with numinous force?

By 1930, African rhythm—not African beats, but

European beats transformed by the African—had entered American life to stay. Which is to say, the *technical language* and the *technique* of African metaphysics was a language we were all beginning, wordlessly, to know. America was excited by it. America was moving to it. America was resisting it. American intellectuals were pooh-poohing it. But the dialectic had been joined.

In the thirties and on into the forties, big-band jazz would be the dominant form, both commercially and, for a time, creatively. In Count Basie's band and Jay McShann's, Duke Ellington's and Earl Hines's and Benny Goodman's, many of the soloists who were moving toward modern jazz, *mental* jazz, earned their living, deepened their art, and did some of their best work. But another tradition was going on at the same time that would be at least as important, and again it was going on among the poorest blacks, and again it was a matter of dancing.

This was the blues that was being played in small cramped shacks—honky tonks, juke joints, barrel houses —at the edge of nearly every small town in the South, west into Texas, and north to Chicago. When white intellectuals started to discover rural blues in significant numbers, in the late fifties and early sixties, they were discovering it out of context. On records or in "folk music" settings, for them, it was strictly a music to be listened to. In the joints where it was played in its heyday, it was a dancing music. Sometimes it was a piano, sometimes a combination of instruments, and often just one man with a guitar, but people came to mingle, to gamble, and to dance. The relationship of musician to dancer was exactly the same as the relation of drummer to dancer in Haitian Voodoo, where a drummer worked closely with the dancer and could often evoke possession at will. Texas barrelhouse piano player Robert Shaw put it this way much later: "When you listen to what I'm playing, you got to see in your mind all them gals out there swinging their butts and getting the mens excited. Otherwise you ain't got this music rightly understood. I could sit there and throw my hands down and make them gals do anything. I told them when to shake it and when to hold it back. That's what this music is for."

Music historians have usually treated jazz separately from the stream that combines blues, rhythm and blues, and rock 'n' roll, so they've failed to see the full scope of what happened musically in the years after the Second World War. In jazz, the big bands faded quickly after the war was over. There were no longer millions of lonely boys to be entertained everywhere, so the big bands became too costly to keep up. Only the most famous survived, and not in the manner to which they'd been accustomed. Radio and jukebox fare thinned as a result. It was mostly insipid show music now, not the full-bodied jazz people had danced to so furiously during the war. At the same time, the new jazz of Charlie Parker, Thelonious Monk, and their cohorts, was a complex, intense music that was listened to, not danced to—the first African or African-influenced music ever primarily for listening. In this sense (and in this sense alone) it was as non-African as Mozart. Yet, unlike European music, rhythm was its core; melody and harmony were played almost as an aspect of rhythm. Many melodies, and virtually all the improvisation that made up the body of the music, were generated by the rhythm. It was as though the African metaphysic, in order to continue itself, now needed to meditate upon itself—to explore its own complexities in a way that the religious music of Africa could not do (it hadn't developed forms with which to meditate upon *itself,* as Western music had, and this was what jazz was now doing). In modern jazz more than in any previous form, improvisation would take the role that possession by the god had once taken, solos would be longer, more intricate, and less and less dependent upon laws of harmony and melody—a true entering into, and remaining in, another state of being, and *thinking* musically within that state. By the early sixties artists like Cecil Taylor and John Coltrane would be openly insisting that such meditation was precisely the object of their music.

To play for dancing was to focus on the listener; in this new jazz, for the first time, the focus was entirely on the musician. Ideally, the listener listened intently enough to join the improviser's trance. That was understood as the listener's job, the listener's act of creation. This made possible a depth of thought—thought expressed musically but thought nonetheless—fully the equal of European musical thought, but with the intensity, the rhythm and the constellation of meanings that had come out of Africa; and the "subject matter" was purely twentieth century. I submit that if you want a commentary on, say, James Hillman's book *The Dream and the Underworld,* listen to Cecil Taylor's *Live in the Black Forest,* Miles Davis's *In a Silent Way* or *Bitches' Brew,* Charles Mingus's *The Black Saint and the Sinner Lady.* Conversely, if you want to delve into that music verbally, even interpretively, read Hillman's book. Ornette Coleman and R. D. Laing, Rahsaan Roland Kirk and Joseph Chilton Pearce, Charles Mingus and William Irwin Thompson, Thelonious Monk and Robert Bly are brothers, dealing with the same subject matter in different mediums.

But these musicians paid a price for the tremendous concentration they achieved. They had largely left the dance behind. And, leaving the dance behind, they'd left the dancers. Not the dancing artists, who spent all their energies on their dances, but the rest of us, who, both knowingly and unconsciously, were still yearning for the dance to take us up and return our bodies to our hungering spirits. So it is no coincidence that the very same years—the mid-forties—that modern, mental jazz first got recorded were the years that rhythm and blues made its appearance. The dance *would be danced*. It would not be denied or stopped. It seemed to have a will of its own.

People who complain that amplified music is show-biz hype overlook the fact that the first musicians to start playing electrically amplified instruments regu-larly were backwoods, rural-blues players. Arthur "Big Boy" Cruddup was the first to accompany his singing on electric guitar for a record, in 1942. Over the next sev-eral years he made very popular "race" records, doing electrically the rhythms and feels that Robert Johnson had recorded acoustically in 1936. (In 1954, Elvis Pres-ley's first recordings would be Big Boy Cruddup num-bers, often imitating Cruddup's delivery note-for-note.) Sonny Boy Williamson, Professor Longhair, Pete John-son, Big Joe Turner, Muddy Waters, Willie Dixon, Little Walter, and Clifton Chenier, among others, would by the late forties have created the lineup that would be a rock 'n' roll band: electric guitar, drums, bass, har-monica and/or saxophone, and occasionally a piano. Those men made a wild, haunting music—the long snake moaning plain.

Theirs was the music, in those little sweaty juke joints, that Elvis Presley, Jerry Lee Lewis and Carl Per-kins, among others, sneaked off to hear when they hit their teens in the late forties. These and the others who would first play what came to be known as rock 'n' roll were claimed by this music, this insistence by the dance itself that it survive. "Best music in the world," Lewis would say later. "Wilder than *my* music."

These young white men were living more primi-tively than most people can imagine now. The main street of Lewis's hometown of Ferriday, Louisiana, wasn't paved till 1951; and he didn't live in a house with electricity and running water till he began to sell records in 1957. These young men attached themselves to this music against redneck strictures that we tend to brush aside now, but which took no small courage to transgress then. They had all been raised to think this was the Devil's music, and they pretty much believed that. They had all been raised to be deeply bigoted, and they believed in that too. Yet they sat at the feet of blacks whom they wouldn't sit with at a lunch counter, because they couldn't get enough of black music. Most of them never reconciled these contradictions in their personal lives, yet that didn't stop them from transmitting the raw elements of the music to white people with a force, and on a scale, that any sane person would have thought unimaginable before Elvis had his first number one record in 1956.

Stating it with no holds barred: the moment this black music attracted these white musicians was one of the most important moments in modern history.

How typical that the best writers on these men—see Greil Marcus's crucial chapters on Elvis Presley in his superb *Mystery Train,* and Nick Tosches's biography of Jerry Lee Lewis, *Hellfire*—virtually ignore the importance of how these men *moved.* Elvis's singing was so extraordinary because you could *hear* the moves, infer the moves, in his singing. No white man and few blacks had ever sung so completely with the whole body.

Elvis before the Army, before 1959, was something truly extraordinary: a white man who seemed, to the rest of us, to appear out of nowhere with moves that most white people had never imagined, let alone seen. His legs weren't solidly planted then, as they would be years later. They were always in motion. Often he'd rise on his toes, seem on the verge of some impossible groin-propelled leap, then twist, shimmy, dip, and shake in some direction you wouldn't have expected. You *never* expected it. Every inflection of voice was matched, accented, *harmonized* by an inflection of muscle. As though the voice couldn't sing unless the body moved. It was so palpably a unit that it came across on his recordings. Presley's moves were body-shouts, and the way our ears heard his voice our bodies heard his body. Girls instantly understood it and went nuts screaming for more. Boys instantly understood it and started dancing by themselves in front of their mirrors in imitation of him.

Nobody had ever seen a white boy move like that. He was a flesh-and-blood rent in white reality. A gash in the nature of Western things. Through him, or through his image, a whole culture started to pass from its most strictured, fearful years to our unpredictably fermentive age—a jangled, discordant feeling, at once ultramodern and primitive, modes which have blended to become the mood of our time.

It is not too much to say that, for a short time, Elvis was our "Teacher" in the most profound, Eastern sense of that word. This is especially so when one recalls this Sufi maxim: "People think that a Teacher should show miracles and manifest illumination. The requirement of a Teacher is, however, only that he should possess all that the disciple needs at that moment in time."

Blacks pretty much ignored him—they knew precisely where he was coming from (he was coming from them) and they didn't need to be told what he was saying, it was all around them and always had been. As for white mainstream culture—nobody knew what to do. An official culture that had become an official culture through the act of separating one thing from another (instead of unifying them), couldn't then process Elvis or the rock 'n' roll, black and white, that he was forcing on them. Yet Elvis was the first product of African metaphysics in America which the *official* culture could not ignore. The various American establishments—political, intellectual, media—had successfully ignored American music since Buddy Bolden (who was only mentioned in a newspaper once in his life, when he was arrested during what we might now call his first nervous breakdown). But they couldn't ignore Elvis. And they weren't going to be able to ignore American music ever again. They could co-opt Elvis, as they finally did, but they couldn't rationalize him. And they couldn't stop him. Within months of his first hit, black artists as wild as Little Richard, Fats Domino, and Chuck Berry would be heard on white radio-stations for the first time, due to the demand Elvis had created for their music.

It is important to recognize that when whites started playing rock 'n' roll, the whole aesthetic of Western performance changed. Wrote Alfred Métraux of Haitian Voodoo dancing: "Spurred by the god within him, the devotee . . . throws himself into a series of brilliant improvisations and shows a suppleness, a grace and imagination which often did not seem possible. The audience is not taken in: it is to the *loa* and not the loa's servant that their admiration goes out."

In American culture we've mistaken the loa's servant for the loa, the horse for the rider, but only on the surface. We may have worshiped the horse, the singer-dancer, but we did so because we felt the presence of the rider, the spirit. John Sebastian of the Lovin' Spoonful said it succinctly in one of his lyrics:

> *And we'll go dancin'*
> *And then you'll see*
> *That the magic's in the music*
> *And the music's in me*

The Voodoo rite of possession by the god *became the standard of American performance in rock 'n' roll.* Elvis Presley, Little Richard, Jerry Lee Lewis, James Brown, Janis Joplin, Tina Turner, Jim Morrison, Johnny Rotten, Prince—they let themselves be possessed not by any god they could name but by the spirit they felt in the music. Their behavior in this possession was something Western society had never before tolerated. And the way a possessed devotee in a Voodoo ceremony often will transmit his state of possession to someone else by merely touching the hand, they transmitted their possession through their voice and their dance to their audience, even through their records. We feel a charge of energy from within us, but it is felt as something infectious that we seek and catch and live. Anyone who has felt it knows it is a precious energy, and knows it has shaped them, changed them, given them moments they could not have had otherwise, moments of heightened clarity or frightening intensity or both; moments of love and bursts of release. And, perhaps most importantly, we could experience this in a medium that met the twentieth century on its own terms. So we didn't have to isolate ourselves from our century (as the "higher" art forms often demanded) in order to experience these epiphanies.

And for all this the body is the conduit. It is no coincidence that the first generation reared on rock 'n' roll is the generation to initiate the country's widespread aerobics movement. As distorted by image consciousness as that movement is, it shows a new emphasis. We feel our bodies, have an awareness of our bodies, that is new in Western culture. In the light of the music we've saturated ourselves with, this should come as no surprise.

The steady stream of mixed black and white rock records played on the major radio outlets began with Elvis Presley's "Heartbreak Hotel" in 1956. Within only two years, dancing in some neighborhoods was already going beyond the lindy, that patterned dance of our Western past. "Let your backbone slip," is how many lyrics put it. Or, as Jerry Lee Lewis instructed in the spoken riff of his classic "Whole Lotta Shakin' Goin' On":

> *Easy now . . . shake . . . ah, shake it baby*
> *. . . yeah . . . you can shake it one time for me*
> *. . . I said come on over, whole lotta shakin'*

> *goin' on . . . now let's get real low one time . . .*
> *all you gotta do is kinda stand . . . stand in*
> *one spot . . . wriggle around, just a little bit*
> *. . . that's what you got . . . whole lotta shakin'*
> *goin' on . . .*

It is not only that he's describing exactly the dance that George W. Cable and others described in Congo Square; it's that, as Lewis says, "we ain't fakin'." The measure of how much we ain't fakin' is that you can see in Maya Deren's 1949 footage of Haitian Voodoo dancers exactly the same dancing that you've seen from 1958 to the present wherever Americans (and now Europeans) dance to rock 'n' roll.

Which is not to say that rock 'n' roll is Voodoo. Of course it's not. But it does preserve qualities of that African metaphysic intact so strongly that it unconsciously generates the same dances, acts as a major antidote to the mind-body split, and uses a derivative of Voodoo's techniques of possession as a source, for performers and audiences alike, of tremendous personal energy.

Texas singer and songwriter Butch Hancock comments on Presley's historic appearance on the "Ed Sullivan Show": "Yeah, that was the dance that everybody forgot. *It was that the dance was so strong it took an entire civilization to forget it.* And ten seconds on the 'Ed Sullivan Show' to remember. That's why I've got this whole optimism about the self-correction possibility of civilization. Kings, and principalities, and churches, all their effort to make us forget the dances—and they can be blown away in an instant. We see it and say, 'Yeah—that's true.'"

Greil Marcus speaks of "the energy in popular music that usually can be substituted for vision." His book *Mystery Train* lives on that insight, and it is the single most important insight of any of this music's commentators. The tremendous energy of rock 'n' roll has been so intense from its beginnings to this day that, while rarely articulating a vision for itself, it can't help but spark visions as it passes.

When Elvis Presley hit the charts in 1956 there was no such thing as a "youth market." By 1957, almost solely through the demand for his recordings, there was. It was a fundamental, structural change in American society. In a few years we would learn *how* fundamental, as that "market" revealed itself also to have qualities of a community, one that had the power to initiate far-reaching social changes that seemed unimaginable in 1955. The antiwar movement, the second wave of the civil-rights movement, feminism, ecology, and the higher consciousness movement—and there was little distinction between them all when they were beginning at roughly the same time—got their impetus from the excitement of people who felt strong because they felt they were part of a national community of youth, a community that had been first defined, and then often inspired, by its affinity for this music. *That* was the public, historical result of those private epiphanies of personal energy we'd felt through the music's form of possession.

The thread that ran through all those movements of the sixties, and continues in their derivatives now, is a fundamental challenge to the old Western split between the mind and the body. More than any other single concern, this challenge defined the *mood,* if not always the issues, of the sixties. As William Irwin Thompson once put it, "The rock music of the sixties came close to being so powerful as to uproot a whole generation from one culture and socialize it completely in the new [New Age] one." The socially furious music of the punks, the sexually explicit music of Prince and his contemporaries, carry that on. And all this was implied in the music's African roots from the beginning.

As Duke Ellington put it in his libretto to *A Drum*

Is Woman (a libretto in which he makes clear that he means "a drum is a goddess"):

> *Rhythm came from Africa to America.*
> *Do you know what it does to you?*
> *Exactly what it's supposed to do.*

I haven't meant to imply that either jazz or rock 'n' roll is a greater or more socially significant music than the other. They are both faces of the same music. Within each is the holy drum. Rock takes the stand and recreates every night the terms of our survival, part ceremony, part cavalry charge. In all its genres it is Whitman's barbaric yawp amplified across the roofs of the world, making so much *possible* that had been so long lost. And it has to be done every night because, as one wise nineteen-year-old girl told me long ago, "There are things that have to be learned all over again, every night."

Jazz also must take the stand every night, recreating and regenerating its forms, but contemporary jazz comes after what's lost has been discovered again. Jazz is the subtlety of feeling, the swiftness of thought, always implicit in the true freedom that we all say we seek. It's the suppleness of existence itself. It is change itself, flux itself, and the intelligence that seeks both to remain true to its source and to change. Even jazz at its wildest suggests a focused inner meditation that rock knows nothing about. Jazz mothered rock, and yet rock is earlier, more primitive. If rock is ceremony, jazz is knowledge. It is the initiate's knowledge that the ceremony exists both to celebrate and, in distilled form, to preserve. We must remember Coomaraswamy's thought, that "so long as the material of folklore is transmitted, so long is the ground available on which the superstructure of full initiatory understanding can be built."

Music can be understood by the body instantly—it carries so much history within it that we don't need history to understand it. But a culture as a whole, a country as a whole, cannot be understood by the body alone—at least not anymore. The history of America is, as much as it is anything, the history of the American body as it sought to unite with its spirit, with its consciousness, to heal itself and to stand against the enormous forces that work to destroy a Westerner's relationship to his, to her, own flesh. This music, largely unaware of itself; carried forward through the momentum of deeply rooted instinct; contradicting itself in many places; perverting its own purposes in many instances; sinking many times under the weight of its own intensity into a nether world of hate and confusion and bad trips; and trivializing its own meanings at many a crucial turn—this music yet rushed and rushes through every area of this country's life in an aural "great awakening" all its own, to quicken the body and excite the spirit and, quite literally, to waken the dead.

From the first the music has felt like an attack on the institutions—actual and conceptual—that it was, in fact, attacking. From the first it moaned and groaned furiously all the length of its great long snake, and has never been afraid of venting its own fury—often resulting in its own destruction. "If I told you what our music is really about we'd probably all get arrested," Bob Dylan told an interviewer in 1965. Angry enough, often enough, the music has frightened its very dancers, so that many don't want to be challenged in that way for very long and they let the music become merely a memory of their youth. But it is a music that won't stop and that will not leave us alone. It speaks through the body and invokes the spirit. And some of us have felt, since the first day we heard it, that this is the aesthetic we have to live up to. No matter how the deal goes down.

It's fitting to end with the superb New Orleans

musician Sidney Bechet's definitions of the music he
helped give us:

> *It's everybody's who can feel it. You're
> here ... well, if there's music, you feel it—
> then it's yours too ...*
>
> *Oh, I can be mean—I know that. But not
> to the music. That's the thing you gotta trust.
> You gotta mean it, and you gotta treat it gen-
> tle. The music, that's the road. There's good
> things alongside it, and there's miseries. You
> stop by the way and you can't ever be sure
> what you're going to find waiting. But the
> music itself, the road itself—there's no stop-
> ping that. It goes on all the time. It's the thing
> that brings you to everything else. You have
> to trust that. There's no one ever came back
> who can't tell you that.*
>
> *After emancipation ... all those people
> who had been slaves, they needed the music
> more than ever now; it was like they were try-
> ing to find out in this music what they were
> supposed to do with this freedom: playing the
> music and listening to it—waiting for it to
> express what they needed to learn, once they
> had learned it wasn't just white people the
> music had to reach to, nor even to their own
> people, but straight out to life and to what a
> man does with his life when it finally is his.*

Bibliography

What follows is by no means a complete bibliogra-
phy, but lists the books most referred to, most of which
can be found by going to not more than three or four
well-stocked bookstores, though some are out of print.

The list of recordings includes several representative selections of the artists mentioned in this chapter (the well-known rock 'n' roll titles are not listed, as they can be found anywhere).

Adams, Henry. *The Education of Henry Adams.* (Various)

Baldwin, James. *Go Tell It on the Mountain.* New York: Dell, 1952.

Baldwin, James. *The Devil Finds Work.* New York: Dial, 1976.

Baldwin, James. *Nobody Knows My Name.* New York: Dell, 1961.

Bechet, Sidney. *Treat It Gentle.* New York: Hill & Wang, 1960.

Blesh, Rudi and Harriet Janis. *They All Played Ragtime.* New York: Oak, 1971.

Bookhardt, G. Eric and Jon Newlin. *Geopsychic Wonders of New Orleans.* New Orleans: Contemporary Arts Center, 1978.

Deren, Maya. *Divine Horsemen: The Living Gods of Haiti.* New York: MacPhear and Company, 1953.

Guralnick, Peter. *Feel Like Going Home: Portraits in Blues and Rock 'n' Roll.* New York: Vintage, 1981.

Hentoff, Nat and Nat Shapiro, eds. *Hear Me Talkin' to Ya.* New York: Holt, Rinehart and Winston, 1955.

Hentoff, Nat. *Jazz Is.* New York: Avon, 1976.

Hurston, Zora Neale. *Tell My Horse.* Berkeley: Turtle Island, 1983.

Lomax, Alan. *Mister Jelly Roll.* Berkeley: University of California, 1973.

MacManus, Seumas. *The Story of the Irish Race, Revised Edition.* New York: Devin-Adair, 1944.

Marcus, Greil. *Mystery Train: Images of America in Rock'n'Roll Music.* New York: Dutton, 1976.

Marquis, Donald M. *In Search of Buddy Bolden.* New York: DaCapo, 1978.

Métraux, Alfred. *Voodoo in Haiti.* New York: Schocken, 1972.

Oliver, Paul. *Songsters and Saints: Vocal Traditions on Race Records.* Cambridge: Cambridge University, 1984.

Rose, Al. *Storyville.* Alabama: University of Alabama, 1974.

Tallant, Robert. *Voodoo in New Orleans.* New York: MacMillan, 1946.

Thompson, Robert Farris. *Flash of the Spirit.* New York: Vintage, 1984.

Tosches, Nick. *Hellfire: The Jerry Lee Lewis Story*. New York: Dell, 1982.

Turner, Frederick. *Remembering Song: Encounters With the New Orleans Jazz Tradition*. New York: Viking, 1982.

Williams, Martin. *Jazz Masters of New Orleans*. New York: Viking, 1967.

Recordings:

Coleman, Ornette. *Free Jazz*. Atlantic. 1364.

Coltrane, John. *A Love Supreme*. Impulse. A-77.

Cruddup, Arthur "Big Boy." *The Father of Rock'n'Roll*. RCA. LPV-573.

Davis, Miles. *The Complete Birth of the Cool*. Capitol. M-11026.

Davis, Miles. *Bitches' Brew*. Columbia.

Davis, Miles. *In A Silent Way*. Columbia. PC 9875.

Ellington, Duke. *A Drum Is a Woman*. Columbia, JCL-951.

Ely, Joe. *Live Shots*. MCA. 5262.

Jefferson, Blind Lemon. *Black Snake Moan*. MLP 2013.

Joplin, Scott. *16 Classic Rags, Dick Hyman, Piano*. RCA. ARL1-1257.

Kirk, Rahsaan Roland. *The Inflated Tear*. Atlantic. 90045-1.

Mingus, Charles. *Reevaluation: The Impulse Years*. Impulse. AS-9234-2.

Monk, Thelonious. *Thelonious Himself*. Riverside. RLP 12-235.

Monk, Thelonious. *Genius of Modern Music, Vol I-II*. Blue Note. BST 81510.

Morton, Jelly Roll. *The Library of Congress Recordings, Volume Five*. Swaggie. S-1315.

Oliver, Joe. *King Oliver's Jazz Band 1923*. Swaggie. S1257.

Original Dixieland Jazz Band. *Original Dixieland Jazz Band*. RCA. 730 703/704.

Parker, Charlie. *The Very Best of Bird*. Warner Brothers. 2WB 3198.

Shaw, Robert. *Texas Barrelhouse Piano*. Arhoolie. F-1010.

Wild Tchoupitoulas. *Wild Tchoupitoulas*. Island. LPS 9360.

THE GREAT WALL OF HOLLYWOOD

Once upon a time in L.A., where Hollywood Boulevard meets Sunset in the neighborhood of Los Feliz, before any house now standing was built, there was a wall. Drive east today on Hollywood, and just where you cross Vermont to merge into Sunset you'll see on your right a shopping center. I'm told that where the Safeway is now is where the Great Wall of Hollywood once stood.

It was built by D. W. Griffith in 1916 as the Great Wall of Babylon for *Intolerance*. *The Birth of a Nation*, originally entitled *The Klansman,* had been released the year before. This son of a Confederate cavalry colonel, born into Reconstruction Kentucky, and a "liberal" by the Southern standards of his time—and it is fair to judge him by the standards of his time; few of us could stand to be judged by any future—had made a movie that had singlehandedly ignited the long-defunct Ku Klux Klan. A movie, that would, yes, kill people, terrorize, haunt, and give America the indelible image of the white-hooded, white-robed men standing beside their burning cross. What a fitting thing for them to burn. Everything it symbolized was already burning them from the inside, so why not make their smoldering inners a symbol of terror?

We forget how primitive a world was watching movies in 1915. Very few streets in that United States were paved. Very few houses had running water or even gaslights. Many citizens couldn't read.

Slavery had been over for just fifty years and most living blacks had either been slaves or were the children of slaves, living beside their old masters and *their* children, and only Faulkner has gauged the enormous tension they each took as a matter of course every day, a tension livid beneath their slow southern ways. For such raw psyches, still living nineteenth-century lives, the new form of film was more powerful than I think we can imagine now. Not that Griffith and his film aren't to be held accountable for the role they played, but it wouldn't have taken much to ignite reaction—hence the power of *The Birth of a Nation* must have been felt as a deluge. The measure of Griffith's horror was that, his success assured if he only followed the formula of *The Birth of a Nation* (as Cecil B. De Mille, his contemporary, did), he chose instead to risk everything to make *Intolerance*.

Everyone interested in movies has seen the famous photograph of Griffith's Wall of Babylon teeming with extras. It was ninety feet high, and could and did support thousands on its parapets, as well as statues and goddesses that were each five times the height of a man. Griffith's cinematographer Billy Bitzer made it look like stone but the wall was wood and the fire department declared it a hazard. Griffith managed to keep it up anyway. A Santa Ana wind almost blew it over; Griffith's people climbed the swaying wall and tied it down as though the set were a great drydocked ship. The wall held. When you see Griffith's battle scenes, with their furious mayhem, hundreds jumping, screaming, grappling, and many carrying torches, it's impossible that some weren't injured and it's a miracle the wall didn't burn.

Intolerance cost half a million 1916 dollars, enough to make forty features of that day at their average cost of $12,500. It doesn't matter what such a thing would cost now because now no one would permit it. If the fire department didn't nix it the insurance companies or the unions would. Anyway, no studio would okay it, which, from the studio's point of view, would be correct, because *Intolerance* lost money. Movies are incendiary, and it is hard to *incite* people to peace. That was Griffith's intention, and the inherent contradictions, combined with his gambles with form, left movie audiences baffled (we take cross-cutting in time for granted now, but Griffith's audiences, seeing it for the first time, simply didn't understand it). Yet *Intolerance* gave more than it lost. It gave the film industry the capacity to make more money than it had previously dreamed of, because it gave them the sophistication of the tracking shot, the first use of crane shots, intercutting in time, an unheard-of sophistication in editing, and the first large-scale night sequences. But its greatest innovation was to show on what *scale* a movie could be accomplished, what hugeness "the screen" could encompass. *The Birth of a Nation* had proven that a movie could shake the world. *Intolerance* proved that a movie's capacity to *create* a world was virtually limitless. And so "the movies" truly began. In just thirteen years since the first eleven-minute feature in 1903, the technical and conceptual foundation of "Hollywood" had been achieved.

Griffith's actual wall stood into the 1920s, slowly crumbling. Finally, it was torn down. By that time silent Hollywood movies had become the experience that most Americans had most in common—more in common, for instance, than their language. Hundreds of thousands in the cities spoke little or no English, and regional accents were so pronounced that some of our rural peoples, especially, could barely be understood even 150 miles from their homes. "Local" *meant* local. This isolation is what made the lynchings and terrorism of the day possible. It would be movies, radio and television that would finally unite these United States. We are a media country in part because media gave this sprawling amalgam of places its most coherent sense of *being* a country.

In this sense media is our *roots,* more than we've considered or admitted. What other word is there for the channels through which we came to have and to feel an identity as a people?

We forget how awed and stupefied were the rest of the arts at the speed and completeness with which the movies took over. We take movies for granted now, but Nathanael West didn't. F. Scott Fitzgerald didn't. Movies were an inventor's toy when the two were born—Fitzgerald in 1896, West in 1902. By the time these men were in their teens, movies were *the* popular art of the Western world. They had usurped the public's interest in the arts as a whole and in literature especially. The men who had made a toy into an empire had, in effect, caught these writers in a maze. By 1930, the consciousness of the American writer had become trapped on a movie set.

No one was admitting it, however. Did the technique of Ezra Pound's *Cantos* owe a debt to the technique of film editing? How much of Joyce's stream-of-consciousness had a source in the motion-picture language of stream-of-images, which he no doubt paid close attention to when he managed a chain of movie theaters in Dublin in 1909? Or the photographic technique of Ernest Hemingway's prose, with its mastery of the "close-up" effect and of the "cut"—very different, say, from the descriptive effects of Conrad—why hadn't these been employed before 1915? Nobody asked these questions.

With the exception of the poet Vachel Lindsay, who wrote the first book of film criticism, the movies were more feared than considered.

What *was* discussed was how the movies had taken over huge tracts of what had been the novelist's territory. Fitzgerald, for one, expressed his panic and dislocation graphically in *The Last Tycoon* (written after Fitzgerald had read and praised West's *The Day of the Locust*). He had his fictional studio head, Monroe Stahr, give a guided tour of the studio to a visiting Scandinavian prince. In the studio commissary they see an actor costumed like Abraham Lincoln:

> *Then [the prince] saw Abraham Lincoln, and his whole feeling suddenly changed. He had been brought up in the dawn of Scandinavian socialism when Nicolay's biography [of Lincoln] had been much read ... now seeing him sitting there, his legs crossed, his kindly face fixed on a forty-cent dinner, including dessert, his shawl wrapped around him ... Prince Agge, who was in America at last, stared ... This, then, was Lincoln ... This, then, was what they all meant to be. Lincoln suddenly raised a triangle of pie and jammed it into his mouth, and, a little frightened, Prince Agge hurried to join Stahr.*

Lincoln is Lincoln, and Lincoln is not Lincoln, and most of all: Lincoln works for Stahr. Fitzgerald knew how much had been stolen from everybody else. He knew he would never be able to write a Lincoln in a novel or a history that would have the power of the studio's Lincoln, who, regardless of what words they put in his mouth or to what ends, could get up and *be* Lincoln, before millions. We were still forty years away from when Lincoln and Washington could be used in commer-

cials to sell pizzas and used cars, but Fitzgerald had understood. The images would become so worn that our
history would lose its power to teach us anything. We
would come to live in a present that included the *images*
of all eras while forgetting their histories.

Perhaps it is not accurate to say that we take
movies for granted now. Rather say that Fitzgerald's
sense of being overpowered by media has become such a
fundamental part of our experience that we take such
impotence for granted. Fitzgerald felt shock at his di-
minishment; we are not shocked at ours. We know the
screen is not real, yet we feel unreal beside it. Our moments of love, trembling between fear and grace, are not
"true love"—we've seen what that looks like on the
screen. Our hesitant speech, with its painful silences,
isn't good dialogue. Our desperately awkward acts of
survival are not real physical bravery. We are like
people who've combed their hair in a magic mirror. The
mirror shows only a state of idealized perfection, while
we grow older and our hair is thinner and longer. No
wonder, after dressing before such a mirror for eighty
years, we look a little strange.

In *The Day of the Locust* West had already gone farther than Fitzgerald would live to go with *The Last Tycoon*. West wasn't a writer to be much afraid of anything, but he had a great respect for monsters and he
knew what century he was in. Unlike most major writers of his time—the year *Day of the Locust* was published also saw the publication of *Finnegans Wake*, *The
Wild Palms*, *Tropic of Capricorn*, *The Grapes of Wrath*,
The Big Sleep, and *The Web and the Rock*—West dis-
played little nostalgia for the nineteenth century. Since
that was a dominant literary tone in his era, it's not
hard to decipher why his novel failed to recoup even the
miserable $500 of his advance.

West followed the spectacle of Hollywood into something Fitzgerald didn't live to get: a vision. He expressed that vision in a stunning passage that has to be given in full for its power to be appreciated. Tod Hackett, a painter employed by a film studio as a set designer, has seen the girl he is obsessed with—the Jean Harlow–like Faye Greener—pass by his office window in an extra's costume. He follows her:

> *The only bit of shade he could find was under an ocean liner made of painted canvas with real lifeboats hanging from its davits. He stood in its narrow shade for a while, then went toward a great forty-foot papier mâché sphinx that loomed up in the distance. He had to cross a desert to reach it, a desert that was continually being made larger by a fleet of trucks dumping white sand. He had only gone a few feet when a man with a megaphone ordered him off.*
>
> *He skirted the desert, making a wide turn to the right and came to a Western street with a plank sidewalk. On the porch of the "Last Chance Saloon" was a rocking chair. He sat down on it and lit a cigarette.*
>
> *From there he could see a jungle compound with a water buffalo tethered to the side of a conical grass hut. Every few seconds the animal groaned musically. Suddenly an Arab charged by on a white stallion. He shouted at the man, but got no answer. A little while later he saw a truck with a load of snow and several malamute dogs. He shouted again. The driver shouted something back, but he didn't hear.*
>
> *Throwing away his cigarette, he went through the swinging doors of the saloon. There was no back to the building and he*

*found himself in a Paris street. He followed it
to its end, coming out in a Romanesque
courtyard. He heard voices a short distance
away and went toward them. On a lawn of
fiber, a group of men and women in riding
costume were picnicking. They were eating
cardboard food in front of a cellophane
waterfall. He started toward them to ask his
way but was stopped by a man who scowled
and held up a sign—"Quiet, Please, We're
Shooting." When Tod took another step forward the man shook his fist threateningly.*

*Next he came to a small pond with large
celluloid swans floating in it. Across one end
was a bridge ... He crossed the bridge and
followed a little path that ended in a Greek
temple dedicated to Eros. The god himself lay
face downward in a pile of old newspapers
and bottles ... He pushed his way through a
tangle of briars, old flats and iron junk,
skirting the skeleton of a Zeppelin, a bamboo
stockade, an adobe fort, the wood horse of
Troy, a flight of baroque palace stairs that
started in a bed of weeds and ended against
the branches of an oak, part of the Fourteenth
Street elevated station, a Dutch windmill, the
bones of a dinosaur, the upper half of the
Merrimac, a corner of a Mayan temple, until
he finally reached [a] road.*

*He was out of breath. He sat down under
one of the poplars on a rock made of brown
plaster ... From there he could see the ten-
acre field of cockleburs spotted with clumps
of sunflowers and wild gum. In the center of
the field was a gigantic pile of sets, flats and
props. While he watched, a ten-ton truck
added another load to it. This was the final*

*dumping ground. He thought of Janvier's
"Sargasso Sea." Just as that imaginary body
of water was a history of civilization in the
form of a marine junkyard, the studio lot was
one in the form of a dream dump. A Sargasso
of the imagination! And the dump grew continually, for there wasn't a dream afloat
somewhere which wouldn't sooner or later
turn up on it, having first been made photographic by plaster, canvas, lath and paint.
Many boats sink and never reach the Sargasso, but no dream ever entirely disappears.
Somewhere it troubles some unfortunate person and some day, when that person has been
sufficiently troubled, it will be reproduced on
the lot.*

It doesn't matter that the great backlots West described are gone, paved over with office towers, condos,
and freeways. His backlot is still very much our environment. You can have an experience very much like
West's in your own home, never leaving your chair, using your remote to flick through the fifteen or twenty-
five or fifty channels on the cable. Most of the children of
America have taken West's trip thousands of times by
the age of five. It was West's vision that the studio
backlot was a better metaphor for the twentieth century
than anyone had yet come up with.

West saw that the new art mirrored its century perfectly, not in its single works but in the monstrous phenomenon itself, "the movies," with their distortions,
their lies, their pathetic ideals of beauty, and their irre-
sistible waves of violence. No single movie ever did it,
but "the movies" became like some gargantuan single
work, savagely if unconsciously satiric, hopelessly ba-
nal, stunningly beautiful, childishly heroic, adolescently
cynical, deeply in love with love, and mowing down in-

digenous Indians, Africans, and Asians for the pure hell of it—a many-headed artwork almost as compulsive and complex as the century it tries both to express and to sell.

West knew that those dreams weren't just being dumped on a field somewhere. They were being dumped on us. As though everything that had once been anchored deep in what Jung called our collective unconscious had been suddenly torn loose by the storm of this century, and was floating haphazardly now on the surface of our lives.

While the hierarchy of the arts, ruled at the time by the major literary critics, kept waiting for the movies to be taken for granted, to die down, to be assimilated, West knew that the movies were assimilating us:

> *A great many of the people wore sports clothes which were not really sports clothes. Their sweaters, slacks, blue flannel jackets with brass buttons were fancy dress. The fat lady in the yachting cap was going shopping, not boating; the man in the Norfolk jacket and Tyrolean hat was returning, not from a mountain, but from an insurance office; and the girl in slacks and sneaks with a bandanna around her head had just left a switchboard, not a tennis court.*

We take *this* for granted now. It is, simply, American. But when West wrote those lines they were true only of Los Angeles. He had the vision to know that Los Angeles, and not New York, was the vanguard city of American culture—which was something else that didn't endear him to the critical establishment, then as now inflating New York and deflating the rest of the country. He saw that Americans would not be living like New Yorkers but like Angelenos. Years before blue jeans, for one, had gone from Western films to juvenile delinquent films to the common casual garb for men and women all over America, then all over the world, West knew that we would wear the movies on our backs.

He was also the first American writer to understand that Americans are unified less as a people than as an audience. Few have understood it since—Ronald Reagan being one of those few. An audience has very different needs, very different values, very different expectations than those of a people. A people is a historical entity, with an identity in place and time. An audience gathers for a show and then leaves, all its parts going in separate directions. We barely have a clue to the *psychology* of an audience, though we have come to know something of their power. America is like one of those slides you see under a microscope with cells splitting, melding, gathering together again, breaking off into clusters. We are a huge gathering of audiences that combine and recombine constantly in different ways for various attractions. We have not yet figured out how to govern something like this. We don't even know how permanent it is.

The audience phenomenon is the Western mind-body split at its most virulent, its most destructive. With an audience the split is complete, for an audience has no body. It is all attention, all in its heads, while something on a screen or a stage enacts its body.

It is no wonder that such a population feels more and more at a loss, groping for anything that will give it solidity or the illusion of solidity. Add to this how little of their own psyches they acknowledge as *theirs,* how little of their own inner multiplicity they're willing to recognize or manifest, and you look upon a people whose human birthright has been shattered.

It may be that computers will network this amorphousness in such a way that the audience will have more capacity to talk back to the screens and so will cease being an audience. That's one dream. But for now we are still what West called us, "the people who stare."

Nathanael West would not have been amazed at an America that could watch the Vietnamese carnage on television every night and still not end that war. West saw no innocuous pastime in "entertainment." He saw masses of bored, unhappy people mesmerized into a unity of wanting. And, because they want what they can never have, what in fact does not exist, he saw that American life was more and more founded on a yearning, a burning, a burning underneath every drabness. That, in this sense, we were already living in the flames. That the Americans most without hope would begin to set flames to their own houses (the ghetto riots); and that the Americans most without vivacity would consent to dropping those flames on far-off children—is no surprise to this vision. If your own body becomes progressively more unreal to you, how can you be expected to believe in the reality of anyone else's?

That we have come to live every day with the threat of the most deadly burning ever conceived—would have made sense to Nathanael West. To the invention of the television, the dream factory inside every home, West would have made a gesture of recognition. Hollywood is inside us. This, he knew. It was only a matter of time before we took it inside our homes where it belonged.

But what Hollywood produces are not quite dreams, and he was mistaken in calling them that. We've devalued our dreams, frightened of what they might tell us. Hollywood's products are fantasies made from the fragments of real dreams, hence expressing those dreams inadvertently, powerfully, and often in reverse. So we live in the psychic country of the photographic negative, exposed to our inner messages not in themselves but in the way we camouflage and distort them through "entertainment's" constant environment of fantasy.

So they swirl around us now, fragmented dreams

and inflated fantasies, everywhere we look, almost every room we enter. It is difficult for an American to go anywhere in the world, into the wildest wilderness, on the highest mountain, or on the bottom of the sea; into any neighborhood of any nation anywhere; or out beyond the rings of Saturn—it is difficult for an American to go anywhere that has not been the setting for some fantasy seen once, or twice, or in various versions, with every conceivable ending, with every variety of situation. The world has become a set.

Even the Himalayas, even the galaxy itself, are small in the shadow of Griffith's wall. What changed with "the movies" wasn't simply a way of telling a story. What changed was the scale on which we judge a human event.

Which, in itself, is a human event of the first magnitude.

We have not learned how to live with this. We overvalue the public event, undervalue the private event, and rarely see the connective tissue between the two. This, coupled with the speed of information, the capacity of any shred of event or speculation or concoction suddenly to occupy the center of our lives or to surround us, assaults us anew every day so that every day is a coming to terms. It could take another century or more for our thinking to adjust to such a massive shift in scale.

"All the world's a stage" no longer applies. "All the world's a set" is a very different notion. A stage is something that is always with us, upon which sets move. But a set? A set is hardly there at all. A set changes with each scene, and can even change many times within a given scene. What with everything changing so drastically every year, and with simultaneous realities and unrealities demanding our attention literally on pain of death, to live all our lives on West's backlot is our collective fate—a fate where houses and apartments are only dressing rooms for work and entertainment, with views from our windows that might as well be backdrops for all that they seem "natural" to us anymore, with radios and stereos constantly playing our very own private soundtracks, soundtracks that we hear too often and too loudly, to cover a silence we cannot bear: the silence of insubstantiality that descends on a set when the cameras aren't running, the head-throbbing silence of West's man in the middle of the lot, utterly unable to *know* what's going on though he can *see* it, unable to predict or control or map it, unable to absorb its variety, unable to shout it down or talk to it, making his way across it with the vaguest of purposes, the Everyone, the citizen of the twentieth century, trying with all his distracted strength to be steady and to hold to whatever "brave" might mean to people lost on God's own backlot.

WE ALL LIVE
IN THE SOUTH BRONX

We all live in the South Bronx. For the image of that neighborhood has taken residence in America's consciousness—it is the newest extension of our American dream: everybody's nightmare of the future.

In fact, it's the only American place in many decades to become truly mythic. New York City as a whole became mythic around the turn of the century, and by 1930 it had generated the submyths of Greenwich Village, Park Avenue, Broadway and Brooklyn. By that time Hollywood was also mythic, casting a reflected myth on Los Angeles that had nothing to do with reality and still doesn't. (For instance, the film industry employs 22,000 Angelenos, while the aerospace industry employs 416,000, but that has nothing to do with the image of "tinseltown.") In any case, since World War II America has lost more mythic places than it's engendered.

It lost "the South" for instance. The South was a myth, necessary to keep firmly in place the accompanying myth that racial discrimination existed only there. White people used to actually tell themselves this. The civil-rights movement disposed of these myths, both by destroying the older order in the South and by revealing the depth of bigotry everywhere.

Texas is trying hard to remain a myth, but losing a bit of its mythology almost every day as more and more easterners—still called Yankees there—populate its cities, and as its economy depends more and more heavily on Yankee-dominated banks. In a little over a decade Texas has moved from a rural-dominated to an urban-dominated state and is expected to become as populous as California in the next fifteen years—which means that most Texans will not *be* Texans. And its old myths are also crumbling in the face of Hispanic urban majorities that are harder and harder for the Old Texas–dominated media to conceal.

The South Bronx has replaced the South as the place of national evil, and it's replaced Texas as the place where the wild roam free.

For a short time it had rivals for its new place in American mythology. Haight-Ashbury (when suburban children were sleeping in its doorways) and Watts (when it was on fire) became notorious, but they were never truly mythic. People were not intensely aware of what these neighborhoods *looked* like, for instance. It took only a few years for them to lose their notoriety. Nor did Haight-Ashbury and Watts ever have a notoriety that was more than rhetorical. That is, the names of both neighborhoods became buzz-words in the rhetoric of various factions trying to get what they wanted in various arenas.

But not the South Bronx. It's too hot to handle with rhetoric, as Jimmy Carter proved when he stood on its gutted streets and promised a change. That bit of vaudeville notwithstanding, the cityscape of the South Bronx is now known by sight everywhere in America, precisely because it is the place where American civilization has stopped.

We all live in the South Bronx because that neighborhood is the unavoidable proof that American civilization *can* stop. It can stop literally right around the corner, and if it does nobody can do a thing about it. Americans know this and are obsessed with it. Almost every new movement, and certainly every public institution, is focused on *not* becoming the South Bronx (as opposed to movements in the sixties which were focused on becoming something new and unheard-of). We live in the first phase of American history not obsessed with progress but with survival.

The hip health movement expresses this as bodily survival, the religious fundamentalists as moral survival, while the media are (rhetorically) concerned with the survival of freedoms, the police with the survival of public safety, the schools with the survival of basic reading skills. The Reagan administration has channeled this national obsession into its massive defense spending, survival again the only justification; and the only justification for paring weapons spending even a fraction is the survival of the economic system itself. The forces that oppose the administration, both within and without the country, also oppose it on grounds of stark survival. Every level of our culture today focuses its strongest energies on the terror of dissolution.

And our most potent image of what this dissolution will look like is the South Bronx.

Hence its mythic power. If America wasn't obsessed with fear of its own dissolution, the South Bronx would be merely an ignored anomaly, the way the millions of Americans ill with near starvation during the fifties were an ignored anomaly—they didn't fit into the nation's image of itself, and they still don't fit into our cherished image of that time, so it's as if they never existed. In contrast, the South Bronx is the most powerful *visual* image America has fixed on since the images of Woodstock and of the mass demonstrations of the sixties and early seventies.

Which brings us to the subject of film, because it's as a visual image that the South Bronx has exerted its power. So: how has our most powerful visual medium dealt with this ineradicable image?

It's to be remembered that this image did not become well known through the movies. It got into the movies because it had already become well known. Such has been its power.

First let's discount the motley sex-and-death exploitation films that use the South Bronx as the set for apocalyptic Westerns. Moronic films like *The Bronx Warriors,* or even rather well-done films like John Carpenter's *Assault on Precinct 10* (a recasting of the Howard Hawks Western *Rio Bravo),* need for their contrivances a setting in which no rules need be observed, and the South Bronx serves well. John Carpenter's *Escape from New York* postulated that we officially incarcerate all undesirables in a South Bronx–like Manhattan, neglecting to mention that the unstated (but not unofficial) policy for doing precisely that is working quite efficiently now in most urban centers. Walter Hill's *The Warriors* is a South Bronx–inspired fantasy, wonderfully filmed, which comes out of the streets but never deals with them except to stage chases. Phillip Kaufman's lovely tale, *The Wanderers,* shows how much the nice Bronx fears the South Bronx, but never confronts what this means. And one could make a good case that without the South Bronx as inspiration, *Mad Max, The Road Warrior,* and even *Blade Runner* might never have been conceived, but that takes us far afield. There are four films that deal with the South Bronx directly, and that both intentionally and unintentionally reveal a great deal about both the place and we who look at it from afar: *Fort Apache, the Bronx; Wolfen; Koyaanisqatsi;* and *Wild Style.*

   Fort Apache, the Bronx (1982, directed by Daniel Petrie), a police drama, gives us Paul Newman, Ed Asner, and Ken Wahl as cops running around the neighborhood trying to solve an interconnected web of crime. The film presents the South Bronx as primarily a police problem. That's handy. That means, by implication, that the residents of the South Bronx are criminals. The film bends over backwards to show two or three who are as law-abiding, at least, as the filmmakers, but it has to strain so hard to do this that the very strain casts the residents in a guilty light. That, at least, is the effect. Hence, they've brought this stage of affairs on themselves and they deserve what they get. It's *their* fault that landlords torch the tenements for insurance write-offs rather than pay for renovation or property taxes. And, righteously, this criminality extends unto the seventh generation— the children are clearly as culpable, and at least as criminal, as their parents, and they deserve what *they* get.
   This is clearly the view of most Americans right now.
   The movie's rhetoric denies this. But every scene depends on these assumptions, and a few isolated speeches to the contrary can't compete with the structure and cinematography of what we see for two hours. Hollywood films often base their premises on assumptions that the film claims to deny by a few scraps of dialogue, but the picture's emotional force and financial profit bury its well-meaning, carefully isolated words. In *Fort Apache, the Bronx,* with noted liberal Paul Newman as a policeman and loudly liberal Ed Asner as his chief, the fundamental assumption is clear: in the long run, citizens, the authorities have your best interests at heart, and you may trust the authorities to get you out of this

mess. This message carries another one in its pocket: don't trust yourselves.

Fort Apache, the Bronx, is a movie that begins and ends with the concept of powerlessness: the police are (temporarily, to keep the plot going) powerless; the residents are powerless; and you, the audience, are powerless to change the situation. Everybody is nicely off the hook. Especially you. End of picture. End of the Western world.

End of the Western world, that is, if you believe this stuff. For that the police are powerless is a vicious lie; that the residents are powerless is an authoritarian wish (who knows what might happen if the residents decide they're *not*?); and convincing you, the mainstream audience, that you too are powerless is the glue that holds all this in place.

Wolfen (1981, directed by *Woodstock* director Michael Wadleigh) went for bigger game, literally: *Wolfen* postulates mythic creatures, wolves with godlike powers, who live in the ruins of the South Bronx and prey on the decay of the city, on the decay of our civilization. The only people aware of them are some American Indian shamans who work in high-rise construction. Again, the only white people who can deal with this are the police, but Albert Finney plays a cop capable of understanding notions that Paul Newman's cop couldn't spell. As Finney discovers more and more about the wolfen, he is drawn further and further from the police worldview. When he comes face to face with the wolfen at the climax, he accedes to their powers and their rights, and the wolf-gods spare his life. Finney comes to agree with the shamans, that this civilization is doomed by the same primitive forces it has unleashed. Only doom can restore the natural order of things and put man back in his rightful place.

Again: end of picture, end of the Western world. Again, all the characters (and by implication, all of us) are assumed to be powerless. But *Wolfen* postulates a greater power, the primitive force itself, with its unerring instinct for attacking our weaknesses. The clear implication is that this force is powerful enough to create a new, better order after ours is destroyed.

There is a lot to admire in *Wolfen*. It's a picture that plays for keeps. *Fort Apache* merely reinforces our sense of powerlessness; *Wolfen* states the terms of that powerlessness (at least, according to Wadleigh) and doesn't let us squirm out of facing a very possible doom.

Koyaanisqatsi (1983, directed by Godfrey Reggio) is a New Age film by a New Age thinker in a New Age form—neither fiction nor documentary, it is like the *Roma* of Fellini and the *F for Fake* of Orson Welles: it's an impressionist essay in which ideas themselves become characters. There is no story, no human personalities to identify with, no dialogue and no narration. The film takes us from America's desert to its cities, holding our attention by the sheer force of its photography. In this sense it is one of the purest films ever made. While never uttering a word, *Koyaanisqatsi* broods on doom with the sonorous righteousness of an Old Testament prophet. For its first half hour I was no less than awed. Reggio photographed *the planet itself* as a character—an incredible achievement. It was something more than his time-lapse photography and his thrilling sense of light. It was that—especially in Monument Valley and the great American deserts—he let the land be felt visually as one can sometimes feel it in meditation. No one had ever done this with film before—at least, no one had ever done it to me.

After this outer and inner spectacle, Reggio literally flies to the South Bronx. He hovers over it for quite some time—almost all the shots are from the distance and safety of the air. We have to consider the musical score here, by Philip Glass. Ponderous, suffocating, operatic yet electronic, it blasts down over the South Bronx as it did over Monument Valley, as manipulative as any score Hollywood ever conceived, intended to limit your response to a solemn, sober spectrum—a disturbing contrast to the wilderness photography that is so sweeping and free. Over Monument Valley the score says "Majesty!" Over the South Bronx: "Repent!"

The South Bronx serves as an introduction to Reggio's city, and the city of Reggio is not human, not even (like *Wolfen*'s) animal, but insect. An ant-heap. Reggio's high-speed photography (counterpointed now and then with slow motion) portrays us as masses of frantic ciphers walking convulsively and driving convulsively, pointless blips on a massive video game that's about to blow its fuse. End of picture, end of the Western world.

Koyaanisqatsi spends the better part of an hour making the same visual point again and again in the same way with virtually the same footage. A tirade is a sure sign of a poverty of ideas. Reggio's overstatement undercuts his proofs. He begins by saying that the city is crazy and ends by showing only that it drives *him* crazy. He not only loses his cool and his taste, but his integrity. Because, first off, an artist using high-level technology to reach his audience ought to have something more to say about the fountainheads of that technology—the cities—than a simple "Repent!" Secondly, it is no secret that rocks live on a different time scale than people. Speed up the view of a rock and you get lovely light effects. Speed up people and you can't see them, or they look stupid. If you showed the Hopi village at Second Mesa in fast-time, they too would appear crazed and silly.

Lastly, there is the use of the Hopi themselves. Reggio quotes them, rolling their words across the screen and using their language in choruses scored by Glass, as his ultimate authority. "Koyaanisqatsi" is a Hopi word meaning, roughly, that a life out of balance leads to disaster. His clear intention (like Michael Wadleigh's) is to oppose our civilization to the American Indian civilization and find ours wanting.

That our civilization is, in a word, fucked, is evident to virtually everyone not legally dead. That we have a great deal to learn from American Indians is obvious enough that even John Wayne said it in many an old Western. But I don't know anyone who would want to be a woman in *any* Indian tribe, Hopi included. And some of their tribes had no better luck with their cities than we've had with ours. Not far from Santa Fe, where Reggio is based, are the Chaco Canyon ruins. There, in the seventh century A.D., the Anasazi built what was for a long time the largest city in North America. A single building is thought to have housed a thousand people. The city stretched for miles, and, with its suburbs, supported at least 25,000. This is as big and bigger as some of the Mesopotamian cities where "history" is said to have begun.

The area is totally arid now, but archeologists believe it couldn't have been barren then, or it could not have sustained all those people. On the contrary, its construction shows that there were once forests nearby, and near enough irrigation and drinking water for everyone for some 400 years. But it seems the Anasazi overpopulated the land and denuded it. Wild animals deserted the area. Heavy foot traffic and bad farming ruined the topsoil. With lack of vegetation, water sources dried up. Eventually Chaco Canyon had to be abandoned, and in the thousand years since that landscape has never recovered. Chaco Canyon is an aboriginal South Bronx. These are Indian stories we are rarely told.

So *Koyaanisqatsi* is as simplistic in its way as *Fort Apache*. Reggio's camera lingers over the ruins of the South Bronx with the love of a satisfied hate, as though to say: "This is your city and it serves you right. Watch how beautifully the buildings fall. Their fall is more beautiful than you."

Which is not to say he's wrong. It may be true. But

if Reggio had walked those streets he might have over-
heard someone saying, "That's death, bro, that is *death*."

Meaning: "That's beautiful, man, that's intense."

A usage that should make us hang our heads. Death
has been visited upon these people so intensely, in so
many forms—sudden and slow, painful and numbing—
that language, the task of which is always to transform
raw situations into the building blocks of continuing
life, tries to save their lives by transforming the word
"death" into the word "beauty."

It is by such alchemies that we live.

Which brings us, finally, to what *Wild Style* (1984,
directed by Charlie Ahearn) is all about.

So far, in roughly six hours of footage—*Fort Apache,
Wolfen,* and *Koyaanisqatsi*—we haven't been introduced
to one soul who actually lives in the South Bronx. We
haven't heard one voice speaking its own language.
We've merely watched a symbol of ruin: the South Bronx
is the last act before the end of the world.

And then *Wild Style* comes along like a train car on
the elevated, sprayed with primary colors in dancing designs. The film is almost as illegal as graffiti itself, in
that it was shot for the almost unheard-of sum of
$75,000 and completed (editing and labwork) for another
$125,000. With today's prices, that is the filmic equiva-
lent of taking some spray-paint cans and sneaking into a
railroad yard at night to paint a mural on a subway car.

Like *The Harder They Come, Rockers,* and *The Cool
World*—the only movies with which it can be compared
—*Wild Style* stars the people of the street. Graffiti painters, rap singers, hustlers, crazies, and hoods play themselves. The South Bronx becomes not buildings but
faces. When Hollywood looked at the South Bronx, it
found powerlessness. When Santa Fe looked at the
South Bronx, it found doom. When in *Wild Style* the
South Bronx looks at itself, it finds, living deep among
the squalor and the meanness, what John Coltrane once

expressed in capital letters as: "ELATION—ELE-GANCE—EXALTATION."

What we fear for the future is already their past. And it is their continuing present. Poverty, violence, chaos, and illiteracy are the *givens* of *Wild Style*. American civilization has most definitely stopped, and where do we go from here? Is beauty still possible? Is celebration feasible? The question the picture implies is:

Can we Americans live without "America"?

Its answer is that Americans are more than America, and that to survive they need not to defend but to create. Beauty is their weapon and beauty is their creed.

While the media and the government have written off these people as functional illiterates, they themselves have developed "rapping," where the "emcee" or singer speaks in rhymed couplets of his own composition (sometimes composed on the spot), and the rhyming goes on and on while the music plays in the background and the people dance. You're an emcee if you're exceptionally good at rapping, but you hear it everywhere.

While mainstream artists are begging the government for NEA grants, the graffiti painters of these streets have for years been risking jail terms and beatings to make their murals on the subways and other forbidden surfaces. *Wild Style*'s character Zorro is played by Lee Quinones, a legend among "the graffiti writers," as the painters are called ("to write" in their slang means "to paint"). Quinones says in the picture, in his own words: "Being a graffiti writer is taking the chances and shit. Taking the risk. You gotta go out there and rack up, go out and paint, and be called an outlaw at the same time ..."

To which Grand Master Caz, a major South Bronx rapper, says:

> *Let your mind be pure and free to create*
> *With the beat in your heart dare to be great*

To powerlessness, to hopelessness, to doom-guilt, Zephyr Witten, another true-life graffiti artist, says: "I came to paint not to bullshit. So fuck you."

> *You got to start from nuthin'*
> *and then you build*
> *Follow your dream until it's fulfilled*

So the Grand Master Caz rap goes. But don't confuse the energy of *Wild Style* with easy optimism. Hope, creation, beauty—these are deadly serious concerns. The picture's major characters (Lee Quinones, and the woman who plays his ladylove and fellow artist, Pink Fabara, like Quinones a real-life graffiti artist) smile only once in the picture. Amazing, when you think of it. They try a few guarded, shy smiles here and there—beginnings that are soon halted. But only one full flat-out leap of a smile. And their joy is not felt as a private, personal commodity—as joy is usually felt in virtually all American films. Their joy is only felt when the entire community is having a party, when the dancing and rapping are in full swing against the backdrop of a mural—people joining together in a blast of the energy that lets them survive.

(It's also worth mentioning that when we think of the South Bronx we usually and automatically think "black," but *Wild Style*'s principals Quinones and Fabara, are Hispanic, Grand Master Caz and Fab 5 Freddy are black, and Zephyr is white, and they are all South Bronx people.)

The story is too slight, the balance between fiction and documentary too delicate, for me to give anything away for those who haven't seen it and might hope to catch it at some revival house or on video. But the point here is that, deprived of any access to legitimate art, these people made their own. Deprived of formal education, they created a medium of rhymed chanting that can be danced to—an incredible, instinctual fight to preserve the integrity of language by people who for the most part can barely read. And in break dancing—which spread from the South Bronx to the whole country—they created a vivid form being imitated at all levels of the dance world. *Their* world has been sentenced to death by the artists of America as well as by its politicians, but these South Bronx artists have swallowed that sentence and spit it back as rhyme and design and movement. There is nothing hopeless, hollow or snide about their work, as there is in the art and music of the well-off urban and suburban young. The mainstream artists can, both literally and figuratively, afford to be hopeless and snide. These street artists of *Wild Style* know that beauty is a matter of life and death—that beauty calls out from within to be expressed against all obstacles because beauty is absolutely necessary to human life.

It is the wisdom of the street that the word "death" must be transformed into the word "beauty." The South Bronx reminds a nation obsessed with survival that we cannot survive this era unless we transcend it.

CITIES OF PSYCHE

It is scarcely possible to conceive of the laws of motion if one looks at them from a tennis ball's point of view.
—Bertolt Brecht, *Brecht on Theater*

To live in a city is to be hunted. And to hunt. When the anxiety and danger of the hunt lives in the very air of a place, we call that place "a real city"— New York, L.A., Houston. A sense of danger in the streets is the least of it. A sense of danger in concepts, in desires gone beyond their limits, resources governed by fantasy instead of need—this is what makes our cities dangerous. A sense that somewhere in the city there are *always* people awake, and some of them are way over the edge. In Hemingway's phrase, they are "out beyond where they can go." Whether they're bag ladies, dopers, or subway painters; whether they're musicians, vice cops, or computer obsessives; whether they need to party all night or write all night or sit wide-awake at their windows; or even those who call in on the late-night call-in shows; and of course the muggers and break-in artists, who have an almost official status, whose dedication we all honor with the gesture of checking the locks before we turn out the lights, *if* we turn out the lights—raw nerves, raw nodes, in a system that one can't help but become a part of just by moving in and setting up shop.

It is not merely the danger of losing your soul in such a place. You can lose your soul anywhere. It is that in a place with this quality of "city," soul is the medium of exchange. Whether or not you admit it, whether or not you want it, you are hunting and being hunted, creating and consuming and being consumed, in terms of the deepest, quickest and most gleaming area of your identity. That is why the exhilaration can be so great and the despair can be so crushing. That is why stunning things come from places like this, stunning things and slews of inner deaths.

But it is plain that we can no longer confine such an atmosphere to the New Yorks, the L.A.s. What's scary and exciting about America now is that, communications doing what they do, the entire country is taking on the mood of such a city. Now, for instance, you can stay up and watch TV all night nearly everywhere in the country. Not exactly a stunning cultural achievement, I agree, yet isn't it odd, to say the least, that it's profitable to beam all-night programming into the average American home? With cable, satellites, and cassettes, one of the final distinctions between big town and small town has gone down. Little Bible-belt Clarendon, Texas, which still doesn't allow liquor to be sold within the city limits and where the churches discourage dancing, can be exposed to the same full-strength dosage of media as New York. While CNN, cable's twenty-four-hour-a-day news broadcast, has deflated the power of local television news and newspapers in which it can still be virtually impossible to see or read significant national or international news. And television expansion is just one example.

With these developments, the most crucial distinction between big town and small town—the amount and range of available stimuli—is no longer as distinct.

And then there is merchandising. The K-Mart in Fredricksburg, Texas, sells the same stuff as the K-Mart in L.A. It is no longer easy for local powers to keep, say, music which they consider outrageous out of their territory. They need the new K-Marts and Gibsons too much because of the employment situation, and it is very hard for them to put personal pressure on the chain-store decision makers. (It's virtually impossible, in fact, without national campaigns that are difficult to organize and usually ineffectual.) The small town is now like a single street in a larger city.

Some may wax sentimental about these developments, mourning the passing of the small town, but those places are usually so bitter, bigoted and confining that it's hard for me to join in their grief. Let Prince and Cyndi Lauper be sold in a chain store in Sweetwater. There are people who need them there.

The words "urban," "rural," and "suburban" are less distinct every day. L.A. is less a contained area than it is a sprawling neighborhood, and just down the street lies Albuquerque, nearer by plane than Pasadena is by car from Santa Monica in traffic. And Albuquerque is merely, in turn, an overgrown shopping mall for Santa Fe and northern New Mexico, which is another neighborhood, not "the country" at all. It is commercially dependent on Texans and Angelenos and New Yorkers who see its sights and buy its art. Where is the "urban" and where is the "rural" in all this? For with such a direct dependence on Texas, California and New York, a rural area like Santa Fe–Taos can't be said to be separate anymore. As a result of its new proximity, its real estate prices go up, its rents go up, and its social divisions are exacerbated. There is no separate entity. In the same way, with so many northerners and so much northern money determining the growth of Texas, there is no way anymore to separate Texas as a culture from the north as a culture, as there was even ten years ago—

they are neighborhoods of the same interconnected city.

The Grand Canyon is a park. Culturally, that is. Its ecology is no longer determined by God but by policy in Washington. New York's Central Park is wilder, certainly much wilder at night—only the desperate would camp out there, so which is wilderness? With our airplanes and our communications network, where does any one place stop and another begin? Or are the differences becoming no greater, really, than those of mood and climate, and even climate changes drastically now, while the trademark of our culture everywhere is sudden shifts and shatterings of moods. L.A. or New York may be more geared to such a density of life than Austin or Denver, but that is quickly changing. Austin's traffic problem is fast becoming as critical as L.A.'s and Denver's air pollution is worse. While the Minneapolis area is producing more exciting artists these days. And when creators or even politicians become significant in one place, everyplace else soon hears of them. There is more available in the classic big cities, but the smaller cities are no longer that much more peaceful. The differences blur more and more each day, each place a neighborhood in relation to the others.

Which is to say: "America" has become the name of a city.

It was once common for major cities to be surrounded by great protective walls. That was when each city was virtually a separate government resisting all other control. The rise of nationalism changed all that in the West and the walls either came down or, as the cities grew beyond their old fortifications, were never rebuilt. But until recently a city has been defined by where its buildings ended. That is still true as far as our laws and our governing facilities are concerned—they will likely be the last to catch up. But we are not a city of walls any longer. We are a city of screens.

Which isn't to say we're a city of movies, quiz shows, newscasts and computer displays. They occupy the screens, but each is a momentary passing presence upon a huge thing to which we are far more vulnerable and which we are not trained to perceive as *a thing: millions of screens surrounding us everywhere.*

The walls go up and down, poorly built, more shoddy every year, almost arbitrary—for more and more Americans it is unusual to live within the same walls for more than a few years. But the screens are constant. Built better every year. And the screens are uniform. They're everywhere. They are a reality, an environment, that the English-American language is not equipped to handle; they are a many-headed but incredibly unified object that we haven't the words, yet, to recognize, re-cognize, think about.

What does it mean, that our walls change but our screens don't? Is it possible that our walls change now *in relation to how our screens don't?* Because we can make any new room the same as one we've left by simply turning on the television, activating the computer? Yet we manage to concentrate on each ghostly image as it passes, and not the true network of glowing walls that is our new city.

To recognize that the screens are immensely attractive is not to address *why* they're attractive. Certainly a great deal of it is our restless need to project ourselves out of our bodies, to leave our bodies at all costs, and focus our awareness on the screen, letting the screen do the embodying. (We Westerners are *that* uncomfortable in our bodies.) But it goes both ways. We go into the screen, and the screen goes into us. We are assimilating, ingesting, digesting—what? "Information" is too crude a word, but it camouflages the word "form," and, even more significant, the word "formation"—and this holds a clue.

What America is, and what the rest of the world is

fast becoming, is an enormous and constantly shifting juxtaposition of every *form* humankind has ever known or imagined. It is in the throes of a compulsive act of formation, a wild and instinctive and brutal clash and combining of forms in a mass effort at metamorphosis into the forced formation of a world we can all live in.

If this only involved a clash of opposites we wouldn't be so confused. We'd just take sides and have at it. In fact, it involves so many sets of fundamental opposites whirling around each other in so many furious swirls, at so many purposes and cross-purposes, with so many conscious and unconscious intentions, at such speed, with such force, that words like "political" and "psychological" and "economic" and "religious" and "scientific" and "artistic" grow every day more pitifully inadequate, more obviously limited, and we grope staggering toward a worldview that could include all the old words without being classified and confined by any of them.

This explains the screens. And our fascination with them. And their central place in our homes, and how they have redefined our cities, becoming the most constant feature. For there on the screen is where we see the many surfaces of this enormous process that we live our part of each day. And it doesn't matter very much if it comes in the form of sitcoms or commercials, news shows or old movies, fundamentalist preachers or rock videos, because everyone enters this kaleidoscope on whatever level they're capable of at the moment and it's hard to watch a little of it without getting some of all of it. Every element on the screen tends to refer at frequent intervals to every other element, and this is as true of the sitcoms as it is of the preachers and the rock videos. They talk about each other, display each other, interpret each other—*become* each other. Turn down the sound, and the preacher Jimmy Swaggart, with his screaming and his crying, could easily be performing a rock hit, while the Coca-Cola commercial could just as well be advertising *est*. Leaving off the sound just takes an unconscious identification into consciousness.

And what is a modern shopping mall but the same thing projected into three dimensions? It is no wonder that the young gravitate to them and feel most comfortable there. Artists and intellectuals can say what they want about shopping malls and such places, but the young go where they can "play," and play, in mammals, is *always* an instinctive effort to learn something necessary for survival. The young go to such places because how to be at home in this cacopohony of forms is what they most desperately need to learn, and they are not learning it in school. We are profoundly more uncomfortable in the world than they are. What they seek is not something we know how to teach them.

And so "information" is a buzz-word for "formation," the task of formation being much too scary to contemplate outright. And one of the things we are forming, in anticipation of the enormous population we are going to have to sustain, is an urban culture spread over a continent and spreading over the world—not the pastoral image of a "global village," but the funkier image of a global *city*.

L.A. or New York or New Orleans, Santa Fe or Austin or Boston, in this sense no longer exist. They are the names of malls in this immense city—a city studded with mountains and widened by deserts—called the United States of America.

But let's look in detail at this process of formation, and the meaning of this playing. We'll take the most primitive sort of screen there is, an arcade of them to be found in every mall: video games.

Our boy Brendan got me into video games—a boy who is much in my thoughts as I write of a world which will be even more dangerous for him than it's been for us. I met him when I married his mother. We laugh together, we joke each other roughly, we remind each other constantly whose turn it is to do the dishes. We talk about movies and about the Bible and about World War I ace Billy Bishop; we talk about Jack London and the Ku Klux Klan and music; and we have fierce arguments, fiercer as he gets older, about what are and aren't his responsibilities, mine, his mother's, who's right, who's half right—all those intense ceremonies of his self-exertion that are our culture's ritual of initiation, played out ad nauseum from roughly the age of ten to whenever a boy is finally a man. And the flashes of understanding and comradeship in between that make it all worth it. I say all this so you'll see that I didn't get into video games lightly. Brendan got me there.

It was because I was frightened at how enthralled he was with them, while at the same time I knew that when I was his age it would have been useless to try to keep *me* from them. And his mother, wise woman, said that we just didn't *know* about them—didn't know what their purpose was in the evolution we are all enduring now. For there is nothing without its seed for the future —an invigorating and terrifying thought. Anything that can grow cannot be wholly without its seed. Jan's thought is that the work of life is to keep your spirit while you try to face the nature of what grows, be it arsenals or children.

A frightening woman, my wife.

So there was nothing to do but go with Brendan to Captain Video, the arcade where the kids hang out, and get to know the games. And now my high score at Zaxxon is 91,750. Which, believe me, is pretty good.

What was immediately obvious is that this was not just a place where "the kids" hang out. It was mostly kids, but people of all ages came there regularly, including adult couples on their way to and from the nearby

movie theater, and even adults by themselves. Boys
were a majority, but not a great majority. And there was
every race.

With the mixture of sexes there was, of course, a
pick-up scene. Say you're playing Zaxxon, concentrating
on flying your fighter through the maze, destroying installations that are curiously unpeopled. ("You bomb
targets, kid," the games teach, "not people.") So you're
into it, and pretty good, and suddenly your eye catches
somebody's reflection on the screen—a reflection carefully positioned so that her face is clear and eyes meet
eyes, her face like a cloud your war is fought within. So,
hey, you get a little nervous, it becomes an act of theater, you react a little more vocally when you miss,
when you hit, when your fighter explodes. And when
you're flying through the calmer zones you check out her
reflection, and she knows it, that's why she's standing
precisely there.

Which is to say that the games are quickly adapted
to purposes similar to any generation. A bit comforting,
that.

But the strangest thing about the games is that actually they have only one rule: *there will be no winning*.

For those of you too fastidious for video games, they
go like this: the vast majority of them involve some kind
of combat, and in virtually all of them you simply try to
amass the highest number of points until you are finally
killed. It's the ultimate no-win situation. If you are one
of the ten top scorers of the day, your score (body count?)
appears on the screen and you get to code in your ini-
tials, or whatever nickname you can make up, using no
more than three letters. (When I get a high score, I usually code in WHY.) But the point is that at no point does
the (war) game say, "You win."

"Like Vietnam instead of World War II," novelist
and TV producer George Howard told me. Just like.

This may be new. Can you think of a culture, an

era, when a craze developed for playing games that can't be won? Even with the pinball machines you can win a free game, but not with the video game. Here you play your damnedest till you get killed, then a computer (the media?) totes the score. It's as though our kids are learning the proper mindset, if there can be said to be one, for limited wars—wars in which there are no clear-cut winners.

Or "wars" like Grenada, which was very like a video game in form. A certain number of points for hitting the beach, for evacuating the students, for fighting Cubans, for avoiding Russians, for capturing generals, for keeping the news media stymied, and when it's over you have a score and you've gotten a thrill but you can't really call it a victory, yet Americans approve. Haven't they been pumping billions of quarters into the same sort of activity?

Forty-odd wars are being fought as I write this evening.

Fifty thousand soldiers died last year. There is no count for civilians.

The United States is supplying more than twenty of those wars.

At item from the *Los Angeles Times:* "The eighteen and nineteen year olds currently entering the Soviet armed force have been drilled in the virtues of combat heroism from the day they began primary school. By the end of the ninth grade they knew how to disassemble, assemble, and fire an automatic rifle . . . a majority have taken part in realistic war games for young adolescents . . . the military indoctrination of Soviet youth is without parallels in the industrialized world since [Nazi] Germany . . ."

The *Los Angeles Times* doesn't take video games very seriously. Or toys. Or TV. Or football. Or the commando-khaki clothing that so many kids and adults wear these days. The dumb Soviet government spends a fortune organizing and supplying their kids; in America, what we loosely call the entertainment industry lures citizens into *paying* to train their own kids. What our training lacks in thoroughness it makes up for in subtlety and technology.

The MACH 3 laser-disc game. You sit in a cockpit simulator faced with a high-speed movie that gives you a fairly realistic visual of low-level flying. You strafe ground installations, blow bridges, dodge heat-seeking missiles, and bomb cities. You look "down" and you're over *freeways* with cars moving on them, and when you miss your designated targets your bombs often fall on the wee moving cars. And that doesn't hurt your score.

Those Soviet kids just train for ground warfare, which is certainly useful, but how frightened their leaders must be that we are not only creating the new technology but are schooling our children by the millions in the rudiments of electronic weaponry. Our *real* tanks, artillery, ships and planes are equipped with computer video screens for targeting, and already our children are swift in the ways of the screen. They are athletes in their ability to gauge the speed of thirty, fifty blips at once. While the Soviets are training their kids to refight World War II.

That's one level of the video-game phenomenon. It is part of our enormous culturization for war. And the children flock to it, especially the boys, because they don't need to be told that more of the world's resources are spent on war preparation than on anything else. That fact is in the very air they breathe, and through their play it is a fact that they try to take in and live with. That's their way both to prepare and to be less frightened—which also means to be less feeling, but how can we blame them? To feel at all means to open oneself up to terror now.

That's what's obvious about video games, but there is also something much more subtle going on—the true seed Jan sensed when she spoke of not knowing what place these toys might have in our evolution.

One evening the Zaxxon was out of order. It had been taken apart, opened. Inside, the circuit board was visible. The remarkable thing was that the geometrical pattern of the printed circuitry (which looks like a city's grid from the air) *was the same sort of pattern used in the visual graphics* of the game! I know enough about video to know that the pattern of its circuitry does not dictate the pattern of its graphics. So, these designs are choices. I walked from screen to screen, game to game, amazed at how many of the "games" are played out on a graphic that's only a slightly disguised image of a printed circuit. Pac Man is the most obvious—no wonder it swept the country. The games are enacted on images of what amount to magnified computer chips.

So what *is* the standard video game once we strip it of the idea of "game"—for while the most obvious areas of the mind are reacting to the surface game, the player's consciousness is, as always, doing something much more elaborate. The players are projecting their personas, their egos, their presences, into a blip, a fighter, a car, a figure; and then *they journey into the computer chip*. To be tested.

This goes on on one level while the culturization for war goes on on another. Repeat: it's become the instinct of the race to magnify the computer chips *and play in them*. I doubt that the inventors of the games, programming fanatics all, had a conscious sense that their imaginations were literally entering into the chip itself, to play there like children. But "play" is a way things enter the psyche, or reenter it after having sprung from it. Some part of the player's psyche learns to *move* within the computer chip, within its dimension of inner space, agilely, with great speed.

So, truly, a seed: the computer chip, so foreign to my generation at first, has been internalized by Brendan's generation through the very disciplined concentration that playing a video game demands. A fascinating progression: first the human psyche concocts the computer chip; then it makes the chip do work; but it is bewildered, both by the chip and by the chip's work—by the chip's place in the human scheme; so, frivolously, in play, the psyche magnifies the chip through fantasy; then uses fantasy *to enter its own magnification of its own creation,* so that the chip can be immersed in raw psyche again, and once more *become a part of nature.* For it began in the psyche, which is a part of nature.

A fact which is too often forgotten. The forces of nature created the mountains and the seas and the computer chip. For if the psyche is not a natural force, then what is it?

Humans, especially ecologists—and I say this while supporting the ecology movement to the hilt—tend to project a human morality onto natural forces. But this is a thought process that paradoxically separates "nature" from "human," because the pattern that generally results from this projection is that "nature," as given, is "good," and "human," in relation to "nature," is generally "bad." But the human psyche *is* a natural force, and an immensely powerful one. In this sense the computer chip is as organic a work of nature as a leaf.

Technological civilization, a product of the "nature" that is human "nature," is "natural." But it's unbalanced. There are many classically "natural" ecological situations that also cause ruin because they're unbalanced. The Ice Age was "natural," and it, too, decimated countless species of plants and animals. We don't really even know what "unbalanced" means in these contexts. Does what appears to be unbalanced in our view actually balance quite nicely in some larger, universe-oriented view? Do we have enough information to make such judgments? Obviously we have so little information on a universe-scale that anything we suspect must be tentative one way or the other. Including the notion that technological civilization is "unnatural." A computer chip is no more unnatural, certainly, than a poem or a drum. It may be that the human psyche has invented such a thing in profound vexation at being unable, for reasons we can't even guess at, to use all of its actual brain capacity; hence it projects that capacity in a concrete form that can be manipulated and controlled. Or so they devoutly wish. But control, in any ultimate sense, is not a human possibility—and that, too, becomes more and more evident with computers. In fact the most sophisticated chips have an electrical charge so delicate that they're affected by the full moon! So the circle comes round again.

We cloak much of this activity as "entertainment," but our psyches are never at rest. *All* of oneself is present in *any* activity. While "entertainment" occurs on one level, formation occurs on another, and perhaps combat training on yet another.

To return to video games (and national attendance at the arcades has gone down in rough relation to the rise in home computer sales, so the phenomenon hasn't diminished but has shifted screens and become more complex): they are one way that our minds are literally *eating* the computer chip; chewing it; digesting it; turning it partly into waste (i.e., the games train for war), but also partly into something with the capacity to nurture. For that is what the psyche does—its impulse is to turn *everything* into an element toward some future growth. The chip came out of us, but that doesn't mean we can understand it. And so we take it back into ourselves in play, to let it marinate there, nonverbally, as we try, as a culture, to grow into the demand for understanding that it forces upon us. To face that demand is probably why we invented it in the first place.

It's probably why we invent anything.

I think of Brendan, sleeping as I write this, and all of this swirling in his now eleven-year-old mind. He may, as an adult, buy the idea that these manifestations

around him are wholly unnatural—at least for a time.
But right now it is his given world, and he accepts it on
its own terms while trying to figure it out on his; and he
finds its "nature" deeply exciting. They're building a
mall a few blocks away, and he and his friends can't
wait. That is where they'll prove themselves in each
other's eyes, as we did and as all kids must. I have on my
wall a homework assignment he wrote a year or so ago,
and it shows me a mind that *sees* everything it looks at,
so I don't worry about the mall much. The assignment
was to make sentences of his spelling list, underlining
the spelling words. He called his "Simple People," and
this is his whirling, his impulse to join us all together,
his sense of the blending of the forms around him, exactly as he wrote it:

> *Some* people *are* simple, *some* people *are*
> evil, *one person may be an* uncle *and own a*
> temple, *some people may* settle *and may also*
> travel, *one person might be a* mammal *and*
> *be* single, *one person might have a* nickel
> *with a* beetle *on it, and some* people *may*
> *have* maple *syrup in the* middle *of their pan-*
> *cake and some may have it on the side, some*
> *people may have their water in a* bottle *and*
> *some people may have it in a* kettle, *some*
> *people may have the entire top* level *of a*
> *building and some may have just a* sample.
> *Some people may prefer a* handle *or a* pedal
> *on their bike and some may prefer none at all.*

When we use the term "inner city" we don't mean
the city as a manifestation of what's within us, but perhaps we should. It is very difficult to locate the gates to
such a city. Once cities began to spread out to cover the
world we stopped building individual gates. Now we
have interfaces instead of gates, between city and not-

city, and they become more and more vague. Yet in some places there are still the relics of gates, or rather the impulse toward gates, if you look not directly but out of the corner of your eye.

The gates to L.A. from the east are beauties: two huge, swept-lined, breathtakingly graceful overpasses where Interstate 15 meets Interstate 10, marvelous sculptures of many roads balancing each other, so large that the cars become incidental. Forget it's a freeway, look at it purely as design, and you see in its lines precisely the freedom and sense of style that the city would most like to be known for. They suit the dream of the place—there's nothing quite resembling them anywhere else; they've been formed here because of how the highways drop out of the mountains to I-10.

It's not in the style of such gates to have decoration, statuary, or symbology, yet the highway itself is not without them. Long before you get to the first of those overpasses, as the road climbs out of the Mojave and as the desert very gradually becomes an irrigated suburb, you can see them. Say there's a windstorm—there often is—and you're driving through a light but gritty cloud. It is not quite dark, it is summer, and you're still more than three hours from Los Angeles but the highway has changed from two lanes a side to four, signaling the real entrance to the city. The edges of the pollution layer have seeped out to Palm Springs. These are the best conditions to see the creatures.

If the dust is right, they'll seem real just a moment, lit by neon and looming on your right. Bigger than they were in life, molded fairly accurately, in a parking lot by the side of the highway, lit by a truck stop's neon: tyrannosaurus rex, and great brontosaurus, standing patiently, waiting for you. Someone thought you'd enjoy eating badly prepared food if you were watched over by dragons.

Dinosaurs in the parking lot. Video games in the

lobby. It is a fitting terminal through which to pass to such a primitive and Day-Glo place as L.A., where Hollywood concocts its fantasies and the defense industry concocts *its* fantasies as thousands of Latin-Americans swell the city more each day with a desperate purpose that is caught somewhere between hope and the sweatshop. At sixty-five miles an hour there is an instant when those dinosaurs look natural, and you may have the sense of being greeted—with a show of teeth, and a roar, and the psychic wash of dragon breath. Welcome to L.A.

You hit the city during one of those inexplicably sudden rush hours that can occur around 1 A.M. Joining the swirl of lights, you try to adjust from open highway to zigzag freeway, and you're about to miss your exit. Say you've been playing a cassette of Thelonious Monk. You put it on somewhere around the Salton Sea. Fault-line music. You chose Monk because the desert and the dinosaurs reminded you of those odd, stonelike tones he could get out of a piano, and the way his riffs hover over bottomless rhythms that shift slowly and unpredictably and inevitably.

You're listening harder than you know, and about to miss your exit, because, as I said, your freeway timing is off and you've been more aware of Monk's dream-state timing, and now, to make your exit, you glance over your shoulder and gauge speeds of every vehicle you see, hit the gas, zig into the next lane, brake a little, zag into the next, hit it, you're on the exit lane, brake slow now, and you're on the ramp, *and all the while you've been paying attention to Monk's solo "Ask Me Now,"* and more than this: *one part of your brain has been watching you do it all,* amazed that you could do the calculations implicit in the highway move while listening hard to Monk's ideas.

This is an event. How many parts of you are functioning at that moment at speeds and complexities (complexities of function if not of depth) undreamed of ninety years ago? It is an event as important as any war, as any legislation, as any shift in global weather—not in itself but in its nature, because something very like it happens to tens of millions every day, all day, all night.

Brain exercises. If you were doing something as complex with the rest of your body you'd expect a medal. We are being trained? Perhaps the purpose of the modern urban environment is to train us? For we must never forget that it is we ourselves who dreamed up this maze that we run. If this twentieth century we have created is *not* purely accidental and negative, if that's even a possibility, then: why? For if the universe can be said to have a purpose, then this too must.

Not one purpose, of course, but a purposeful momentum of cross-purposes.

What distinguishes the twentieth century from all others? The speed and force of its unique technology. In every other century we know about there was an obvious separation between what's called the "subconscious" and the "conscious"—individual daily life was more or less ordered, however unjust or distasteful, and cacophonous cross-purposes were left to be slept through in dreams. But in the twentieth century, our technology has produced an environment *that duplicates many of the conditions of dreams*. Technology has projected the subconscious into *things,* legions of new *things* that take their sudden shape every day around us, one invention after another piling up so quickly that it is almost as if each thing is metamorphosing into the next, as though "thingness" is actually alive and changing, like the growth of a jungle seen through time-lapse photography.

So, what distinguishes the twentieth century is that each daily life is a progression through a concrete but fluctuating landscape of the psyche's projections. The surreality, simultaneity, and instantaneous change that occur in our dreams also occur all around us now, as they did *not* in the European towns where our ethics were codified or in the Stone Age encampments where our nervous systems evolved.

So the condition of our subconscious is now also the condition of this physical environment we've built for ourselves. No wonder our cities barter in souls. It's as though we're all living inside one massive model of the individual psyche.

Might this be the purpose of this environment? To revivify the psyche by making it deal with its immense physical image at every turn? For each of our psyches is far huger than the individual who lives in it, in that we have manifested in action only a small part of what occurs in our psyches. So we've created this bewildering, multifarious modern world in order finally to learn to *live* in and to use our own immense and cacophonous psyches.

An incredibly dangerous venture, this literal "state" (as in "political state") of mind. We're all terrified. Nuclear bombs had to exist in the psyche before they could exist in daylight. The bomb is so monstrous because it is the thing created by our own psyche's fear of itself.

So you drive in from the Mojave during a sudden rush of traffic sometime after midnight, jockeying for your exit while listening to Monk or Springsteen or Stockhausen. The cloverleaf loop has become the most common feature of every city all over the world. The rectangular monoliths called "office towers" *must* be circled by the loops, is what we seem to have agreed upon. How might this architecture be read in a depth-sociology of the future? That on this planet intelligent life began to ring its cities with structures on which individual psyches could continually circle, night and day, every city and town ringed by fantasies, by thoughts, by furies, by wistfulnesses, by passions, for what is it you do with your mind while you drive? Go to the store, go home, go out on the town, every drive is soaked through with daydreams and mentations of every sort, and most are accompanied with music to egg them on—people taking for granted, now, how consciously they pick the soundtrack to accompany their mode of musing on any particular outing. Fantasy saturating any temporary intention, each mind in each vehicle churning out reels of disembodied psyche, in a moatlike circular pattern of roads, and at speeds, and in numbers, that have never before ringed human cities. As though there had been a decree: we will form and dissipate and form our mentations like a ring of clouds around these places—fantasies beginning in signals of light and trains of thought ending in screeches of brakes, a living whirlwind of raw psyche.

Stonehenge. We have not forgotten. Erase the city, see only the highway, the grace of its arches; forget the awkwardness of the word "overpass," "turnoff", "exit," and see the swirl of stone. A ring of psyche-soaked stone circling the city, the nation, and slowly the entire world. If psyche has raw power, as the ancients taught, then who has begun to calculate the effect of these rings of constant emanation around our homes and work areas? It is no wonder these places become so highly charged, so much more electric than they once were.

This century is only as frightening as the psyche. It is not "out there," happening *to* us. It is a racial effort surging from within to manifest the psyche in every conceivable form, an obviously desperate evolutionary thrust—no one can say why—to leap past the limits we have lived with for thousands of years into an utterly different state of mind—a technologically hallucinogenic century, in which we have created a waking world that behaves with the sudden dynamics of our dreams.

As agri-culture was the root of America's original democracy, and as factory-culture was the root of both socialism and capitalism, so the structures that will transform the twenty-first century will be based on techno-culture. People who think that technology is a dirty word are not going to be able to forge the techno-culture into a nurturing, sustaining *home*. (Neither are techno-crats, who think that technology is the *only* word.) But first we must recognize that the human psyche is one of the great forces of nature, and that what is most frightening about urban technology is that it exposes us to this force as nothing else ever has. We are standing in the storm of our own being, and it is just possible that we have created this storm in order, finally, to know ourselves.

PREDICTIONS: THE NEXT 200 YEARS

There is more to history than politics. Politics is to civilization what the ego is to the self.

—William Irwin Thompson,
At the Edge of History

First some preamble, then some predictions.

At the turn of the century Henry Adams, a man good at predictions, wrote in *The Education of Henry Adams:* "At the rate of progress since 1800, every American who lived into the year 2000 would know how to control unlimited power. He would think in complexities unimaginable to an earlier mind. He would deal with problems altogether beyond the range of an earlier society. To him the nineteenth century would stand on a plane with the fourth—equally childlike—and he would only wonder how both of them, knowing so little, and so weak in force, should have done so much. . . . Evidently the new American would need to think in contradictions . . . it would require a new social mind."

The America of the 1980s is trying very hard to put off acquiring that "new social mind." Of course, we can't put it off. We struggle against ourselves. For we live in a consciousness-expanding society whether we like it or not. All our economic and cultural efforts are bent on creating a society teeming with myriad and often contradictory stimuli that provoke precisely the "new social mind" that we, at the same time, are trying to resist.

Resistance is high at the moment. The fundamentalist movements all over the world have essentially the same appeal: to turn back this terrifying onslaught of cacophonous stimuli that's expanded our awareness so far beyond the old limits. Not only the religious fundamentalists of the United States or Iran, but capitalist fundamentalists, Marxist fundamentalists, technocratic fundamentalists, East Coast liberal fundamentalists, New Age ecological fundamentalists—they all spend a tremendous amount of energy trying to turn off the stimuli, or rather; selecting from the stimuli what benefits their particular platform, and trying to turn off the rest. Their aims are opposed on specific issues, but the basic pattern of their purpose is phenomenally alike. Each group insists on protecting its own favorite stimuli while curtailing the stimuli of the others. This is at present called "politics."

If we look at the events of our era politically, we are left thrashing about between inadequate alternatives, like our politicians. If we look at our era personally, with reference only to ourselves, we feel dwarfed. And if we deny our urges to act "in our time," we feel useless, because we are built to act. How can we relate ourselves to history in such a way that action is conceivable within a personally sane framework? And what do we act *in* when we act in history?

One obvious answer is that no matter what we do we act historically. History is not a spectator sport. There is not you *and* history. There is you, in which history lives. And there is history, in which you live. If you are concerned about Nicaragua, that produces history; if you are unconcerned, that produces history. There is no way you can be ineffectual.

Yet virtually everyone feels ineffectual. Media reproduces "world-class" events magnified in scope and compressed in time, distorted out of human scale. People feel distant from the events when they are actually feeling distant from the distortion. So instead of feeling our integral connection with events and through events, we feel a tremendous anxiety at being surrounded by distortions. This anxiety has become our connective tissue. We are connected neither by a shared worldview nor common goals, but by a common and thorough anxiety.

Yet in a consumer society certain connections should be obvious enough, at least. When you decide what to buy at the supermarket and what to buy at the health-food store, you are deciding between a revolution in agriculture and its counterrevolution. Neither can exist apart from you. If you own a computer you are turning the world of your parents on its ear. Television, the car, air travel—the examples are legion. They are important historically insofar as they have become important to you. You and I are the terms of history.

Which is to say: history is the psyche writ large. It can't be something unimaginably beyond the power and scope of the individual when we make history every day with everything we say and do and dream. We are history. Our psyches are tumultuous. History is tumultuous. Where is the surprise? And where is the "problem" to be "solved"? One does not solve one's nature, one lives it out. One struggles with it, and for it, and against it. One succumbs. One transcends. Sometimes both in a single breath.

Within any hour we can be enmeshed in a nineteenth-century idea of the family, a first-century belief in a divinity, a prehistoric instinct for danger, and a twenty-first-century technological skill. We are subject to, and expressive of, many histories at once because we are composed of many selves at once and are constantly trying to decide between various dominants among those histories and selves. What is an *event* but the eruption into a particular time and place of these uncountable impulses, reactions, dreams, selves? Events are a crude notation of the intricacies of consciousness. "One group may be in power, but all are in consciousness, and it is consciousness that creates culture." So wrote William Irwin Thompson in *Passages About Earth,* and we have always lived that sentence.

What is plain, when you come to the end of this train of thought, is that we do not know where the human individual ends and the human race begins. We have never known. Democracy, fascism, monarchy, and socialism are four models of how it *might* be, and they are all inadequate. And if tribal life had been enough it would have stayed enough. We remain confused about the relationship of the one to the whole. But it *is* plain that in the way that individuals organize their lives into projects—career, marriage, raising children, hobbies, what-all—the race as a whole takes on what could be called "historical projects" as if by mutual consent.

For instance, the people of Europe didn't get together and decide to dominate the rest of the known world. Until 1492 only a handful believed that there even *was* any more world. Yet, without new technologies to spur them on, suddenly, in the 1500s, they pretty much stopped building cathedrals and devoted their surplus resources to discovering, occupying, and milking the rest of the planet. Everything that has changed drastically since 1500 has changed because of that historical project. What we call "technology" is its direct result, and now with this technology we are setting out on new historical projects.

We do not announce these projects, they announce themselves. We do not decide on them, yet as a race we devote our best energies to them. When I said I was going to try my hand at "predictions" I was using a hyperbolic word to say that I was going to try to identify what the new historical projects have become and where they might take us—since the sensation definitely is that we *do* them but they *take* us. What has humankind mutually, unconsciously, and nonverbally decided to embark upon, and how long will these new voyages take? We cannot "see" this future when we look through the eyes of personal, ambition-oriented, lifespan-limited time—one's personal scale is too small. Nor is vision possible through the eyes of political, issue-oriented time—historical projects contain all the issues, but they are far more than the sum of their parts. But historical time, like the time of the Freudian/Jungian psyche, contains all sides and contains all time while being suprapresent: all-at-once. Seeing through the immediacy and eternity of historical time, we can see a long way and yet remain on a human scale.

So what are the historical projects we are embarking on now? The most obvious, the one that contains all the others, is the crystallization of a planetary culture. Not the *formation* of one. That's already happened. We have a planetary culture right now. Tehran, Los Angeles, Rio de Janeiro, Moscow, Sydney, Peking, Jerusalem are next-door neighbors, borrowing each other's tools, gossiping about each other, sleeping with each other's spouses, carpooling, and watching their kids play and fight together. But that image is far too peaceful, of course, because this planetary culture is in a state of anarchy. Order is not about to collapse; order has collapsed.

No culture presently existing on earth is applicable on a planetary scale. Period. And that's what all the fuss is about.

Because we're not just going to be neighbors. *We're going to be each other.* The new technologies make separation ultimately impossible.

Since we are already living on a planetary scale,

this means that every existing culture has been rendered obsolete. Russia, North America, Europe, the Islamic nations, China, the Third World—all are getting more and more frantic as it becomes more and more obvious that their present ideas and customs can't cope with, hence will not dominate, the coming planetary civilization. Neither the Bible nor the Koran, nor *Das Kapital*—the three books that everyone is at present hitting each other over the head with—is capable of the flexibility demanded by an instantaneous planetary civilization. And yet the struggle between Judeo-Christianist capitalism, Moslem nationalism, and socialism *is* what we call "politics" on a world scale. Which dismisses politics as the place to look for resolutions.

None of these systems will win. What they will do for the next hundred years is exhaust themselves in continuous conflict, while the new crystallization of planetary culture, the new human order, takes place far beneath them, so to speak—under the brouhaha, within the ever-widening cracks in their social fabric. The prevailing powers will be displaced *from the inside*. Orientation toward a true planetary culture will happen everywhere, at varying rates, connecting up slowly until the prevailing "great powers" of nationalism and commerce will simply fade out and/or join up. This is hardly farfetched. Precisely the same general schemata was played out when the Church gave way to nationalism 500 years ago; and again 1000 years before that, when the Roman Empire gave way to the Church. I don't mean to suggest that just because one can state it succinctly the process will be peaceful; it will be messy. Very. The Inquisition, the massacres of the Provençals, and the religious wars that wracked Europe for two centuries and more were all part of the hysteria of the Church giving way to nationalism. We mark the dates of the wars but we can't really mark the date when the Church's opposition to the new order ceased to be a critical factor.

In these huge transformations there is never an exact date of "revolution"; instead, things inexorably revolve.

The crystallization of our planetary civilization will have five basic themes:

> *1. The creation of a world economic system.*
> *2. Advances in cybernetics, biology, space, and brain research.*
> *3. The empowerment of brown, black, and yellow peoples.*
> *4. The equalization of men and women.*
> *5. The creation of a new cosmology that will replace Judeo-Christian-Moslemism.*

They are interwoven, of course, but for the sake of discussion let's take them theme by theme:

The creation of a world economic system. "To incorporate" means literally "to inhabit a body," "to embody." Stretch it further: to create a body. Like it or not, and for good or ill, multinational corporations are the first entities operating coherently on a world scale. In much the same way as the New World was explored and settled first by traders and slavers bent on exploitation, the skeleton of the next stage of planetary culture is being created by the corporations. New Age advocates are loathe to admit it, radicals and liberals are furious at it, national governments are outmaneuvered by it; nevertheless it's happening, and there's nothing anybody can do to stop it.

Right now these corporations are performing the first essential steps toward a world community; they are taking jobs and dollars out of the United States and rooting them in other parts of the world. A crucial step in a world in which 6 percent of the population (the United States) consumes 80 percent of the resources. Before the year 2000 a catastrophic depression, possibly ignited by the ripple effect of nations' deficits or the default of Third World loans, will cause the corporations to institute the equivalent of a world currency. The destabilization of existing currencies, some artificially low and some artificially high, will demand this if world trade is to continue. This will not solve many problems in and of itself, because the *system* now functions as a world currency anyway, though it wastes a great deal of energy in the awkwardness of dealing with particular currencies; and a new system would have to make provisions to enable the various major nations to finance themselves by printing their own money; nonetheless, that can't get any more awkward than the present system. But the institution of a world currency or its equivalent, a huge simplification of the current system, will significantly weaken nationalism and *that* will be important.

If the major nations are battling a depression, they will have to accept any feasible proposals that multinational corporations offer. As nationalism weakens, a world economic system will grow more quickly. No one can say what that will be like. Some insist that all future economics will, or indeed must, be based upon ecology; others say the corporations will strip the planet of resources before we can achieve the world economy. What will likely happen is an interplay back and forth between these poles of possibility. What is certain is that to settle into a workable and more or less equitable (or it would not be workable) economic world order will take at least a century. Probably longer. We are just at the beginning of the sorting-out process.

Advances in cybernetics, biology and space. The leaps in biology and the militarization and exploration of space are wild cards. Will we be able to create new human beings, and will they really be all that new? (They, too, will have tumultuous psyches.) Or will the unused portions of our brains wake up? Will we be able to develop and harness the psychic, "extra-sensory" or psi powers that we see in many individuals in our culture and in whole tribes in aboriginal cultures? Will that help the integration of all our various parts? Will it make a difference to have missiles in space stations instead of submarines? What is certain is that these developments will put a tremendous strain on the Judeo-Christian-Moslem cosmologies through which most are viewing reality. A view of the infinite such as only mystics once had will increasingly become the stuff of news broadcasts, and the present cosmologies will seem increasingly claustrophobic.

The advances in cybernetics and electronics are networking the world. Humans have an impulse to gather in cities so they might continue to do it anyway, but because of computers cities are no longer necessary. Cities are for storing information, that has always been their power; but with computers, any place can have an instant access to any information; any place can be a center. The answer to overpopulation may live in this fact. There is a great deal of unused space on this earth, and cities don't have to be the nodes of massed humanity that they are now. When you see a satellite dish beside a trailer in the middle of the Mojave, you are seeing the beginning of the end of cities as we've known them for the last 10,000 years.

But it is easy to overestimate computers. Human beings work with information but they don't dream information. And information is a poor substitute for meaning. And without meaning we become maddened—sometimes slowly but always surely. It will take a new cosmology, beyond what we've known, to make this information explosion meaningful. And making it meaningful is all that will keep us from being mad.

The empowerment of black, brown and yellow peoples. White-dominated corporate capitalism is at present trying to control, to stem the tide of, the empowerment of nonwhite peoples. Rhetoric aside, that is much of what Vietnam was about and that is most of what our Latin American involvement is about. Our military-economic machinations are causing massive suffering not because they're working but because control is not possible. The attempt simply causes chaos.

The forces that will empower what Jesse Jackson calls the rainbow peoples are more inexorable than politics or economics. The white peoples have stabilized their population growth while the rainbow peoples are growing at unimaginable rates. Their growth is too fantastic for the present famines, and even the worse famines that threaten, to prune them down to white levels. The machinations of the West caused the population explosion by upsetting the careful centuries-long balance of indigenous peoples. Now that explosion will swamp the West. Is swamping it. Cheap foreign labor produced by overpopulation is taking thousands of jobs from the United States every year.

Within thirty to fifty years the United States will become a Latino-dominated country. Whether or not Latins become a majority (and even that is conceivable) they will be our most culturally cohesive faction, the deciding factor. It will utterly change the valence of North American thought. Who knows what we will be like when our fundamental racial connection is not to Europe but to Latin America? Meanwhile the planetization of the world's economy will take more and more money from the white masses. Whites sense this now in the United States, and that is one reason why they seem to care for nothing anymore except prosperity.

This process will be *messy*. The white race is already the most despised on earth, so who knows what will happen as other races begin to have the clout to match their hatred? As James Baldwin once put it, it is "remarkable that a people so quick and proud to boast of what they have taken from others are unable to imagine that what they have taken from others can also be taken from them."

The equalizaton of men and women. This movement is taking root everywhere. In Latin America it invigorates the revolutionary movements, while in Islamic countries it drives the fundamentalists into frenzies. There seems to be a real difference between the masculine and feminine ways of carrying out tasks and perceiving gestalts, but these effects are the least predictable. Here is where the future goes past anything we know. The fundamental unit of civilization is not the individual but the family, so the equalization of men and women is changing civilization at its root. This literally changes our dreams. This is the change that must absorb all the other changes. We know from what we see around us in relationships and marriages that in the end this is the hardest change, the change that effects people most intimately. It means that the future of the world is the future of the heart—as it has always been. It means that our capacity for love will ultimately have more effect than our capacity to store information. For the family is the crucible in which the psyche takes form, and history will continue to be the psyche writ large.

The creation of a new cosmology that will replace Judeo-Christian-Moslemism. This is the most subtle, and possibly the most drastic, change that faces us. As Judaism, Christianism, and Moslemism become more and more politicized, which is to say power hungry, they lose their moral authority. They are agendas now, not religions. They are no longer channels between the individual and the infinite, they are political parties. The Judaist faith is so tied up in the Judaist state that they are no longer perceived as separate. Moslemism is frantic in its inflexibility and is exhausting itself in wars. Whether or not these wars are lost, they cannot be won.

Moslemists will not achieve their goal of keeping the rest of the world out, especially as they are fighting with the rest of the world's weapons. Another decade or so of increasingly insane warfare will exhaust not only the people but the faith. This is not apparent now because the only people who get into the media are extremists. But there are also millions who want only to live normal lives. It is a question of their inertia and suffering pitted against the zeal of the fundamentalists, and the two cannot coexist indefinitely. If the region weren't being artificially stimulated by massive armaments supplied by East and West, it would already be dropping with exhaustion into *de facto* solutions.

As the world economy progresses it will no longer be advantageous to East and West to continue the arms flow, and the region will cool. The faiths of Moslemism and Judaism will be the final casualties. The way the Crusades were the beginning of the end for the authority of the Roman Church, so these wars would be draining these faiths even if the world weren't outdistancing their concepts.

But the most desperate religion today is Christianism, partly because it is so dependent on the very systems that are subverting it. The Christianist revival in the United States is a media phenomenon. It couldn't exist without high-tech concepts and skills that can't help but perpetuate—even among the fundamentalists —the very things they deny.

Desperation can bestow an attractive glow, however, so its very desperation is giving Christianism a surge of power in the United States. But with all the hoopla it is easy to overlook the fact that the New Right is not trying to initiate anything—it hasn't got that sort of intellectual power or flexibility; the New Right is expending all its resources in attempting to roll back what others have initiated.

The cultural seesaw between Right and Left now camouflages a planetarily ineffectual administration that is completely in the hands of the multinationals

(128 of the top 500 U.S. corporations paid no taxes during '83–'84, so efficiently is our government serving their needs); and the corporate agenda has nothing to do with the New Right's. While the American people fight among themselves over who gets what civil liberties, how much money can be spent where, and whether a woman can control her own body, the multinationals solidify positions that are fundamentally subversive to American nationalism and that will ultimately result in the disintegration of American influence as the planetary economy begins to gain strength. The jingoistic Bible fundamentalists are being duped on a grander scale than they are duping.

But it is the *faith* of Christianism that is fading. Its influence was fading more and more, everywhere, and had been fading steadily for several centuries, before the increasing obsession with Armageddon of the last twenty-five years. First the atomic bomb, then the apocalyptic fervors of the sixties, then the deterioration of the international situation ever since, have revived not so much belief in Jesus as belief in the Book of Revelations. Revelations is the foundation for American fundamentalism. The present fervor is being drummed up by Revelations' assertion that these disruptions presage the Second Coming. Analyzing this, it is helpful to think back to the year 1500. Like the year 2000, the year 1500 was a magic number for Christianists. Mystic intellectuals as brilliant as Hieronymous Bosch believed, with many peasants, rulers, and clergy, that Christ would return in 1500 and it would be the end of the world. When this failed to happen, faith and thus the authority upheld by that faith diminished. At the same time, Columbus changed the popular conception of how the world itself was structured. By 1517 Luther could nail his proclamation to the door of a church and make it stick, cracking Christendom in two, spurring the nationalism that was already deflating the Church, and giving

a religious basis to the capitalism that was to become
the new order. By 1543 Copernicus could publish his
thesis that the sun was the center of our solar system
and that the earth revolved around it, as opposed to the
whole universe revolving around the earth, which was a
central thesis of the Church. From that point the Church
was, conceptually as well as politically, in retreat.

Christianism survived that blow essentially by becoming more secular and decentralizing. When Jesus
fails to arrive in the next twenty-five years, what's left
of Christianism will be shaken to the core. Unable to
accommodate the massive world changes, and no longer
being fueled by an apocalypse that never showed, its
psychic residues will continue for ages but its force will
be quickly dissipated. For we have now what they did
not have in 1500: a new, utterly different cosmology
growing in strength and faith, manifesting everywhere,
and ready to become the dominant mode of thought as it
becomes more unified. Call it New Age, call it what you
will, it combines Eastern thought with relativity physics
with cybernetics with Sufic and Franciscan and Hasidic
and Zen mysticism with pagan animism with astronomy
with biology with Hellenic polytheism with tribal ritual
with Jungian and Freudian and Gestalt psychology with
ecology with the arts with African aesthetics with Jefferson with Marx with ... Well, the point is that one of
the historical projects in force now is a planetary movement to form a new faith out of what's applicable in
many old thoughts and what is fresh to our time, a new
faith that can handle the complexities of a planetary culture.

This movement is doing precisely what Christianism once did. It is blending the newest thoughts with
what has gone before, alchemically transmuting the
used ideas along the way. In this manner, 2000 years
ago, the early Christians blended Judaism with the Isis-
Osiris mysteries of Egypt with Roman law with Greek

philosophy with the pagan shamanism of Europe, and included all in disguised form within the Church.

Right now the new cosmology is showing many faces. It can take on the corporate mask of *est* or the authoritarian mask of so many gurus. It is playing with forms. They are everywhere you look. For me, its most appealing are in the explorations and meditations of people like Robert Bly, James Hillman, Joseph Chilton Pearce, Ilya Prigogine, Buckminster Fuller, Gioia Timpinelli, Lewis Thomas, Cecil Taylor, William Irwin Thompson, Miles Davis, Doris Lessing, Gabriel García Márquez, Thomas Pynchon, Marie-Louise von Franz, Lawrence LeShan, Antonio Machado; or it is in the quiet, nondoctrinaire mystic communities like Findhorn; and it is reaching mass form in films like *Poltergeist, Close Encounters of the Third Kind, The Last Wave, My Dinner with Andre,* and the *Star Wars* trilogy, and with the entire literature of science fiction, an enormously potent force for getting new thoughts out there amongst us all —science fiction is a new generation of Arthurian-like stories in a relativistic context. In short, the spiritual issues that in the West have been the exclusive province of Judeo-Christian-Moslemism for a thousand years are being explored now all over the world with hardly a reference to standard Judeo-Christian-Moslemism.

This cosmology is chaotic and contradictory now, as Christianism was in the first century after Christ. The slow unification of Mediterranean Christianists during the first century wasn't very interesting to the Roman population either. They thought of it as a novelty, as a crazy cult. The new cosmology is at the same stage. It is not news, it is not politics, but it *is* history. The news and the politics will follow. The coherence of the world a century from now, its very ability to support life, probably depends on how successfully this new cosmology will articulate itself.

Carlos Fuentes has reflected that instability "comes when societies cannot see themselves reflected in their institutions." It is being demonstrated every day that the institutions our planetary civilization needs cannot be supplied by our present forms of government and thought. This demonstration is what we call "news" and we watch it every night. But there will slowly grow a unification of the new modes of thought and consensus about them, and this will express itself in the *form*-ation of the new societal forms, the sustaining culture, that we need. For the sustaining culture that we seek is at the other end of these changes. But it is not a pot of gold at the end of the rainbow; if it's not made every day in our vision as we go day by day through this dangerous time, then it will not be. We may not live it but we *must* see it. Only the act of envisioning can one day become an embodiment.

The crises of our world express themselves as political crises but they are without political solutions. This drives everybody concerned with solving them quite crazy. The only possible solutions are cultural, and cultural solutions can't be legislated and they usually can't be willed. Cultural solutions evolve.

And people are hard put to explain *how* they evolve. What is merely an idea in one century becomes a powerful institution in the next. That's why expressing ideas is so important. Nothing happens without them.

Culture proceeds out of the necessity of private, individual yearnings, decisions, and attempts; first and last stands taken alone, yet growing out of and feeding into a sometimes real and sometimes merely envisioned community. Buddy Bolden's community was real. Walt Whitman's was envisioned. When the community is real, the effects go taproot-deep and spread wide and are virtually impossible to eradicate until they've run their course. Buddy Bolden's music may have been despised or ignored by the dominant mainstream culture, but fifty years later it had become the mainstream's music. This wasn't willed. And not only did nobody legislate for it, many tried to legislate against it. It wasn't supported by governments or by the rich. But it happened.

When the community is envisioned, the individual's work can attract a community-in-spirit if the work is strong enough—almost all that is greatest in American literature has followed in Whitman's path, has been attracted to Whitman's community, and this was his stated goal from the beginning. The same might be said for Einstein, Freud and Jung. These private and intimate decisions, intentions and stands—relating to, depending on, either a real or envisioned community—are finally the only way to redefine and redirect any culture.

We shy away from this thought because we have been spoiled into expecting large and fast results, but that, too, is media conditioning—an emphasis on the grandiose that keeps us from deep change. Yet Whitman just wrote a poem, Einstein just conceived a brief mathematical formula, Freud and Jung and Marx just wrote books. Buddy Bolden just played the blues. Jesus and Buddha merely spoke and healed, mostly among very small groups of people. We may be nostalgic about previous mass movements and wish there could be new ones, and there *are* times when our individual, deeply private stands accumulate into mass movements—that's a step in the process. Then waves like "the women's movement," and "the civil-rights movement" arrive from our privacies and lift the culture to new levels of awareness. You'll remember that what sparked the civil-rights movement was an old black woman's refusal in Montgomery, Alabama, to go to the back of the bus—not out of any political stand, not with the intention of starting a mass movement, but because she was sick of being treated badly. And her action inspired her minister, Martin Luther King, to wider action.

But just as often there are times when the mass

movements are reactionary, are the accumulation less of private yearnings than of private panics, and their object is to crush the awareness that has been won. To depend on mass waves is to leave oneself helpless before forces utterly beyond one's control. That passivity is beneath contempt to, say, a Marie Laveau, who coalesced a whole community, the community that would inspire America's world-shaking music, by simply focusing intensely on what she believed and cared about.

This is (1) corny, and (2) terrifying. It is, in fact, corny in proportion to how much it can terrify. For as Confucius really did say, "The way out is via the door. Why is it that no one will use this method?"

It's your own door, to your own life, whether that door is the blues or physics. As long as it's truly yours, the act will have effect.

So, in this light, to cast a vote in an election, say, or to organize or join a demonstration, or to take any overtly "political" action whatever, is not a futile exercise. Issues will come through your door that must be fought for or against, in whatever way, political or otherwise, you can find to fight. But your heart doesn't swell with victory or break with defeat. Instead you are participating in (or choosing not to participate in) a process the limits of which you know in advance, as John Adams and Thomas Jefferson knew in advance the limits of *their* political process, though that knowledge didn't paralyze them. At best such activity, whether as follower or leader, constitutes a cohesion of private passions into a public forum that takes all of society forward into a world where *all* of the many-faceted human psyche will be welcome and useful; at worst, it's a holding action, a skirmish providing you with a Rorschach of the state of flux. But this overt political action is only a fragment of your true historical action; your true historical action is the force of your entire life within the emerging pattern, a pattern that you influence even in your dreams. Which is to say: what goes on in your head is connected to the future of the planet.

A future being worked out, in broad terms, in the huge historical projects I've tried to describe—the creation of a world economic system; the advances in cybernetics, genetics, space and brain research; the empowerment of brown, black and yellow peoples; the equalization of men and women; the creation of a new cosmology —all constellating as a whole, a planetary culture wherein people view their entire planet as they now view their nation or their city.

There are obvious pitfalls. The worst is the possibility of a homogenous planet, as Americanized as the Western cities are now, under a world government that enforces its will through satellite laser weapons. That's the most paranoid mix of possibilities, but there are many more. Yet even in a planetary culture, Brazil and China and New England will never be alike. It is important to remember that historical projects on this scale are not deterministic. For instance, even on the comparatively unified scale of the eastern half of North America, European dominance expressed itself one way for New Orleans, one way for Atlanta, another for New York, another for Boston. Which is to say, we can name the overall movements and their elements, but no one can predict culture. Nobody in the rabidly racist America of 1950 could have predicted that white children would, without "intention," transform black music into a unified youth culture—a culture which, from roughly 1958 to 1972, would feel purposeful enough to be the catalyst for the antiwar movement, the ecology movement, and the feminist movement, and would give tremendous energy to the movement toward the new cosmology. We can see the patterns of what is to come, but we can't dance its dances or hear its music.

And it is important to remember that this historical project of a sustaining planetary culture *will take at*

least a century, perhaps two, to work out. This will be a
time of upheaval. Wars, famines, depressions, and probably a few atomic bombs, probably dropped by and on
Third World countries. The word "panic" comes from the
name of the great god Pan, from the times when he
would suddenly make his appearance and drive people
crazy with ecstasy and terror. Obviously we are now in a
state of panic, driven to these projects by who knows
what forces? And we do not know if we can survive. I
have not mentioned nuclear destruction because it is
plain to everyone that in panic at these changes we
might emulsify ourselves. We also might not. Ecological
disasters will also no doubt occur. They might finish us.
They also might not. The planet may have its own
projects, for which it does not need us. But why would
we be here if it did not need us? "What to do then?" the
poet Antonio Machado asked. And he answered his own
question with "Weave the thread given to us, dream our
dream and live; it is the only way we can achieve the
miracle of life."

There's a century or two to survive, and even with
all the poetry we can bring to our lives this will be quite
a prosaic task. In such an era, if one judges one's state by
personal time, one can't help feeling caught naked in a
massive storm. If one judges by political time, then the
issues offered are frustrating and elementary, however
necessary it may be to engage them. But if you look at
your life on the level of historical time, as a tiny but
influential part of a century-long process, then at least
you can begin to know your own address. You can begin
to sense the greater pattern, and feel where you are
within it, and your acts take on meaning. Meaning is
the beginning of power.

We have taken on these historical projects, or they
have taken us on, and they are our work for the next 100
years. More like 200. The human being in the year 2200
will consider our era to be as primitive, as dark, as

chaotic, and no doubt as romantic, as we now think of the Middle Ages—though perhaps some of them will know that some of us were trying to build their world, even now, and that without our commitment to what *could* be, they wouldn't have any world. But we don't know if they'll be thanking us or cursing us. For myself, I like to think of the words of the physicist Niels Bohr: "The opposite of a correct statement is a false statement. But the opposite of a profound truth may be another profound truth." We are moving from one constellation of profound truths to another. And as we make that movement, we are how history breathes.

3 A.M. *The darkness of a new age. Survival is a frightened word, but, for this interlude at least, you are not frightened. You go to the window and, startled at yourself, you feel a rush of tenderness for the sheer vulnerability of this immeasurable, crass, headlong-rushing, longing world of your fellow creatures. Something sleepless in your heart calls out to what is sleepless in the hearts of the others. And sometimes it happens that in the darkened building across the street, one light goes on. Somebody else is tired of being asleep, but is uncertain of what to do with such uneasy wakefulness. Each of us has turned on a light. Each of us has been, again and again, a lighted and distant window for someone to look toward after they've stepped from a dream. They are looking toward whatever's to come, straight at us. We are looking at them. We are each other's answers. We always have been, and always will be.*

The house is quiet, the street is quiet—for one suspended moment the city seems actually at rest. You can almost hear the music to which, half-unknowing, you've been dancing all along.